Abby's message light was flashing wildly when she entered her apartment. She was almost too afraid to listen to it. She didn't need any more bad news. Reluctantly, she pressed the button while she flipped through the mail.

Tammy checking on her, her mother inviting her to dinner tomorrow night and Dr. St. John's office confirming their arrangements for next week. The last message was brief; *"Hi, I spoke to Sarah today and she told me about the surgery. Everything will be fine. She's very good at what she does. I'll call you afterwards to see how everything went."*

Pressing the button to erase all the messages, Abby thought that Mason certainly was keeping close tabs on her for a person who wasn't ready for an emotional relationship. She tried to ignore the giddy feeling she had gotten from hearing his voice. She missed him terribly but didn't have the nerve to call him. He must have been a little afraid of talking to her personally too, because he could have called the shop if he'd really wanted to speak to her.

UNCONDITIONAL

A.C. ARTHUR

Genesis Press Inc.

Indigo Love Stories

An imprint of Genesis Press Inc.
Publishing Company

Genesis Press, Inc.
P.O. Box 101
Columbus, MS 39703

ISBN: 1-58571-142-X
Manufactured in the United States of America

First Edition

Visit us at www.genesis-press.com
or call at 1-888-Indigo-1

DEDICATION

Abby's story was written before I experienced a life-
threatening hospital stay personally. Picking it up and
reading it again opened so many wounds and healed
countless others. In that spirit, I dedicate this book to
my aunt, Paulette R. Fleet (1943-2003)—a woman who
gave and instilled in her family the value of
unconditional love.

PROLOGUE

"I'm not sure I'm doing the right thing." Tammy paced the floor of her dressing room.

"All the money Daddy's spending for this wedding, you'd better be sure. Besides you and Jeff have been together for four years now, and marriage is the logical next step." Abby tried to ease her big sister's fears.

"Love and marriage do not require logic, Abby," Tammy snapped.

Abby was big on logic and well thought out decisions. She analyzed every aspect of her life, making what she considered the most realistic and appropriate decisions.

She was and would always be the most sensible of the Swanson girls. Tammy had long since claimed the title of reckless and irresponsible. Marrying her off to the son of the richest family in Manchester was a definite kudo in the opinion of construction worker Jim Swanson and his wife, Anna. However, Abby wished it weren't this particular family her sister had chosen to marry into.

Abby, herself, would probably remain single for the rest of her life—and that suited her just fine. She had no wish to cater to any man. Her life was her own and she intended to keep it that way.

Slowly, Abby walked down the aisle in the stiff, mint green creation Tammy had picked out for her. The dress was hideous and Abby had made no bones about it when Tammy had first showed it to her. Still, a sister was a sister and she'd swallowed her bile and was wearing the noisy, crinkly garment, all the while praying for the moment she could rip it off and push it as far back in her closet as it would go.

At the altar four men stood elegantly garbed in Armani tuxedos. Green bow ties and cummerbunds matched the revolting bridesmaids' gowns perfectly. The two guys on the end shifted uncomfortably and Abby felt their pain. She'd met them last night at the rehearsal. They had both gone to school with Jeff and seemed pleased to be asked to join his wedding party, but hated having to wear the dreaded "monkey suit," as they called it.

Tammy's two girlfriends stood off to the side prettily, waiting for Abby to take her place in line. They smiled like supermodels, their lips glossed and eyes shadowed with intense color. The photographer enjoyed every shot he took of them. A person would have thought a celebrity was standing up there with all the flashing that was going on. When Abby approached, the flashing lights all but stopped. If it weren't for the fact that her father was paying him, Abby was sure the photographer would have ceased taking pictures altogether as she approached the altar.

Abby was no fool. No matter how pretty the dress, which in this case didn't help her situation, or how much make-up she wore, which was always minimal, she would never be beautiful. That fact she had accepted a long time ago.

Her too round face and dull brown eyes would never make her a party stopper. Tammy, on the other hand, had hazel brown eyes and a shiny black mane which she had recently, against her mother's wishes, tinted with auburn strands. In fact, Abby was the only one in her family with her particularly drab coloring. Her parents, who were both direct descendants of the Senaca Indians, had beautiful bronze complexions and midnight black hair, but not Abby.

Every person in the sanctuary stood as Tammy made her grand entrance. Abby smiled at the sight of her father, as handsome as ever, walking Tammy down the aisle. It was a refreshing change to see him in something other than overalls and plaid shirts. Her daddy, the apple of her eye, the only man she'd ever allow herself to love, was tall and strong, and his broad shoulders squared when he walked. He was brimming with pride and clung to the daughter he was preparing to give away. A part of Abby gave in to the envy that gnawed at her.

When the minister began to speak Abby let her thoughts drift to something more satisfying, something she was good at, her job. Mary Fellowes was having her baby's room decorated by Corel Designs, the firm where Abby interned. She had lots of ideas and couldn't wait for the chance to see the space she would be working with. A color palette had already been selected and pieces of furniture waited to be ordered. She became so engrossed in thoughts about her work that she didn't hear the minister request the rings.

"The rings?" the minister repeated. "Please."

Thrust back into reality by one of the bridesmaids poking her bouquet into her back, Abby blinked, only to find everyone staring at her, including the best man.

Mason Penney was Jeff's older brother and had left Manchester to go to college in Boston almost twelve years ago. After becoming a doctor, he had gotten a job at Boston General.

This was his first visit home since then.

Abby hadn't really known him. He was her senior by seven years so they hadn't exactly run in the same circles. In fact, she didn't remember much about him and Jeff didn't talk about his family much. Abby understood why. The hostility the Penneys felt toward the Swansons had existed a long time. Among other things, the Swansons were outside the elite society circle of the Penneys. Although they were far from starving, the Swansons were nowhere near as well off as the Penneys.

After she managed to slip the shining gold band off her thumb, the only finger it would fit without tumbling to the floor, Abby's eyes shifted in apology to the congregation.

Pauline and Stanford Penney sat in the old church looking as if they were receiving a death sentence. It was a sad sight; still, Abby couldn't muster up any pity for them. After today they'd have no choice but to accept the union, for better or for worse.

Mason stood at the altar next to his brother, looking solemn and depressed. Abby figured he probably shared his parents' feelings about the wedding. For all the excitement he was showing, he could have stayed in Boston.

His cool gray eyes were set deep into a finely sculpted face. His nose was slightly crooked, probably from being broken a time or two, but he had a strong jaw line and full lips. His ears were a bit too big, but not horribly distressing.

It took a minute before Abby realized that those chilling, smoke-colored eyes were staring at her as intensely as she'd been staring at him. Heat rose to her cheeks and she prayed the blush wasn't evident. *Abigail Mae Swanson, you are not blushing because some man is looking at you.* She scolded herself because that's exactly what she had been doing. Beneath his steady gaze she felt self-conscious. She wanted to look away but something deep within those serious eyes held her.

CHAPTER 1

September, four years later

"Come on, Tam, push as hard as you can." Abby released the leg she'd been holding in the air and wiped the sweat from Tammy's forehead.

"I am, dammit! I am," Tammy groaned.

The warmly decorated birthing room was full of noise and excitement with Jeff and Abby standing at Tammy's side as she lay in the hospital bed that had quickly been transformed into a birthing bed. A burgundy floral border and thick brocade valances accented walls painted a muted tan color. There were a television and a dresser for the expectant mother and newborn's clothes as well as a roomy closet for visitor's coats. All of this had been designed in an effort to produce a relaxing mood for the birthing experience. In Tammy's case, it had failed dismally.

Acknowledging birthing experiences to now be a family affair, the hospital allowed up to ten people in the birthing room, according to the mother's wish. Even younger siblings were allowed to share the experience.

As a result, Jim and Anna Swanson sat on the couch near the window, while Jeff's mother, Pauline, stood rigidly in the corner closest to the door. Melissa, Tammy and Jeff's firstborn, stood beside her maternal grandparents clapping in exuberant anticipation of the newborn's arrival.

"Okay, Tamara, here comes another one." Dr. Craig sat on a

stool at the end of the bed, his gloved hand assisting the newborn's descent. A glance at the fetal monitor told him he needed to get the baby delivered soon, before concerns for the baby became an issue.

As if she sensed his concern, Tammy's scream vibrated off the walls. Melissa's tiny hands ceased all movement, her face crumpled and she began to wail as loudly as her mother. Anna pulled Melissa onto her lap, cradling her in her arms. Jeff cringed from the pain of Tammy's nails digging into his flesh. Abby placed one hand behind her sister's back and with the other pulled Tammy's left knee as close to her chin as she could and began counting.

"We've got hair! Tammy, give me another good push. Just like you're having a bowel movement," Dr. Craig encouraged.

"This is one hell of a bowel movement!" Tammy growled.

"You're doing great, baby, it's almost over," Jeff whispered close to her ear.

"One more good push," Abby prodded.

"What do you mean *good*? They've all been...aaahhhggg..." Tammy pushed with all the energy she could muster after nine hours of labor.

With a bright red face and a scream as loud as a banshee, the latest addition to the Penney family made her debut. Melissa broke away from her grandparents to greet her little sister. Anna prayed in her corner and Abby spotted a glistening sheen of tears in Pauline's eyes. *Well what do you know, she's human after all,* Abby surmised.

Being held by one adept arm, the baby squealed and cried against Dr. Craig's ministrations. Covered in blood and other guck, she flailed and whined as the suction was plunged into her throat for the third time. As Abby watched, she felt an undeniable twitch in her stomach, an all too familiar feeling as of late. Almost as if everything in her life were about to change and her body was preparing for that transformation. That was silly, she knew. Still, she couldn't quite identify what she was feeling at this very moment. All she knew was that she didn't like it and more than anything else, she wanted to be out of the birthing room as quickly as possible.

More specifically, she wanted to be out of this rut she had slipped into. Since Tammy's pregnancy, Abby had felt unbearably jealous of her big sister and the life she'd made for herself. It wasn't that she didn't love her own life, because she did, or at least she thought she did. Her career was going great. Business was good and she was making a name for herself in the design industry. But something was missing. Something she had previously thought she could live without. Something that Tammy had.

"You did good. She's beautiful." Abby kissed her sister quickly on the forehead. If she didn't leave this room soon, she'd be bawling uncontrollably. Then everyone would wonder what was wrong and she would finally voice what she'd been denying for so long. With everyone engrossed in the new addition to the family, she figured now was a good time for her escape.

"After all that hard work I think I need a drink. I'm going down to the canteen. I'll be right back." Abby dragged the back of her hand across her brow as if to emphasize all the hard work she had spoken about.

"Okay, I'll be here." Tammy's eyes never left the baby that lay quietly in her arms.

Stepping into the hallway, Abby removed the silly little green hat she wore, wishing she could also be rid of the matching over-sized pajama costume she had donned to coach Tammy.

Standing with her back against the wall, she replayed what had happened prior to the miracle she had just witnessed. Tammy had called her at her office earlier this morning to say that she thought her water was leaking. Abby quickly made the drive to Tammy's house.

By the time she had gotten there, the contractions had started and Tammy was attempting to pack herself a bag. She opened the door for Abby with her bag and nightgown in her hands.

"What are you doing?" Abby screeched. She walked briskly through the door, grabbing the items out of Tammy's hands.

"I'm trying to pack a bag," Tammy said, the strain in her voice apparent.

"You should have already had this packed," Abby scowled. "Go sit down. I'll finish this and then we can go to the hospital." Abby was finished in under five minutes. Not only was Tammy's bag packed, Abby had grabbed Melissa's toddler luggage and thrown some clothes in there as well.

"Have you called Jeff?" Abby asked when she was back in the living room scooping Melissa off the couch and into her arms, pausing briefly to kiss her niece's chubby little cheek.

"No, not yet. I'll call him in a minute," Tammy hissed through the pain of another contraction.

"I'll call him. You just come on before I have to deliver that baby right here in your living room." Abby moved to the door and pulled it open.

"You don't know how to deliver a baby," Tammy groaned when the pain had subsided.

"Exactly! So hurry up."

They arrived at the hospital safe and sound, despite Abby's erratic driving. Once Tammy was admitted and hooked up to all types of monitoring gadgets Abby called Jeff and her parents. She didn't bother calling Jeff's mother. Jeff would have to do that himself; she had no intention of dealing with Pauline today.

"Emergency c-section in room 409," a male voice yelled, snatching Abby from her reverie. She envisioned yet another woman about to meet the child she had carried for nine months and felt a wave of depression.

How would it feel to give birth to her own child? She closed her eyes to the haunting thought, hoping it would go away. *Well, you aren't getting any younger, Abigail,* she could clearly hear her mother saying.

She didn't want any kids; she had never wanted kids. She'd decided that long ago, Abby reminded herself. But she couldn't deny the yearning burning deep inside. The desire to hold that tiny life in her arms and to know that it was all hers. *This too shall pass*, she thought. At least she hoped so.

"Is it over?" a deep voice inquired from behind.

Abby took a deep steadying breath, trying to regain her composure, before responding to the stranger who had spoken to her. "Is what over?" The words were muttered before she had turned completely. Before her eyes locked with his twinkling gray gaze.

He wore a crewneck sweater which molded attractively over thick biceps and broad shoulders. Her breath caught as her eyes roamed over the delicious package he presented. He stood only inches away from her, so close she could smell him and her mouth watered at his scent. She couldn't believe it! Watered.

Over a man—Lord, she must be desperate. Whatever this funk was she was in must be diminishing her good sense.

He stood with his hands in his pockets his feet spread slightly apart, his forehead crinkling in response to her question. "The delivery. Did she have the baby?" He spoke slowly, as if she were a dunce.

The way she stood gawking at him, she couldn't blame him; she would have thought the same thing herself.

"Oh yeah, she had another girl." Abby was about to ask who he was when she saw Pauline approaching them.

"Your first time seeing a baby born?" One thick bushy eyebrow rose in question. His voice was deep, smooth and intoxicating.

"Oh, no. I was there when Melissa was born but it's amazing just the same." He looked vaguely familiar but she couldn't quite place his face. He was damned fine though; she knew that without a doubt. His dark chocolate complexion combined with those sexy gray eyes was wreaking havoc on her already emotional state.

"You don't have kids of your own?" He wasn't sure why he continued the conversation; she was evidently shaken up by the birth. He should have just gone into the room and left her alone.

"No." *Not yet*, she thought wistfully.

"Mason?" Pauline touched his arm and ignored Abby.

"Hello, Mother." Mother? *This* was Mason Penney. Damn, he looked even better than he had four years ago at the wedding. She watched as he hugged his mother and they chatted about him being back in town. Abby felt like the proverbial third wheel so she turned to walk away.

"Abigail, don't be rude." Pauline's snide tone stopped her in her tracks. "You remember Mason, don't you?"

Turning slowly, Abby answered her question, biting back the smart remark she wanted to say instead. Pauline grated on her nerves. The sound of her voice, the look in her eyes, her mere presence bothered Abby. She had never liked the woman and as much as she tried to be a fair person, Abby didn't think that would ever change. Old family feuds had a tendency to linger from generation to generation.

More than thirty years ago Pauline and Anna Whitehead had been in love with the same man. Stanford Penney.

The three of them had gone to school together. Anna's parents had struggled to pay the tuition in the private school while Pauline and Stanford's wealthy parents had barely noticed the exorbitant amounts. Against his parents' wishes, Stanford began to date Anna, feeling an irresistible bond with her.

It was then that young Pauline set her sights on Stanford. When she couldn't turn his head with her own charms, Pauline went to Stanford's parents, spreading vicious tales about the inappropriate relationship he was having with Anna, who was from the wrong side of the tracks. Stanford's parents then forbade him to see Anna again.

Right out of high school Stanford went into the greeting card business with his father and married Pauline. Anna got a job at the ice cream parlor where she eventually met James Swanson. They were married before Anna's twentieth birthday.

The early love triangle created a hostility that Pauline would hold on to for years to come. It didn't matter that Anna eventually married another, one of her own, Pauline had been reported as saying. No, none of that mattered. What mattered to Pauline was that Anna had once thought she was good enough to be with someone as wealthy and established as Stanford Penney. Pauline would forever hold that against Anna and in time, against Anna's children.

"Yes, ma'am, I remember him. It's nice to see you again, Mason." Taking a chance, she looked at him again.

"I didn't recognize you," he lied. He had known who she was from the moment she stepped out of that room. "How have you been?"

Abby frowned. "I'm just fine." Abby felt the heat rise in her cheeks and prayed her blush wasn't apparent.

Jeff came out of the room and joined the family reunion. Abby watched the threesome for a few minutes before making a successful exit.

After slipping into the bathroom to change her clothes, Abby went back into the room to say good-bye to Tammy. She needed to get started on the plans for Melissa's room, which would be even more exciting since she now had to decorate for two girls. The baby suckled Tammy's breast and Melissa sat entranced on the bed beside her.

"Greedy little thing, isn't she?" Abby took a seat at the foot of the bed.

"Hey, girl. I guess we can't name her Elwood," Tammy grinned.

"No, I don't think that's appropriate." Abby touched her niece's chubby little cheek and watched as her eyes stayed fixed on her mother.

"We've decided on Megan Abigail. Do you like it?"

Abby was touched. "Of course I like it. She's so pretty. Not much hair though," Abby laughed.

"I know," Tammy answered. "Ouch!"

"What's wrong? Do you want me to get the doctor?" Abby came off the bed, afraid that something was wrong.

"I haven't had a baby latching on to these in a long time. I forgot how much it hurts." Tammy frowned. Her hair was sticking up every which way.

Reaching down to smooth Tammy's hair, Abby smiled.

"Thanks, girl, I can imagine what I look like."

"Beautiful, as always," Abby said honestly. Tammy smiled into the familiar eyes.

"I'm perty too, Aunt Abby," Melissa said, defiantly crossing her little arms over her chest.

"Yes, you are, sweetie. You're very pretty." Abby scooped Melissa off the bed. The little girl looked just like Tammy. Right down to her long piano fingers. She was so adorable. The distinct stab of jealousy ebbed its way into her mind.

"Aunt Abby has to go now but I'll be back in the morning."

"Grandma said I could stay with her tonight. Are you finish my room yet?" Melissa asked.

"No, sweetie, that's why I need to go home, so I can get started." Abby had told Tammy about the room but Tammy wouldn't have told Melissa. Pauline must have—anything to outshine Melissa's other grandparents, or at least try to.

Abby drove home from the hospital, her mind vividly replaying the events of the day. Tammy had looked so happy feeding her child. Abby flinched as she remembered the alarming jolt of jealousy she'd felt. She doubted that she would ever experience the joys of motherhood. And frankly, she was shocked at how much that realization bothered her.

In her apartment, she sat at the table and began to sketch preliminary plans for the nursery. Somewhere around midnight she dozed off. When her head made painful contact with the table, she figured it was time to go to bed.

Lying in her queen-sized bed surrounded by goose feather pillows, her last thought before entering a serene slumber was of Mason Penney.

Mason sat at the end of the long cherrywood table remembering countless meals he and his brother had shared in this very room. The drapes, heavy gold damask, still hung at the windows. The rug, a rich burgundy and gold creation, still cushioned his feet. Things hadn't changed much in this room. He almost wished things hadn't changed at all.

Pauline had instructed Nadine, the Penneys' cook since forever, to cook her son a good breakfast. Nadine had cooked for an army. He had eaten all the eggs, scrapple and pancakes he could store for the moment and was enjoying a cup of coffee when Jeff walked in.

"There you are. I should have known you'd be wherever the food was. What's going on?" Jeff was full of cheer. Mason envied him.

"Hey, congratulations again!" Mason stood and gave his brother a bear hug. It felt good to be home. It felt safe. "You have a beautiful family," Mason complimented before taking his seat again.

Jeff picked up a plate and began scooping a little of everything onto it. Mason watched the boy who had grown into a man. Jeff, always tall and lanky, hadn't changed much.

"Thanks. I'm glad you finally got around to visiting."

Mason detected a note of hostility but quickly dismissed it; after all it had been almost four years since his brief stay at Jeff's wedding.

"So how does fatherhood feel?"

"It's cool except I haven't managed to produce a son yet. But I'm still young. I have plenty of time." He took a seat across from Mason.

"You've got two beautiful girls. What more could you want?"

"You know how hard it's gonna be trying to live in a house full of women? I'm going to need a lot of help."

"Yeah, I hear you on that one."

"So how long are you staying?"

"I've sort of taken a hiatus, so I'm not pressed for time." Mason carefully tucked memories of Boston into the back of his mind. He had come home to escape, not talk about them.

"The hospital let you do that?" Jeff looked up from his plate long enough to see that Mason didn't want to talk about the hospital.

"I'm thinking about going into private practice with a few colleagues so the hospital is pretty much giving me whatever I want to keep me there." Hunching his shoulders, Mason tried to shrug off the indecisiveness that had plagued him these last few months.

He was at the height of his career, in high demand at Boston University. Still, something was missing from his life. He wasn't happy. All the things he'd worked so hard to obtain, the things he'd thought he needed to have complete happiness didn't seem to be enough. His life needed to change and he couldn't figure out what to do. Correction: He knew what he had to do; the trouble was figuring out how to do it.

"That's great. Listen, I have to get over to the hospital to pick up Tammy. Why don't you come over for dinner tomorrow? You could visit with your nieces and we can catch up on things." Jeff stood and stuffed a piece of bacon into his mouth.

"Tammy's not going to want company. She just had a baby."

"Please, she loves having company and besides, I'll cook. All she has to do is sit and look pretty. So tomorrow at seven?"

"Okay, I'll be there," Mason agreed.

Witnessing a normal life would help him keep his mind off the mess he'd made of his own life.

CHAPTER 2

"Ms. Swanson, Dr. Craig will see you now."

"Thanks." Abby was doing what most people hated, getting a physical. She was overdue by a couple of months, having pushed the yearly appointment further and further back. Finally, she figured she'd better go and get it out of the way.

"Hi, Abigail, how are you?" Dr. Craig was a short, fat, balding man in his late fifties. But he was the sweetest man a person could ever meet and he had brought Abby into this world.

"I'm fine. But I think you purposely have your secretary send me all those reminder notices. I don't think your other patients get hassled when they miss an appointment the way I do."

Dr. Craig chuckled and his whole body rumbled. "Just trying to take care of you, Abigail. That's my job, you know. Now just relax, get undressed and I'll be right back."

When he returned to the room, Abby was sitting on the exam table swinging her feet idly. First came the series of questions—general health stuff. Then the physical exam began. Abby had never met a woman who could stand the annual Pap smear. It was, to her, the most degrading experience of womanhood.

"Relax." Dr. Craig said, reciting the words that were always easier said than done. She stared at the ceiling, counting the panes of paneling that were lined in a unique geometric pattern.

"Have you been doing your breast exam monthly like I told you?" he asked before raising her right arm above her head.

"Not regularly. I forget," she answered honestly. He moved to the other side and repeated the steps he had just performed.

"I don't have to remind you of the importance of self-examination."

"No, you don't." Then the room was silent except for the assistant retrieving new supplies for the next lucky woman this would grace that table.

"Okay. We're going to take some blood and then you can be on your way." Dr. Craig turned to leave the room, then as a second thought, turned to her, "And Abigail, I want you to schedule a mammogram."

"But I'm only twenty-eight." Abby was instantly alarmed.

"Abigail, it's just a precaution. You know, better safe than sorry." Patting her hand gently, he left the room.

Just a precaution, she repeated to herself after Dr. Craig was gone from the room. Reaching down, she felt her right breast, nothing. She felt her left breast. Nothing. What had Dr. Craig felt that made him think he needed to take this precaution? Maybe it was something in her family history, she thought. He'd treated all the Swanson women, including her mother, so he probably knew something she didn't.

Hopping down from the table, she decided not to give it any more thought. It was a simple precaution, just as a Pap smear and blood work were. After she was dressed, she stopped at the reception area and scheduled a mammogram for two weeks later. Leaving the office, she decided to head for the mall instead of going back to work. She needed a distraction.

In the car, she thought about Dr. Craig asking her if she needed a birth control prescription. She had been at a loss for

UNCONDITIONAL

words. The last thing she wanted to do was tell her doctor that she had no need for birth control because she had no one in a position to possibly get her pregnant. She suspected he already knew she wasn't sexually active; after all, he was the doctor. In the end, she had accepted the prescription for birth control pills, just as she had done for the past five years. The prescriptions remained stuffed in the bottom of her underwear drawer, never being filled.

Abby felt herself slowly sinking into a state of depression. No man, no babies. What kind of life did she really have? she wondered. Shopping for Melissa always cheered her up, so once she hit the mall she quickly found the nearest toy store. She would buy her a special toy for being a big sister and she'd take it to her when she went to dinner at Tammy's tomorrow. And she would do her best not to think about the fact that it was someone else's child who was the source of her happiness and not her own.

"Hey, Mason, it's good to see you again." Tammy spoke from her spot on the couch. Jeff had helped her out into the living room earlier this afternoon since company was coming.

"Hi, Tammy. It's good to be here. How are you?" Mason leaned over the couch and kissed Tammy's forehead. "You don't even look like you gave birth three days ago."

"Yeah right, tell me another one." They both laughed.

"Mama, mama, you baby is cryin'." Melissa was out of breath from having run from the other room.

"Okay. Why don't you sit and talk to Uncle Mason while I go

20

feed Megan."

"Okay, c'mon, Uncle Mase." Tammy watched as Melissa climbed up onto the loveseat to sit beside Mason

"Do you want me to go and get her, Tammy? You really shouldn't be doing a lot of walking." Mason was on his feet, taking Tammy by the elbow.

"I'm okay. She's right in the dining room. Jeff placed her cradle in there so he would hear her cry from the kitchen, sparing me the trouble of having to get up and get her." She frowned. "A lot of good that did."

"My daddy said you was his brover," Melissa said in her three-year-old language as Mason returned to the couch and sat beside her.

"Yep, I'm his big brother. And you're Megan's big sister."

Her pony-tailed head nodded in agreement. "Yep. Mommy said I can hold her if I'm bery careful." Curiosity drew her attention to his shirt. "You got buttons," she chirped. Coming up on her knees she straddled one of Mason's thighs. "See buttons." She pointed one chubby finger towards his chest until it found the small buttons that lined his shirt. Mason was amazed at her vocabulary; for such a small child, he thought she talked remarkably well. But then he'd never been around a three-year-old before.

Checking her watch to see if she was on time, Abby smiled at the thought of seeing baby Megan again. She would get to hold her and touch her baby-soft skin. And that smell...baby scent

was heavenly and just the thought warmed Abby's insides.

Of course, it would be good to see her sister too, but she'd already talked to her several times during the course of the day. Melissa and Megan seemed to occupy her every thought lately, Abby reflected. Her youthful decision to not have kids was being tested and Abby was afraid it was about to be overturned.

Jeff let her in and quickly informed her that Megan was being fed and Melissa was in the living room. Abby opted to visit with Melissa first, leaving Tammy and Megan to bond. She stopped cold when she saw Mason and Melissa sitting comfortably on the loveseat deep in conversation. They were a sight to see, a replica of a father and daughter spending time together. Mason seemed content and completely captured by Melissa. She watched as Melissa touched the buttons on his shirt, drawing her attention to the massive build of his chest. She felt a strange sensation deep within her stomach. He wore slacks and a casual shirt the same shade of gray as his eyes. Abby's eyes scanned him from top to bottom. Toned, buff, whatever it was she wanted to call it, Mason Penney was a prime example. Even his thighs looked rigid with muscle.

One of Mason's hands rested on Melissa's back for support and Abby imagined the feel of that hand on her skin. Desire swept over her in provocative waves, making her tremble. Immediately, she closed her eyes and dismissed it as hunger.

"Hi!" When she managed to find her voice she frowned at the almost too-perky tone.

"Aunt Abby, Aunt Abby." Melissa ran into her arms, showering Abby with sloppy kisses.

"Hello, Gabby." Mason stood and smiled at the sound of her

old nickname. Oddly enough, he didn't remember it having this effect on him before.

"Abby, please. Nobody's called me that in a long time." She paid an unnecessary amount of attention to Melissa's hair in an effort to avoid looking at him again. She was afraid her lustful thoughts would be easily deciphered. "I didn't know you'd be here too."

"I almost didn't come." Mason shrugged, trying to remain aloof.

Abby couldn't tell if she was glad he'd decided to come or not. She just knew that being around him made her feel things she'd never felt before. "Well, Tammy and Jeff certainly are poor hosts. I need a drink. Can I get you something?" Abby put Melissa down on the couch.

"Yeah, a Coke would be good." For a moment his gaze held hers. They communicated silently, a wordless admission of attraction.

Abby broke contact first, glancing down at a playful Melissa who was now stacking pillows high on the chair and throwing her body against them. "Not in this house. It's strictly Kool-Aid or fruit juice. Which would you prefer?" Abby had to concentrate on not being so nervous around him. She absolutely refused to blush at any time this evening. After all, this wasn't the first time she'd come in contact with a good looking man.

"Fruit juice is fine." He smiled a slow, sexy, toe-tingling grin. Abby thought she would lose her good sense and say something stupid, so she rushed out of the room before she had an opportunity to make a fool herself.

After her departure, Mason let out the breath that he had

been holding since Abby had entered the room. It was strange but he didn't remember Abby being this sexy before, not even at the wedding. He admitted to himself that he had never paid much attention to her as a child, which was what she always seemed to be to him. He used to see her from time to time tagging along behind Tammy at school or at the local hangout. That's when he'd learned of her nickname. Gabigail. Tammy used to complain that she never stopped talking. Mason remembered thinking that it was cute, that the little girl the name belonged to, was cute. Now he was thinking differently.

He saw her differently. The jeans she wore fit her flawlessly. The soft curve of her hips was perfectly outlined as he watched her plump bottom sway out of the room. Her blue shirt clung to firm, full, but not overblown breasts and when she bent over to scoop Melissa into her arms, he was given a pleasant view of the smooth flesh left uncovered by her bra. He grimaced at his burgeoning arousal.

All this *and* she was cute as hell too. Her face was perfectly round with high cheekbones, a giveaway of her Indian heritage that accented the buttery tone of her skin. *Whoa, wait a minute Mase, you can't possibly be interested in little 'ole Gabby.* But she'd definitely gotten his attention.

Tammy and Megan joined Abby in the kitchen just as she dropped ice cubes into her and Mason's glass.

Abby glanced at her niece and saw that her little eyes were open. "Miss Megan, aren't you just gorgeous?"

"Is that for my brother-in-law?" Tammy asked.

"Yes, it is. And you and Jeff should work on your hosting skills. Leaving the poor man alone with Melissa on his first visit."

Tammy laughed. "Weren't they cute? Girl, I think Melissa has aged about ten years since I had Megan."

"She was pulling on his buttons when I came in. You better watch her. She's becoming a hot tamale just like her mother." Pouring juice into each glass, Abby glanced over at her sister, seeking her reaction.

"Shut up," Tammy responded and placed Megan on her shoulder to burp her. "So how do you like him?"

On the way over Abby had figured out the reason Tammy had been talking about Mason so much in the last twenty-four hours. Abby planned to nip this charade firmly in the bud.

"I don't like him any more than I like Jeff and that's hardly enough to start some grand love affair or get me laid, which you think I need so badly. So just squash any ideas you might have in that sordid little mind of yours," Abby informed her matter-of-factly. Then she left the room before Tammy could respond. *There*, she thought, *I told her*. On her way back into the living room Abby mentally prepared herself for the sight of Mason again. For all the confidence she had just displayed to Tammy, this man was having a devastating effect on her hormones. And she felt herself losing control every moment she was in his company. It was probably just a result of the emotional roller coaster she'd been on these last few months and that would fade. At least she hoped it would.

"Here you go. Grape juice. Compliments of the Penneys." If she kept the atmosphere light and friendly, her riotous hormones would calm themselves down eventually. "Where'd Melissa go?"

"She went to get some blocks she wanted to show me. Sit down so we can catch up." Mason had already established his game plan while she was in the kitchen. Watching her move, he was convinced that she would be the best thing to come out of his visit to Manchester. He needed a diversion, something to take his mind off his problems in Boston. Gabby was a pretty fine diversion, he readily admitted.

She sat in the chair furthest away from him, which was probably best since he felt his desire growing with every second she stood perfectly poised in front of him.

"So what have you been doing all these years?" she asked. For some reason, she found herself very interested in his past. But it wasn't because she was interested in him in any way, other than as a part of the family. No, that was out of the question.

"Just working at the hospital. Not really much time for anything else." He took a sip from his glass. The less she knew about his past the better. He wasn't ready to answer any questions about his personal life back in Boston, least of all from her.

"What type of medicine do you practice?" Abby sat back in the chair, crossing her legs at the ankle.

"Orthopedics. What do you do?" Mason kept his eyes on her every movement. She had thick thighs; he liked that in a woman. His breath hitched at the thought of how voluptuous she was.

"I'm an interior designer."

"That's right, my mom did mention that you were doing some work for her."

"Your mother mentioned me?" Abby was shocked. Pauline regarded her with the barest of tolerance; she couldn't imagine what had prompted her name to be mentioned in a conversation with Mason even though she was doing some work for her.

"Why? Is that a shock?" Mason seemed a little baffled.

"Of course it is. I'm not one of her favorite people, you know."

"No, I didn't know and that doesn't mean you don't know what you're doing. You have to be really good at what you do for my mother to hire you."

"Probably. That and the fact that the only other designer in town wasn't available. Still, only the best will do for the Penneys." She mimicked Pauline's snide voice perfectly.

"And what's that supposed to mean?" Mason tried not to take offense but found it difficult as the underlying meaning in her words hit home.

"It means that despite Jeff and Tammy being married, your stuck-up mother generally has no use for anyone in my family. For years she's given us all grief and suddenly I'm good enough to work for her. It's funny how 'the best' ends up coming from the people you look down your nose at," she said sarcastically, but was immediately sorry for her little outburst. Mason hadn't been home during the last four years when Pauline was constantly making jabs at her family and their social standing. It was wrong of Abby to take her frustration out on him.

"Don't start that. Nobody looks down their nose at you or your family." Mason had heard this song and dance at the wedding and he didn't really feel like going through it again. The old family feud was stupid and he didn't for one minute believe that it was still going on.

"Yeah, well, it would be hard for you to see from Boston, now wouldn't it?" Daring him to disagree, she kept her eyes pinned on his.

Jeff heard the argument and knowing the tempers of both

participants knew he needed to put a stop to it before things got nasty.

"I see our dinner guests have arrived." He strolled in looking, as usual, perfectly dressed and primped. Tammy joked about him taking longer than she did to get dressed all the time. With his entrance Abby made a hasty retreat. She helped Tammy set the table and prayed they were having something quick, like pizza. No such luck. Jeff had prepared lasagna with Italian sausage and garlic bread. She was in for a long night.

The food was scrumptious. Abby probably would have enjoyed it more if Mason hadn't watched her like a hawk throughout the meal. It was disconcerting, to say the least. She couldn't relax, could barely talk or play with Melissa, for fear he was recording every word. Finally, she decided it was easier to just leave.

"Dinner was great but I have to get going. I have a busy day tomorrow." She pushed her chair back from the table and stood.

"Tomorrow's Saturday, Abby. You don't work on weekends," Tammy broadcasted.

"I need to hit a few furniture stores. You know, see if anyone has something I need for the nursery." Abby tossed her sister a nasty glare.

"Pink. I want all pink," Melissa announced.

"I'll keep that in mind, princess." Coming around the table, she kissed her niece soundly on the cheek and made her way to the door.

"I'll walk you out," Jeff offered.

"Mason, why don't *you* walk Abby to her car so Jeff can clear the table. I'm going back into the living room to lie down,"

Tammy announced, her intentions so blatantly clear Mason almost laughed himself.

Before Abby could rebut the statement, she saw Mason rising from his chair. Tammy quickly averted her head from Abby's heated glare. Fine, she'd get her back tomorrow.

"You ready, Gabby?" Mason asked when he stood beside her.

"It's Abby and yes, I'm ready. Goodnight." Shooting Tammy's retreating back another heated gaze, she walked toward the door. Thank goodness her car wasn't parked far from the house so their time together would be limited.

Tammy yelled goodbye but didn't dare turn to see what she knew was a nasty look on Abby's face.

It was early fall but already the air held a crisp bite. Mason walked close to her as they traveled down the driveway and onto the sidewalk. The street where Tammy and Jeff lived was generally very quiet, especially in the evening. Streetlights illuminated their path as the two figures walked in silence.

"Look, Abby, I'm sorry if I got a little agitated with you earlier. I was out of line. I really don't want this old feud to be between us." He'd wanted to say this to her throughout the meal but had decided against because of Melissa's presence.

"Yes, you were out of line. Now here's my car. Thank you for your assistance. Goodnight." She fiddled around in her purse trying to find her keys.

Mason smiled at her curt dismissal. "How about I take you to dinner tomorrow night to make it up to you?"

"Didn't you hear when I told Tammy I was working?"

"Stores will close around dinner time if I remember Manchester correctly. We could have a late dinner. Around seven-thirty?"

"I'm sure I'll still be busy. Probably at the shop," she snapped. She was suddenly very angry but hadn't a clue as to why. She finally found her keys, but that didn't change her mood. Mason was too close, and he was talking too much. Why couldn't he just let her get in the car and go on about his business?

"Or I can bring dinner to you." One eyebrow rose as he dared her to come up with another excuse.

His eyebrows were thick and dramatically neat. She quickly admonished herself for noticing such a thing. "No, I work better without interruptions." She noticed that with every exchange between them he had moved a little closer to her so that he now stood only inches away. Actually she could feel his breath on her cheek. His lips were slightly parted, his eyes hooded, as he gently tucked a wayward strand of hair behind her ear.

Abby shivered. "It's cold out here," she whispered.

"I'm pretty warm myself," he answered. "I can spare some body heat."

His hand caught her chin, tilting her head until her lips were inches way from his. Her eyes sparkled beneath the luminescent streetlights. Before he could stop himself, he touched his lips to hers, ever so softly at first, then in response to a burning desire applying a hint of pressure. Her body was in agreement, even if her mind wasn't, he thought as he felt her lean into him. She permitted his tongue to gently explore the depths of her mouth. Innocent acquiescence aroused him like never before.

At the sleek velvet touch of his tongue Abby's eyes fluttered shut and she felt as if she would melt from the intense heat soaring through her body.

She couldn't believe she was kissing him. Actually, there was nothing else she'd rather be doing, and still she couldn't believe it. Just a few minutes ago she couldn't wait to get away from him and now she was afraid she would never get enough. His mouth possessed hers with an aggressive display of strokes and sensations. Her thoughts began to scatter—nothing else existed, not the cars that drove by, not the moon high in the sky above. Her mind was completely full…of Mason.

Mason ended the kiss hesitantly, careful not to break the contact of his body against hers.

"I'll meet you at your shop at seven-thirty." His voice was gruff, his eyes dark with desire. He walked away before she had a chance to come up with another argument. If he had stood there holding her, kissing her for another moment, he would have burst. He was sure of it.

Baffled and thoroughly pissed off at her momentary lapse of judgment, Abby got in her car and pulled off before she was tempted to call him back for an encore.

At seven o'clock, Abby toyed with the idea of going home. She didn't want to go to dinner with him. *Yeah, right, who am I fooling?* She'd taken extra time to dress this morning in anticipation of this very moment. Still, she was hesitant.

She hadn't been on many dates in her twenty-eight years and the ones she had been on hadn't been with Mason Penney. She wondered if it was just his name, and all that went with it, that intimidated her. He was her brother-in-law's brother, for goodness sake. That was weird enough without her feeling all jittery inside whenever he was near her.

And that kiss last night had killed any hope she'd had of getting a good night's sleep. She had tossed and turned all night, remembering his smell, the soft touch of his lips, the way he'd mastered her mouth.

Slamming her hands down on her desk, she sat back in her chair and let her head rest against the soft leather, trying like hell to clear Mason Penney out of her mind.

Chimes sounded, signaling someone had come into the store. Looking up, she saw him. *There goes my chance to escape*, she thought cynically.

Her office was towards the back of the store. It wasn't enclosed so she could see the comings and goings in the store. She saw him walk in, then quickly put her head down to give the impression that she was working. Mason wandered through the showroom, stopping briefly to pick something up or flip through the sample catalogs she had on display. She grew particularly tense when she glanced up to see him flipping through her portfolio. His face was set so she couldn't tell if he liked what he saw or not. It didn't matter anyway; she didn't need his approval. Her work was good and that was that.

He put the book down and started towards her. Her anxiety climbed another notch with the knowledge that in a few seconds they would be face to face again.

"Good evening." His voice preceded his arrival.

Abby looked up to see him approaching her desk in long, slow strides. She drank in the sight of him. Brown slacks hung expertly over long muscled legs; a beige polo shirt was neatly tucked in while the coco brown suede jacket hung loosely over broad shoulders. His eyes glistened in the fading sunlight that streamed through the front window and his full lips turned in a slight smile. She was in deep trouble.

"I didn't think you'd show." Trying to be flippant, Abby shut down her computer and grabbed her purse out of her desk drawer.

"You lie." Sitting on the edge of her desk, Mason caught a whiff of her perfume. Something floral, he figured, and sexy as hell. "You wanted me to not show."

She lifted a brow and shrugged. "You're right." Standing, she slipped the strap of her black Coach bag over her right shoulder and walked around the desk.

Reaching out, he grabbed her arm, pulling her until she stood between his legs. "No such luck."

Mason held her there for a moment. She was agitated, he could tell, and he liked it. Her soft brown eyes glared at him and steam fairly oozed from her. "Do I make you uncomfortable, Abby?"

"No. Why would you make me uncomfortable?" Abby lied. *Badly.*

"I don't know. But you seem a little uptight. Would you rather not go out with me?" He didn't know why he'd offered her a chance to bail out but prayed she wouldn't take him up on it.

"I'd rather you let me go so we can get this over with." Desperately fighting the urge to kiss him, Abby tried again to walk away. This was an impossible situation, she knew. She liked Mason a bit too much, if she were honest with herself. And she couldn't truthfully say that the thought of sleeping with him hadn't crossed her mind. But sleeping with a person was not a casual circumstance for her. It needed to mean something to her. Especially now since she'd finally decided to reverse her decision not to have kids. She needed to focus on finding husband material.

And Mason didn't appear to be that. Not that she didn't think he'd make some woman a good husband some day. But he lived in Boston. His life, his job, everything was in Boston. And she definitely was not leaving Manchester. Besides that fact, he was a Penney and while Tammy and Jeff seemed to have overcome the family feud, Abby wasn't sure she was up for the challenge.

"Well, as long as you're agreeing to go along with this, you might as well know that I like touching you. And I plan on touching you a lot." He stood, keeping her close so that she had to maneuver her feet to keep from falling. Dropping a quick kiss on her forehead, he heard her mumble something.

"Your plans can be changed," she mumbled under her breath.

Mason heard her comment and started to come back with another of his own. But he noticed that his closeness unnerved her. His ego was boosted beyond measure; she liked him. If her discomfort around him was any indication, she liked him a lot. This wasn't going to be so hard after all. Mason had thought that convincing her to have an affair was going to be hard but maybe not. Her passion simmered just beneath the surface. All he needed to do was push the right button.

Dinner wasn't so bad. Mason was actually very entertaining. And Abby had managed to relax enough to enjoy herself—at least until he took her back to the store.

Against her earnest arguments, Mason insisted on walking

her to her car. She knew it was the gentlemanly thing to do but she honestly didn't trust herself alone with him. Through the course of the evening his attentiveness and charming wit had proved she was terribly attracted to him. She walked fast, hoping he didn't stop to talk as he'd done last night when he walked her to her car. She remembered something else he'd done last night; her lips tingled with the memory.

Mason knew she didn't want him near her but not for the reason she would have him believe. He knew she was attracted to him. Women had been in and out of his life since high school, so at thirty-six he thought he knew enough to know when a woman wanted him.

But Abby was different. She acted as if the attraction frightened her. Mason couldn't figure that out. She'd seemed relaxed and comfortable, as long as the conversation revolved around her work or his work. But when he'd touched her hand across the table, she'd bolted, using the restroom as an excuse.

Now she almost ran to her car in her haste to get away. He wondered if the hurry was to get away from him or the feelings he caused in her.

Without a doubt, Abby stirred him in a way he was sure no woman had done before. He wasn't quite sure if that was a good thing or not. One thing he did know for sure was that he wanted this woman, he wanted this affair. If he couldn't make a decision about anything else in his life—which apparently he couldn't or he wouldn't be back in Manchester—he was sure about becoming temporarily involved with Abigail Swanson.

Her pace slowed as she approached her car and since she'd already retrieved her keys, she reached forward to put them into the lock. On impulse Mason snatched the keys from her hand.

"Are you planning to kidnap me now?" Her heartbeat accelerated with his close proximity. Mason's eyes burned with something indescribable as he watched her closely.

"Nope. But I am going to kiss you," he announced. He waited a second for her reaction, half expecting her to bolt. He was pleasantly surprised when she simply folded her arms across her chest and glared at him. Her stance, her look, was so sultry, so enticing, he almost begged her to sleep with him.

"And you had to take my keys to do that?" Leaning against the car door, Abby admitted to herself that she had been looking forward to this kiss all night.

"I didn't want you hopping into the car and racing off to get away from me."

"I'm not afraid of you," she lied. He scared her like nothing ever had before.

"No, you're afraid of what you want me to do to you." He'd hit the nail on the head, he could tell.

Agitated that he'd figured that out, Abby dropped her arms and sucked her teeth. "Anyway, can we get this over with? I have church in the morning." She didn't want to discuss her fears with him. Especially since right now he was the one instigating them.

"Now, where's the romance in that? You just tell me to get it over with like it's a horrible deed that must be done." He laughed, a rich, smooth sound that warmed her heart.

Reluctantly she smiled. "Well, you sure are taking your time."

"I have to take my time," he whispered. He moved closer until the tips of her breasts provocatively brushed against his chest.

"Why?" Her throat went dry; she struggled to breathe. When she finally did take a breath, it was only to inhale the complete manly scent that was all Mason.

"So I don't miss anything." His lips touched hers with butterfly softness. The memory of their previous kiss flooded back into her mind. Her palms rested on his chest and itched to move beneath his jacket. Her knees shook and she grabbed his jacket to steady herself. Her knuckles grazed his chest, feeling its hardness vibrating with each breath. Reflexively she licked her lips.

When their tongues reunited, his arms wrapped around her, drawing her closer. She could feel his heartbeat and knew that he felt hers. Tilting her head, she deepened the kiss. His large hands splayed across her back, holding her tightly. Her breasts pressed against his chest, her nipples tingling from the contact.

Mason struggled to hold on to his control. This date had been an experiment, to see if there was any chemistry between them. He'd gotten a taste of her last night, but tonight was to be the deciding factor. His immediate arousal, coupled with the moans emanating from her, sealed the deal.

He was both amazed and confused. She was very intelligent and talented. He'd seen some of her work in the books at her store and the way she talked about her upcoming projects convinced him that she was destined for success.

But besides that, she'd touched something in him. She was a down-home good girl. She visited with her parents on a weekly basis, went to church on Sundays, and babysat for her sister. She was perfect. She was dangerous.

He ended the kiss before was tempted to put her in the backseat of his car and carry her home with him. He wasn't sure he should be doing this right now. He was already going through so much, adding another ball to the bunch would be too much to juggle.

"Goodnight." Abby snatched her keys from his hand. She saw that he was still trying to regain his footing, so she quickly turned her back to him and unlocked the car door.

"It certainly was." Looking at her one last time through the window of the car, he waved and watched her drive away. "It certainly was."

CHAPTER 3

The lobby was filled with women, all waiting for the same thing, Abby supposed. There was no need to be nervous. This was just a precaution. The other women looked similarly placid as they waited for their names to be called. Abby grabbed a *Good Housekeeping* magazine from the table and absently flipped through its pages.

"Abigail Swanson?" The nurse spoke loudly as she walked into the waiting area. Rising from her seat, Abby followed her down the corridor and into the last room on the right. The walls were stark white, the blinds at the window drawn shut. A chair sat by the door and a monstrous-looking machine stood in the corner. Before she left the room the nurse handed her a gown and instructed her to put it on.

Abby worried that the nurse would return to the room prematurely, so she changed quickly and sat in the chair against the wall. A knock sounded from the opposite side of the door and a tall woman poked her head in.

"Are you ready?" she asked.

"As ready as I'll ever be." Abby wanted to hurry up and get this over with.

"I'm Elizabeth and I'll be your technician. I note that this is your first visit so I'd like to explain the procedure to you. There are two types of mammograms. The screening mammogram is an x-ray of the breast used to detect breast changes. A diagnostic mammogram is another x-ray that's used to diagnosis unusual breast changes, such as a lump, pain or a change in breast size or shape." Elizabeth took a much-needed breath and began again. "Have you been experiencing any pain in your breasts?"

"No."

"Have you noticed any change in the size or appearance of your breasts?" she asked.

"No." As she answered, Abby recalled that just this morning she'd thought she felt something.

"Okay, let's get started." She led Abby closer to the machine and instructed her to open the front flap of her gown. Elizabeth's hands were cold as she lifted the left breast and placed it on the platform. Advising Abby to be very still, Elizabeth went behind a partition and began to press buttons. Abby felt as if this machine would permanently flatten her breast—nonetheless, she didn't move a muscle.

"I'll be taking two x-rays of each breast, Abigail." The technician finished with the rest of the x-rays and then left the room. Abby redressed and sat in the chair to wait. A few minutes went by.

"Abigail, you did just fine. I'll be sending a copy of the films to your primary care physician and he'll give you a call with the results."

"So I can go now?"

"Until next year!" Elizabeth said brightly.

Mason was going to church with Abby today and then they

were going to her parents for dinner. The past week had been a whirlwind of new feelings for Abby.

Since dinner at Tammy's, they'd gone to the movies, shopped for furniture for the nursery and had even taken the girls for a few hours while Tammy and Jeff enjoyed a quiet evening at home. Mason was nice to have around. They talked about everything from medicine to architecture. And the times they were alone he'd touch her and she'd melt. He'd kiss her and she'd nearly swoon. He was addictive and Abby knew she should take a step back.

The time had come for her to examine what was going on between them. It simply wasn't in her nature to allow things to progress naturally; she had to figure them out ahead of time. After all, that was the realistic thing to do and she had always been the realistic one. So as she got dressed for church, she began to sort through the events that had taken place so far.

On their last date Mason had kissed her passionately. She knew that there was something else lurking between them, some unchartered territory. And she was afraid of what that something else might lead to. Being with him casually and having a sexual relationship with him were two different things. Or at least she thought so. This was the one gray area in her life since at twenty-eight she was still a virgin, a fact that further inhibited her in the relationship. She wasn't sure if Mason knew that, but she figured men could tell these things. She probably wasn't even kissing him right. What if he were laughing at her every time? That thought was humiliating.

If that was humiliating, just think how she would feel if she allowed their relationship to move forward? And what about commitment? Abby was no fly-by-night girl. Before she decided to go all the way there had to be something substantial there. Something that was capable of being built into marriage and stability. And with Mason she just didn't know if that was what he wanted or not. The doorbell sounded, snatching her from her thoughts. She pulled on her jacket and ran to answer it.

"Good morning." Mason braced his hands about her waist and kissed her until her knees began to shake.

"Good morning to you too." Abby was breathless. Mason had an amazing way of making her feel attractive and wanted. She'd never felt that way before. She was starting to realize that she liked it.

Dressed in a dark blue suit and royal blue shirt, Mason was very formidable. The navy and yellow tie was neatly tied at the crisp collar of his shirt and she could smell the masculine scent of his cologne. Tommy, the mesmerizing scent that stayed with her each night, long after he had gone home.

"Are you ready?" He eyed the red dress and black blazer she wore. Simple, yet arousing.

"Sure am. Just let me get my purse." His eyes followed her into the bedroom. The sway of her hips under the sheer material of her dress was enticing, to say the very least. *Damn!* He had sworn that he wouldn't look at her like that today. He didn't want to see her parents again for the first time in years with a look of pure lust for their daughter on his face. He tried to focus on the ficus tree standing in the corner of her living room, hoping that would offer some distraction. It didn't. Each time they had been together he had wanted nothing more than to simply ravish her. But he knew that was impossible.

The thought had occurred to him that he shouldn't let things go too far with her at all, especially since he didn't plan on staying in Manchester. He knew she had a high moral standard and that she did everything in her power to live by it. He couldn't help asking himself if pursuing her was wise. But for the life of him he couldn't stay away. She was his first thought when he awoke in the morning and always the last as fell asleep at night.

Another problem entered his mind, one that nagged him most of all. Nell. Should he tell Abby? She was only meant to be a distraction during his stay in Manchester so why bother her with small details, he kept telling himself. Besides, she didn't want to know about his life in Boston. She was only concerned with the here and now. Or so he hoped. Once again, he tucked that little tidbit of information safely in the back of his mind. Abby came back into the room and walked past him to the door. He smelled the fresh exotic scent that always accompanied her and groaned.

"What are you wearing?" he asked as he closed the door behind them.

"What?" She frowned, unsure of his meaning.

"The perfume. What perfume are you wearing?"

"It's just some after bath splash I brought from Kmart." Abby felt supremely embarrassed at that admission. "I think this one is Orange Mango." Her lips turned up in a smile.

"It smells great." He had never thought that he would be turned on by a fruit fragrance. But he was beginning to realize that where Abby was concerned, anything was possible.

They sat in the sanctuary listening attentively as the pastor preached the sermon for the morning. It was a powerful sermon about the importance of walking and talking in the Christian way. Mason seemed as absorbed as Abby was. That was a plus for him in her book. She had been raised in the church and therefore would accept nothing less of any man she got involved with. Her parents sat two pews in front of them with Tammy, Jeff and the girls on the other side. Megan was being christened today and Jeff had asked Mason to be godfather. As Abby was already Melissa's godmother, she would have to settle for simply being Aunt Abby to Megan, which was fine with her.

The ceremony was lovely. The preacher also touched on the importance of adults being mindful of what they say and do as children are always watching. Abby agreed wholeheartedly. Mason stood at the altar with the same solemn look he'd had at the wedding. The only difference now was that she knew he was excited as well as honored to be standing there assuming the role of godfather to his niece. He had expressed a lot of remorse for not being home in such a long time. Although he had a full life in Boston, Manchester would always be his home and to Abby this was where he belonged.

Dinner at the Swanson home immediately followed the service. Of course, the older Penneys had other engagements and were unable to attend. But, to tell the truth, no one even noticed. After dinner Abby and Tammy moved into the kitchen to help clean up. As the three ladies worked methodically, Abby knew instinctively that the interrogation was about to begin.

She stood at the sink washing dishes, with Tammy beside her drying. Anna emptied leftovers into containers and put dishes away. This had been a ritual with them ever since the girls had been tall enough to reach the sink.

"Mason is a fine man, Abigail Mae," Anna said. She didn't look in Abby's direction but continued to scoop the last pieces of chicken out of the roaster, placing them gently into a Tupperware container.

"Yes, he is, Mama," Abby admitted. Tammy smiled mischievously.

"And he's not even married. That's a wonder because he's good looking and makes a good living to boot." Anna's graying hair didn't move as she bobbed her head.

"Mama, I know all his attributes. I don't need you to run them down for me." Abby tried to put an end to the conversation. She didn't know where things were going between her and Mason. The last thing she wanted was to discuss it with her mother.

"And your Daddy seems to like him too." Anna was scraping the remainder of the sweet potatoes into the trash can.

"Well, Mama I don't think that's enough. *We* have to like each other. It's simply not enough that you and Daddy like him." Tammy rolled her eyes in response to Abby's remark. Abby responded by flicking soapsuds in her direction.

Oblivious to the antics of her daughters, Abby continued. "I saw how he looked at you at dinner and when we were at the church. That boy's got his eyes wide open and you're the one who opened them. I hope you don't mess things up. I've waited so long for you to find someone." Anna wagged a wooden spoon at her youngest daughter.

"Yes, I know." Abby decided that it was easier to just agree with her. This conversation could go on forever with her feeling one way and Anna determined to feel another.

"I think what you saw, Mama, was just lust," Tammy interjected. I've seen him watch her walk around a room and you can see the heat brimming in his eyes. I think she needs to take him to bed as soon as possible before he busts open." Leave it to Tammy to say something like that and get Anna all riled up. Abby put her head down both to hide her embarrassment and to shield herself from Anna's wrath.

"Tamara Faye! You have the dirtiest mouth. You're not too old for a soap and water rinsing, you know. This is important. It's my grandbabies I'm thinking about, not some horny man." Anna spoke vehemently.

"Just how do you think you're gonna get those grandbabies, Mama, if she doesn't give him any?" Abby had thought the situation could get no worse when, to her chagrin, Mason walked into the kitchen.

His body seemed to fill the room as his eyes quickly found Abby and held. The ladies were silent. Mason looked from one stony face to another.

"Am I interrupting something private?" he asked casually. Abby knew without a doubt that she was blushing. She felt like finding a rock to hide under.

"No, darling, just girl talk. Would you like some coffee and cake?" Anna asked politely.

"No, actually I was coming to see if Abby wanted to go for a ride. I remember the sunset down on the Rubaker property being beautiful this time of year." Mason watched and waited for Abby's reply. He had heard part of the conversation and knew

Abby wasn't too pleased to be a part of it.

"Sure, she wants to go. Don't you, Abby?" Tammy took the dishtowel out of Abby's hand and scooted her toward the door. The last scoot was a little too hard and she ended up against Mason's chest. When his arms quickly folded around her in an intimate gesture her pulse soared. She was losing her battle with morality as she stared into his eyes that glistened with flecks of charcoal. Odd, she thought, she'd never noticed the charcoal before. She wasn't sure watching a sunset with him was what she wanted to do at this very moment.

Mason's body had gone rigid with need at her closeness and his eyes pleaded with her to come with him. He wanted desperately to be alone with her.

In the car Abby's uneasiness grew. Mason was abnormally quiet, giving her time with her own thoughts. She'd never felt this way around a man before and the more time she spent with Mason the more she was convinced that he was an opportunity she hadn't been given before. All she had to do was take a chance. She'd opened her own business in a small town with not much prospective clientele on a chance. Still, she wasn't sure if she was up to this challenge. Mason was out of her league. He'd been playing the game much longer than she had in a big city like Boston. She knew she couldn't compete with the women he'd met there. But what if he was tired of Boston?

Abby sighed. That was certainly wishful thinking. She decided to focus on the here and now, to enjoy whatever time she had with him. The rest she would conquer later.

The Rubaker estate was thirty miles out of the city. Instead of taking the main roads, Mason had decided on the scenic route.

As they drove through the heart of the town, Abby noticed decorations in all the shop windows. With Thanksgiving only a week away the Christmas season was well underway, Abby realized.

During the holiday season Manchester attracted a lot of tourists on their way down south to visit relatives. So attractive window displays would definitely draw the weary travelers out of their cars for a moment of sightseeing and shopping.

"So tell me, Abby, why hasn't some lucky guy snagged you yet?" Mason asked suddenly.

His voice drew Abby's attention from a particularly festive arrangement in the candy store window. "I'm waiting for the right one to try," she shrugged.

"Oh, so you're one of those women on a quest for 'Mr. Right'?" He chuckled.

"Is something wrong with that?" She shifted in the seat to face him.

"No, no. You definitely have a right to be picky. So what are you looking for exactly?" He was curious. It didn't matter if he fit the bill or not, he just wanted to know what she was looking for.

"I don't know. I guess that's what's taking me so long to find him." She bit on her bottom lip thoughtfully. "I mean, I don't have a list of specifications. I just want a good, honest man who wants the same things I do."

"And that is?" he prodded, anxious for more details.

Abby sighed. She'd only just figured out the answer to this question herself a few weeks ago but it was clear to her and came out as if she'd known it all her life. "Kids, career, family, house, cookouts, birthday parties, all that good stuff," Abby said, sounding a bit dreamy.

"The fairy tale," Mason stated blandly, mentally noting that they were on different sides of the fence.

"Yeah, the fairy tale," Abby repeated. "And what do you want?"

"I don't know. I don't think I've figured that out yet," he lied. He knew it wasn't the fairy tale that she had dreamed of. He was definitely not getting married and as for kids, he didn't even want to discuss that.

He parked the car near the makeshift drawbridge. Abby immediately got out to take in the view, and to Mason's relief abandoned the conversation. The sun was indeed beginning to set in a flurry of red, gold and yellow splashing across the sky. A light breeze caused gentle ripples on the surface of the lake. Trees were losing their leaves, coating the grass with a spray of golds and browns. A flock of ducks flew overhead, going south, Abby presumed.

"Pretty, isn't it?" Mason stood behind her, debating whether or not he should touch her and knowing he didn't have a choice.

"Yeah." She felt his body pressing against her back.

Abby sighed inwardly as the warmth of his body lined her back. His arms enfolded her in a circle of supreme bliss. She wrapped her arms around her waist so that they rested on top of his and leaned back into the comfort of his embrace.

"The service was really good today. You never realize how much you miss hearing the Word until you go back to church after a long absence." His breath ruffled her hair.

"You don't go to church in Boston?"

"No, I usually don't have the time. Doctors keep really strange hours, particularly hospital doctors. That's one of the reasons I'm thinking about going into private practice."

"I don't blame you. You can't have much of a personal life," Abby said quietly.

"I guess you could say that, but privacy has its advantages." He turned her to face him. "Who would have guessed that little Abby would grow up to be so pretty?" His hands left her back to frame her face, his thumbs lightly caressing her cheeks.

"Who would have thought anyone would ever notice?" Abby spoke honestly.

"A man would have to be blind or gay not to," Mason chuckled. Abby wasn't prepared for the waves of longing that swept though her like an angry storm. "And I'm neither," he whispered just before he claimed her mouth in a kiss so gentle she wanted to weep with its sweetness. He lifted his head to look at her. The last rays of the sun cast golden streaks throughout her hair. Eyes that he thought were brown turned out to be hazel and glistened with an unfamiliar message. Her lips remained slightly parted and he struggled not to want more. Not to take his fill of this delectable creature.

"Mason."

The sound of his name on her lips was his undoing and he took her mouth again. His tongue stroked hers urgently this time, and her hands went around his neck and pulled him closer, begging for more. He lightly nipped her lower lip, then moved on to suckle her neck. His hands were everywhere all at once. But for Abby that wasn't enough. She needed more, so much more. She felt the volcano inside her threatening to erupt.

"Abby, can you feel me? Can you feel what you do to me?" Mason's voice was a raspy growl.

"I think so," she answered, uncertain.

He knew she was debating, wondering if she should take the chance. He had a funny feeling she hadn't had the complete experience yet. He wanted to be the one to teach her—to show her the marvels of lovemaking. Without thinking of the consequences, he knew that he would make love to this woman. He had to, needed to, for her as well as for him.

Tearing his mouth from hers for what he hoped was the last time he would have to deny himself, he smiled down at her. "Let's go to your place. We're not horny teenagers. Besides, what would your parents say if they knew you were outside necking?" Taking her hand, he started towards the car.

Without a moment's hesitation she followed him. "I don't know, but Tammy would most likely jump for joy." Mason silently agreed with her. He had overhead Tammy's words in the kitchen. A small voice nagged him to take Abby home and leave her alone. But a more persistent voice urged him to continue on his present course.

Mason held her hand throughout the ride home, deftly maneuvering the car without causing any accidents. He knew that she was nervous and the simple touch of his hand would soothe some of her fears.

Once they were at her apartment Abby knew her decision had been made. She had known him all her life but their personal relationship had only begun four weeks ago. She was going to give Mason what she had held so sacred all her life. Not because she was some horny teenager and not because her mother wanted them together so desperately, but because deep down inside she knew that she loved him, though she wouldn't admit it to a living soul because she doubted that Mason was in love with her. But maybe, just maybe, he liked her a lot. And that would have to be enough.

They didn't stop in the living room but headed straight for the bedroom, both of them too far gone to play the stalling game. Mason sat on the bed, drawing Abby onto his lap.

"You have to be sure about this, baby, 'cause once we start, it's gonna be hell for me to stop." His eyes, usually clear and sparkling were now clouded with desire, his voice just barely contained. A rush of excitement hit her with the knowledge that she was causing this reaction in him.

"I've...um...never done this before," she stammered.

"I know. That's why it's important that you really think about it." One hand rested on the small of her back as the other cupped her stocking clad knee.

"It's been the only thing I've thought about since you came back. It's almost like I waited for you." She licked her now extremely dry lips. Mason took her hand and gently kissed her palm, once again ignoring the nagging little voice.

Abby boldly traced the outline of his lips with the pad of her finger. She jumped slightly when his tongue came out and drew its length into his mouth. This was a new sensation. She decided she liked it. When he finished, she lowered her head and kissed him. The heat encompassed her body so quickly and so fiercely she felt as if she were floating in midair. His hands sought one breast covered only by the thin material of her dress and a sheath of satin. She gasped and Mason's tongue plunged deeper into her mouth. He fingered the nipple that puckered at his command. Passion igniting him, he turned her to straddle him. Her dress was becoming a problem so he pulled it over her head tossing it somewhere on the floor. Her plump breasts strained against the thin material of her bra.

"My God," she heard him say. She wasn't sure but she believed he ripped the bra off because in the next moment her breasts were in his hands. Palming the generous weight of each, Mason lavished them with his complete attention. His tongue scalded her skin.

She heard his name being repeated in a voice that vaguely resembled her own. He guided her hand to his chest and she didn't hesitate to follow his lead. The buttons on his shirt were uncooperative but after a valiant effort she unfastened them. Her fingers lightly brushed the hair that sprinkled his chest. She kissed his neck and felt the room spinning around her as he lay back on the bed giving her complete access.

The chest that she had admired on so many occasions was spread before her like unconquered land. Taut muscles bulged from everywhere. She kissed every inch of it, noting consistent hitches in his breath.

"Are you sure you've never done this before?" he asked when she slid her body from his to lie beside him.

"Positive." She smiled at what she assumed was a compliment. He stood to remove his pants and Abby watched him closely.

"It should be a sin to be so fine," she whispered. It was as though the more private part of him took the compliment all to itself, as his penis jutted forward straight and hard. The look of surprise she held did not escape Mason's eyes.

"It's all right, baby. Don't be nervous." He removed her stockings and, lastly, her panties. She lay before him in all her glory, and he was sure he had never seen a more beautiful sight. His gaze rested on the triangle of brown curls that hid her womanhood. He ached to touch her there. Sensing his need, she held out her arms for him to join her.

He tested her readiness first with his fingers before reaching into his pants pocket for a condom. When he was properly sheathed he kissed her and whispered softly, "You are so beautiful, so perfect."

The words registered in her mind just as she felt the pressure of him entering her. The pain lasted the briefest of moments and was followed by a nameless emotion, something akin to absolute bliss. Mason stroked her slowly, moving in and out with long gentle thrusts before passion urged him to move quicker, to go deeper. Abby found herself lifting her hips to meet him. With her legs wrapped tightly around his back, she began to soar, her body quaking with pleasure.

"Abby!" Mason yelled with his release.

They lay together each on separate sides of the bed, for what seemed like an eternity, both afraid of what would come next. Abby finally decided that she needed to know where they stood. She could not survive another second filled with uncertainty.

"So what now?" she said frankly. Her voice was strong but inside her stomach clenched in anxiety about his response.

"You're ready again?" He made a sad attempt at humor.

"I'm serious, Mason."

He knew she was. Draping an arm over his forehead he felt the sting of guilt. "You're too serious, Abby," he said.

"What we just did *is* serious." She felt a mixture of hurt and confusion and anger. She was angry with herself for thinking, hoping, this act would change things.

"I agree." The room was silent again. "Abby, I don't know what it is you want to hear," he lied. He knew all too well but couldn't bring himself to say it.

"Then there's no need to continue this conversation." She rose and padded naked across the floor to the bathroom where she ran hot water for a shower. Beneath the stinging spray of water she let the tears flow. She had known going in that Mason wasn't interested in a commitment. At least that's what she'd figured since they had never discussed it. Still a part of her had wanted to believe that if she shared this coveted part of herself with him he just might change his mind. That had been her mistake.

She remembered reading in novels how after making love the man held the woman, caught up in the intimacy of the moment, whispering of love and commitment. Mason hadn't held her nor had he had much to say.

Turning the water off, Abby pushed the shower curtain back and reached for the towel. She wouldn't regret the act. No matter what came of her and Mason, her introduction to intimacy had been a good one and she would always cherish it.

When she finally emerged from the bathroom, she was shocked to see that he was still there. He sat in the chair across from her bed, a pensive look on his face.

"Come here," he said. She pulled the belt to her robe tight— a little too tight as her breathing was now constricted. Or was that from the sight of Mason's bare chest? Hesitantly, she stood before him. He placed his hands on her hips, pulling her closer.

Resting his head on her stomach with his arms wrapped tightly around her, he tried to tell her what was on his mind. "I don't know what happens now, Abby. Although it wasn't my first sexual experience, it sure as hell was the first emotional one."

She shared his confusion but tried not to take his words too seriously. "I know."

The guilt almost overwhelmed him. He knew that it was time to leave. Time to walk out of her life before he hurt her more than he knew he already had.

And then there was Nell. There was always Nell. He could neither deny nor forget her. But he didn't see that she would fit into Abby's world or her plans for her future.

Still, he stayed.

CHAPTER 4

Mason convinced Abby that having Thanksgiving dinner with his parents was a good idea. He used the fact that Tammy and the kids would be there as his ace in the hole, so to speak. He needed to get back to Boston soon so he wanted to spend as much time with her as possible. Besides, she'd be a pleasant distraction from his parents. Mason sensed a little tension between himself and Abby but didn't want to think about it.

Being with her had managed to put his life in Boston into perspective. But since he had still refused to tell her about that life, he feared she would hate him when he left, a fact that he would have to deal with for the rest of his life. So he was determined to have as many good times with her as he could before then. He would carry those memories back to Boston.

Abby had been skeptical about not being with her parents. It would be the very first Thanksgiving that she had not spent with them. But she promised to have dessert with them—that seemed only fair.

For the dinner with the Penneys, Abby wore a black pantsuit with a silver camisole and kept her jewelry simple with silver studs at her ears and a silver choker at her neck. She wasn't sure of the proper attire at a Penney holiday feast and hoped she'd dressed appropriately. She was driving her own car instead of Mason picking her up so he wouldn't have to leave his family on her account.

As she pulled into the driveway, she saw Jeff's car and realized that she was probably the last one to arrive. Mason opened the door before she could knock. Once again she was swept off her feet. He wore tan slacks, a black shirt and a black tie with Winnie the Pooh and Tigger running across it. She chuckled a bit at the sight of animated characters on a grown man's tie but decided the look definitely worked for him.

"Hey, baby. What took you so long? I was getting worried."

"Procrastinating," she shrugged.

Mason draped an arm around her shoulders for comfort as well as pleasure. She giggled at Pooh and Tigger again.

"What's so funny?" One dark eyebrow rose as he stared down at her.

"This is so cute." She lifted the tie, balancing it on one finger between them.

"It was a gift for the new godfather," he smiled.

She frowned. His smiles alone would haunt her when he was gone. She turned away so that he wouldn't see the change of emotion on her face. She was too late.

With a gentle finger he lifted her chin until their eyes connected. "You okay?"

"No." She blinked as she struggled to get her nerves in check.

"It'll be fine. I promise." As confirmation of his promise he kissed her thoroughly. Pulling back slightly, he stared into familiar eyes that had come to mean a lot to him. "Okay?"

"Okay." He believed she was upset over the dinner. She didn't tell him differently. Her worries were her own. She'd made her choice and she would have to live with it, if she could.

Hand-in-hand, they passed through the foyer headed towards

the living room. Abby was uncommonly nervous. She'd face the Penneys as Jeff's sister-in-law and as a commissioned employee, but as Mason's 'unofficial girlfriend,' it was a whole different ball game.

"Relax." He rubbed her shoulders, sensing her wariness again.

"Just don't leave me alone with them," she whispered.

"I'll stay right by your side," he promised.

"Good."

"Mom, Dad, you remember Tammy's sister Abby…I mean Abigail, don't you?" He sounded like a schoolboy bringing home his prom date.

Pauline sat in an exquisite 19th century Victorian armchair. Abby was immediately entranced. She loved 19th century furniture. Glancing around the room, she saw that the bulk of the furniture was period pieces. Someone with excellent taste and lots of money had decorated this room.

Abby hadn't been granted a complete tour of the Penney home on her consultation visit. Pauline had simply escorted her to the room that would be occupied by Melissa and Megan. She'd even stayed in the room while Abby had taken the appropriate measurements.

Pauline's gaze rested disapprovingly on Abby the moment she stepped into the room. Stanford Penney was more polite in his quiet assessment of his son's dinner guest.

"I'm glad you made it. Mason was about to send out a search party." Tammy came to stand by Abby in a protective gesture.

"Well, I'm here now," she said. "Hello Mr. Penney, Mrs. Penney. Thank you for having me." Her eyes skipped Pauline to rest on Mr. Penney. He was a tall man, broad and sophisticated. Abby wondered briefly how her mother had ever been interested in him. Not that he wasn't attractive, because he had certainly aged well, his graying hair lending an air of distinction to his already important stature. Stanford had inherited his father's money as well as the greeting card business he'd helped build. He was well respected in Manchester and in this house, Abby suspected.

"It wasn't my idea as I'm sure you well know, but since you finally decided to arrive I guess we should eat now." The coldness of Pauline's voice was nothing compared to the piercing stare she gave Abby.

Raised to always respect her elders, Abby's only reply before Pauline could leave the room was, "Nevertheless, it's a pleasure to be here." Mason squeezed her hand with approval and she smiled in his direction.

"Come along, Pauline." Stanford grabbed his wife's elbow, escorting her into the dinning room. They were an odd couple. On the outside they appeared picture perfect but there was something underneath that didn't seem quite right. Abby figured Stanford had quite a handful running a successful business *and* living with Pauline. It couldn't be an easy life he led.

Melissa ran behind her grandparents as Tammy and Jeff followed. Mason shrugged in defeat before leading Abby out of the living room. This was going to be a long meal, Abby thought.

Catered, of course, the meal was fit for a king. Abby doubted that even the pilgrims would have been worthy of this meal. There was enough to feed an army: turkey, ham, candied yams, stuffing, collard greens and much more. Stanford blessed the food and they began to pile their plates. This room followed the same design as the living room and once they were all seated around a beautiful walnut renaissance revival dining table, they began to enjoy the lavish meal.

What could only be described as strained dinner conversation ensued. Pauline's persistent criticism and Stanford's cool annoyance were broken only by Melissa's jubilant toddler talk.

"When will my granddaughter's room be finished, Abigail?" Pauline asked. Her tone indicated that just the sound of Abby's name was annoying.

"The painters are coming on Monday. Perhaps on Wednesday or Thursday we can begin the wallpapering."

"I hope it's worth the money I'm paying for it." Pauline's derogatory tone didn't go unnoticed.

"It will be," Mason chimed in. "I've seen the plans for it. You'll love it."

"Pink. Aunt Abby, I want pink," Melissa chanted.

"I know, sweetie. It will be pink."

"How did you happen to see the plans before I did, Mason?" Pauline asked.

"I was at the shop and Abigail showed them to me," he answered.

"What business would you have at her shop?"

Abby was extremely uncomfortable at the direction this conversation was taking. Tammy, who had been surprisingly quiet until now, decided to add fuel to the already kindling fire.

"They've been spending so much time together lately, I've hardly had a chance to talk to Abby at all." Abby almost choked on the mashed potatoes she had just put in her mouth.

"Mason will be leaving soon and then you can talk to her as much as you'd like," Pauline spat. Abby's already wilted spirits spiraled further downward. Not just because of Pauline's choice of words, more so because Mason didn't deny he was leaving.

The meal progressed with menial chitchat between Jeff and Mason, Jeff and Tammy and at times Stanford contributed a comment or two. He seemed as unhappy as Abby. But Mason didn't say anything to Abby, and Abby ate in silence. Pauline was in her glory; she had won this match and she knew it.

"Do we get cake now, Mama?" Melissa asked.

"We'll get cake at Nana's."

"Yippee, we go to Nana's." Melissa almost bounced right out of her seat.

"Do not yell when you are at the dinner table, Melissa. It isn't polite," Pauline corrected her granddaughter.

"What's polike?" Melissa asked Pauline.

"That's when good, well-mannered people act like good, well-mannered people. It distinguishes us from the people who are not brought up correctly," Pauline explained.

Abby didn't miss the woman's intentional glare in her and Tammy's direction while she explained this point to her grandchild. Melissa simply looked away, her attention being snatched by her father who was making silly faces at her. Abby's attention could not be so easily swayed.

"Thank you for the meal, Mr. and Mrs. Penney, but my parents are expecting me." Abby had endured as much as she could stand. These people had ruined her day and for her own peace of mind she needed to salvage any bit of it she could. She didn't wait for anyone's response, even though she knew Pauline would consider her behavior rude. However, since she already considered Abby one of the people who was 'not brought up correctly,' Abby didn't give a damn what she thought about her at this moment. The sooner she got out of there the better. By the time she reached the front door Mason was on her heels.

"I'll come by later." He helped her with her coat.

"No. Maybe you should stay with your family. This is where you belong." Abby's heart was breaking even as she stared into those dreamy eyes. She didn't think she could stand to be with him another minute, not now that his leaving had been confirmed.

Mason searched her pain-riddled face for some clue as to what was going on. It couldn't simply be his mother, Abby was stronger than that; it had to be something else. In the back of his mind he knew it was most likely his mother's comment about his leaving. This was the beginning of the end, he could tell. Still, he tried to ignore it. "I've been with them, now I want to be with you."

"I don't think that's such a good idea." Abby tried to avoid his questioning stare. She didn't want to make a scene at his parents' house nor did she want to get into the feelings that were running rampant through her right now. She backed out of his reach, not wanting his hands on her any longer.

Mason sighed, thrusting his hands into his pockets. That was the only way he could ensure that he wouldn't touch her. And it was apparent that she did *not* want him to touch her right now. "I know coming here today was hard for you and I appreciate your effort but you shouldn't let her get to you like this."

"She's not the one that I shouldn't have let get to me." Taking a deep breath, Abby took a chance and looked at him. "When were you going to tell me you were leaving? Or weren't you planning to tell me at all? "

He didn't speak. He didn't know what to say. His mother had said that just to get to Abby and it had worked. The problem was it wasn't a lie, so he couldn't use that as a defense. He was going back to Boston. He'd forseen this scene already but a part of him wanted desperately to change the outcome. He didn't want her hating him but didn't really see how he could keep that from happening.

When he didn't answer, Abby turned and opened the door. She walked quickly to her car, refusing to turn back. Mason watched her go in silence. Guilt simmered in his blood, a feeling that was becoming all too familiar to him lately. He had known that it was a mistake to get intimately involved with her. He had known what her expectations were and yet he hadn't been able to resist her. He should have listened to that voice, the one that had warned him repeatedly. Deep down inside he had known that things could easily get out of control. But he had done nothing to prevent it; in fact he'd made them worse.

He had exercised bad judgment once again, this time compromising a woman that he truly cared about. The problem was there was nothing he could do about it. His life in Boston was very demanding as a result of his bad judgment with another woman. He couldn't afford for history to repeat itself. Though the thought of leaving her was painful, it was the only solution. Nell was his priority now.

Abby arrived at her parents' house just in time to help with the coffee and desert. Her father was glad to see her. Her mother, on the other hand, was saddened that she was alone.

"There's my Abby. I knew she wouldn't miss Thanksgiving with her family." He hugged her tightly. With her emotions already in turmoil, she felt the tears threatening to spill and blinked furiously to keep them at bay.

"Daddy, you knew I'd come. I told you I would." Standing beside the old ratty recliner her father had owned for ages Abby felt her heart crumbling piece by piece. It was warm in the living room, the heat from the kitchen engulfing the house. Abby inhaled the smells of home cooking and good old-fashioned apple pie. Anna sat on the couch, a basket of yarn on one side of her as her fingers crocheted furiously.

"I don't know, when a man comes into your daughter's life, her father stops being number one. I understand it but I don't have to like it. Where is your man anyway?" Jim asked the question that had been on the tip of Anna's tongue.

"He stayed with his parents." Abby didn't have the energy to admit that he wasn't her man. They would find that out soon enough. Besides, saying it would mean admitting her mistake and she definitely wasn't ready to do that.

"Oh? Get me some cake and get a piece for yourself too. You're looking a mite skinny there." Her father would never pry. Even knowing that something was wrong with her, he still didn't ask. That was his way. But she knew she couldn't be lucky enough for her mother to afford her the same courtesy. Following her into the kitchen Anna began the assault.

"Abigail Mae, I think it's about time you concentrated on

finding yourself a husband." Pulling two plates out of the cupboard above the sink, Anna placed them on the table with a noisy clank and stared at her daughter.

"I don't need a husband, Mama." She didn't even sound convincing to herself this time.

"How else do you expect to have children? You can't make them by yourself."

"Sure you can, Mama. Science remedied that for women like me." Abby smiled blandly.

"That's not funny, Abigail Mae. Nor is it natural. And I will not have any grandbaby of mine coming from some test tube. That's not the way God intended us to procreate." Anna sliced two healthy chunks of apple pie and placed each on a plate.

"Mama, do we have to talk about this now? Goodness, I'm only twenty-eight and last time I checked it wasn't a crime to be single and childless at my age."

"No, it's not a crime but it sure is a shame. Mason seems like a good boy. Why can't you try harder to hold on to him?" her mother implored.

"I'm not about to try to keep someone who doesn't want to be kept, Mama! If and when I do settle down with a man, you can bet the decision won't be based on my ability to hold on to him or not." Abby stormed out of the kitchen.

Tammy's arrival with the girls shaved some of the tension from the air. Even Jeff looked more relaxed here than he had at his parents' house. Neither he nor Tammy said anything about Mason or where he was. Abby was pleased, or at least she pretended to be.

Why couldn't she have seen it sooner? Why did she have to

wait until it slapped her in the face to realize that Mason was not as emotionally attached to her as she had become to him? At Pauline's tactless mention of him returning to Boston, all hopes of a future with Mason had died. Died before they were born, actually.

They hadn't discussed the specifics of their relationship, she admitted to herself. It was just as much her fault as his, although she would much rather blame him completely. Though she wasn't very experienced with men, she wasn't naïve and she usually knew when a man only wanted sex from her. But as it had turned out, she had apparently been just a diversion for a few weeks. Now Mason would return to Boston as if she had never existed.

No matter how hard it was sure to be, she would forget Mason Penney and resume the solitary life she had been so pleasantly leading prior to Mason. And if she didn't ever get married and have children, then that would be okay too. Her heart burned with that admission.

CHAPTER 5

When Abby walked into her dark apartment, the first thing she noticed was the frantic flashing of the red light of her answering machine. Pressing the butto, she rewound the messages and they began to play while she undressed. General calls, salespersons trying to sell her elaborate computer software and her aunt from Mississippi wishing her a happy Thanksgiving. She was considering erasing the unheard messages when she heard Dr. Craig's raspy voice.

"Abigail, this is Dr. Craig. I need you to call me immediately. It's imperative that I speak with you." She looked at the phone and noted that he had called at two-thirty. It was now almost seven and it was Thanksgiving. Why was he calling her on Thanksgiving? Surely he wasn't in the office working. After the day she had just endured she really wasn't in the mood to return his call. Frowning, she decided to wait until the next day to find out what he wanted. Her iron was probably low again. Anemia was a chronic problem for her. But was it a medical emergency? Abby wasn't sure.

Abby sat in Dr. Craig's waiting room for the second time in as many months. When she returned his phone call on Friday, his secretary had given her the first appointment for Monday morning. This seemed awfully dramatic for a case of anemia. She walked into his office and the first thing she noticed was that he wasn't smiling. Dr. Craig always smiled.

"Hello again," she said cheerfully.

"Have a seat, Abigail." The severity of his tone made her heart race. This was serious.

"I'll get right to the point. When I examined you a few weeks ago, I thought I felt something strange in your right breast. I didn't want to alarm you unnecessarily and I figured it would be best to have a mammogram done anyway." He closed the file on his desk and looked at her for a few minutes. Abby didn't speak. Her throat had suddenly gone dry as if she knew what he was about to say but didn't want to rush him into actually saying it.

"The radiologist called me immediately to inform me that there was a lump of significant concern in your right breast." He waited once again for her to react. She sat perfectly still, knowing there was more.

"It's about the size of a grape, probably 4.5 centimeters in diameter." This time he rose and came to sit in the chair beside her.

"What...what does that mean? Is it cancerous?" Abby spoke in a quiet strained voice.

"We need to find out if it's malignant. I suggest a biopsy as soon as possible."

Something akin to a gasp escaped Abby's throat. This was not happening to her, not now. "Are you telling me that I have breast cancer?"

"I'm telling you that you have a significant-sized lump and it's imperative that we determine its nature. I know this is difficult for you but there is a strong possibility that it is cancerous and that it has already begun to spread to the lymph nodes. We need to find out." Dr. Craig spoke quietly and watched her intently. Reason taking over, Abby stood and walked to the window of his office.

"How soon can it be done?" she asked, her back to him.

With a look of relief, Dr. Craig began to outline a few options. The last thing he wanted was for her to fall apart. He was very fond of Abigail and the Swanson family. His feelings had been just as frazzled as Abby's when he first found out. "There are two routes we can take. One is a fine needle biopsy. That's when a needle is inserted into the breast and a sample of the lump is drawn out. Or we can perform a surgical biopsy wherein an incision is made and we take a sample of the lump, and a few lymph nodes. Considering the size of the lump I would suggest the fine needle biopsy, which we can do as soon as tomorrow. We'll receive the results in a day and then we can decide where to go from there."

"Fine. What time tomorrow?" Turning to him, Abby's face was devoid of emotion.

"Eight o'clock. You can meet me at the hospital."

"I'll be there."

Abby went directly to the shop. She needed to work, needed to find something to occupy her mind. This *thing*, this *lump*, would not bring her down, about that she was determined. She was twenty-eight-years old, for goodness sake; she couldn't possibly have breast cancer. She held firm to the notion that this would turn out to be nothing. Therefore, it would be a waste of time getting upset about it. She had the girls' room to finish and another job waiting in the wings. She was too busy for this to be happening to her now.

At the shop she saw that the deliveryman was waiting for her. The drapes for the room had arrived. She would need to call Pauline to find out a good time to come by and hang them. She didn't look forward to that particular task and decided to put it off until later in the afternoon. After making herself a cup of tea, she inspected the drapes and re-packed them, carrying the box to a table across from her desk. Returning to her chair, she picked up a ring of fabric swatches and began flipping through them absently, thinking of Sarah Byson's home.

Sarah Byson was a very important client. She was almost as wealthy as Pauline, which was the reason for their constant competition with each other. Who had the biggest and most expensive car, the biggest and most expensive jewelry, the best looking home? It was such a headache to have to deal with her but she paid well and the job was almost done. If she could just find the perfect fabric for the window treatment in the living room, she could kiss Mrs. Byson and her thirty-acre estate goodbye. She sipped her cup of tea and allowed her mind to wander through the many patterns and styles. The loud shrill of the ringing phone interrupted her.

"Hello, Gabby." Her pulse quickened at the sound of his voice. She hadn't seen or spoken to him since Thanksgiving a few days ago. She was beginning to think he had gone back to Boston. She wouldn't deny that she was glad he had called but she couldn't afford to have him toying with her emotions again.

"Hello, Mason. What can I do for you?" She decided to stay cool and aloof.

"I wanted to see you. I was wondering if I could come over tonight?" He sounded distant but still too close, if that were possible.

"I'm really busy. Is there a problem?" she asked.

"No," he began. "Yes, there is. We need to talk, Gabby."

She couldn't speak for fear that he would hear the emotion building in her voice.

"Gabby? I know you're there. Forget it. I'll be there at six." He hung up the phone.

This day was getting worse by the moment. For the past four days she had been trying her best not to think of Mason or what she thought they'd had between them. It was hard. She ached for him. Not just physically, but mentally.

He was fun to be around and he always showed genuine interest in her and what she thought. Although he avoided any conversation about serious matters, such as their future, he was otherwise the perfect friend. Besides Tammy, she had never had any close friends. She had always felt so much more mature than others her age. Then Mason had come along and opened the door to something she'd never thought she would have.

She should have been smarter, more realistic about their relationship. She should have considered beforehand that this was not a serious matter for him. But she had been hopeful. She had been ready to take a chance. Hadn't that been the way she'd convinced herself that sleeping with a man before marriage was worth it?

He probably wanted to tell her face to face that he was leaving, to ease his conscience. It would break her heart, but she wouldn't let it break her spirit. A person could still function with a broken heart.

But a confrontation with Mason was not what she needed today of all days. It wouldn't do anything to help the flurry of emotions she was already experiencing. She didn't know if she had the strength to deal with him *and* the worry that she might have breast cancer. Now, for the first time since leaving the doctor's office, she allowed herself to consider seriously that possibility. She wanted to cry. But what good would it do? It wouldn't remove the lump in her breast nor would it soothe the pain in her heart. No, the best thing would be for her to deal with each situation as it came.

She finished going through swatches, selecting three that would match Mrs. Byson's living room. Her next task was the mail. As soon as she began going through the tall stack that had piled up on the floor inside the doorway since last Wednesday, she received a phone call from the real estate agent inquiring as to when she would have a crew available to work on the Rubaker house. She had completely forgotten about that job. As important as it was, she couldn't afford to forget about it. She'd promised them that they could begin construction the first of the year, which meant that she needed to confirm the availability of her father's crew. He had agreed to do the job at the price that had been quoted to Abby by the real estate brokers, which was a blessing because she would have probably lost the bid if her father hadn't agreed to do it so cheaply.

Abby dealt with the real estate agent and then got on the

phone to a furniture store. She was trying to track down just the right crib for Megan when Tammy came in.

"Hi. What are you doing here?" she asked.

"Queen Mother-in-Law wanted her granddaughters to meet her sister, who's in town for the week, so she came by this morning and picked them up." Tammy plopped down into the chair across from Abby's desk.

"You let them go?" Abby was surprised.

"Yeah, girl, I need a break. I've been running nonstop since I got home from the hospital. A few hours of peace will do me some good. And besides, I think Pauline and Mr. Penney are having some problems, so this is a good diversion for her. Why are you so shocked? Melissa's stayed with her before."

"It's just that she's so nasty to us, I'm afraid one day she might take it out on them."

"Now you don't believe that. You've seen her with them. She loves them in *spite* of their mother." Tammy saw something different in her sister today. "What's bothering you? You seem awfully wound up."

"I'm trying to get her room finished as soon as possible, so I won't have to deal with Mrs. Penney. After Thanksgiving's fiasco I can do without ever seeing or speaking to Mrs. Penney for a very long time." Abby spoke in a surly tone.

"Is that all?" Tammy probed.

"Yes, that's all." Abby picked up another envelope and slashed through it with the letter opener.

"Have you seen Mason?" Tammy asked nonchalantly.

The letter opener stilled in Abby's hand; so this was her reason for coming by. Abby's day continued to get worse. She didn't want to have this conversation.

"No, I haven't." Continuing with her task, Abby stuffed the bill for pink paint back into its envelope and pushed it aside.

"Are you upset that you haven't seen him?"

She couldn't lie to Tammy. She never could. "I wouldn't say upset."

"What would you call it? C'mon, Gabby, what's going on with you two? One minute you're inseparable and the next you both go into seclusion. What's the deal?" When Tammy folded her arms across her chest, silver bangles clinked at her wrists.

"I don't know." That was the truth; she really didn't know what was going on.

"You slept with him, didn't you?" Tammy screeched. Large hoop earrings smacked against the sides of her face as she sat bolt upright.

"Do you have to tell all of Manchester?" Defeated, Abby slammed the letter opener on the desk.

"I can't believe it! Abigail Mae Swanson has finally lost her virginity." Tammy was a little too excited, smiling and clucking her teeth.

"It's not a big deal."

"Yes it is, because if you slept with him then things must be serious."

"I thought that things could become serious, so I slept with him. Not one of my best judgments, I now realize. But I don't know what he wants so I've decided to steer clear of him. I can't afford a one way relationship, nor do I want one." Abby felt a surge of strength as she spoke the words, even though they were only half true.

"I think he really likes you. I could tell that on Thanksgiving, the way he was worried about you. You should have seen him; I thought he would wear out that carpet pacing the floor. And after you left, he looked like he had lost his best friend."

That made Abby feel a little better. Maybe he was as miserable as she had been—good, he deserved it!

"Oh, come on, even a dog misses a good bone when it's gone. That doesn't mean he wants the same things I do. I'm not getting any younger, you know. I need to be looking for a suitable husband, not just a lover, regardless of how good a lover he is." She smiled. She had missed the chance to tell her about her first experience but she was going to now.

"Good? What do you mean *good*? Tell me everything and don't leave out a single thing. Not a movement or a moan." Tammy sat on the edge of her chair. They talked for a while longer before Tammy had to leave to go to the market. But she made Abby promise to call her that evening so they could finish talking.

Abby was alone with her thoughts again. Talking about her sexual experience with Mason had excited her. She didn't know that could happen by just talking. Without thinking she reached down to touch her right breast. As if it were scorching hot, she yanked her hand away. The realization that she had a lump in one of her breasts was back. She didn't want to feel it or think about it. She wanted to forget about it. She went into the bathroom to douse her face with cold water. It was five-thirty and she needed to get home. She stared into the mirror a long time. It didn't look like she was sick. She turned to get a sideways view of her breasts. They looked perfectly normal, on the outside.

"Lord, please let this be okay," she prayed.

Within ten minutes of walking through the door to her apartment and putting her bags down, the doorbell rang. She opened it to see Mason standing on the other side. When she let him in, he crossed the room and took a seat on the couch without saying a word. She noticed that he looked really tired—good, he deserved that too.

"Hello, Mason. I see you were serious about us needing to talk." She took a seat across from him and tried to remain calm.

"Don't do that." His words were harsh. Her coldness hurt him more than he cared to admit.

"Don't do what?"

"Don't sit there and act like you don't know what this is about or that you don't care. I know you better than that." His arms rested on his knees and his angry gray eyes glared at her.

"You don't know me as well as you think," she said weakly. Damn, she couldn't even lie to him.

"I know that I hurt you and I want to apologize." His tone changed and his eyes fell to the floor.

She looked at him, really looked at him. He wasn't tired. He was sorry. His face depicted the pain she felt.

"There are things that you just don't understand," he began.

"Apology accepted. Is that all?" she interrupted. It was important for her to make a clean break. She couldn't allow her emotions to rule this time, no matter how strong they were.

"Damn it, Gabby! Are you even going to give me a chance to

explain?" He got out of the chair and crossed the room to stand in front of her.

"No. Any explanations you may have now are too late to mean anything to me." Before he could answer she stood to face him. "Mason, I really don't need any explanations from you and I certainly don't need your pity. If I was foolish enough to believe that we had a good thing going, then that's my problem, not yours. I just wish you could have been a little more considerate about the whole matter."

"What are you talking about?"

"I'm talking about sleeping with me, spending time with me, knowing all along that you never intended for this to be anything except a brief fling until you returned to Boston."

"I never said that's what this was." No, he'd never said it, but he'd certainly thought it.

"You never said it wasn't either. But that was just as much my fault as it was yours, so I'd just as soon get on with the rest of my life without you." She tried to take a step back but the chair stopped her.

"Look, I told you I didn't know where this was leading, I told you that this was the first emotional relationship I had ever had." He tried to make her understand what he was having a hard time grasping himself. She was too close; he wanted to touch her, to hold her one more time.

"Yes, you did. But what you neglected to tell me was that you were too afraid to even give this 'emotional relationship' a try!" Abby yelled, anger refusing to lie dormant any longer.

"What do you want from me?" Mason threw his hands up in the air. He didn't know where to go from here. He couldn't give her what she needed and he couldn't walk away.

"Nothing. I don't want anything from you. So you can take your apology and your pitifully juvenile excuses and get out of my house." Her voice was calm even as her hands shook at her sides.

"Is that what you want?"

Calmly, seriously and hating every syllable, she looked him directly in the eye so that there would be no misunderstandings and said, "Yes, that's what I want."

"Does it even matter what I want?"

"No, Mason, it doesn't. I gave you the privilege of choosing before. I won't make that mistake again." She felt the tears coming and for all her bold talk she was deathly afraid that he would believe her and walk out of her life. He walked to the door and opened it to leave. Abby held her breath, desperately wanting him to come back.

"I wish I could make you understand, Gabby, but I don't know that I can. I'm sorry if that's not good enough." He saw the tears welling up in her eyes before she turned her back to him. She heard the click of the door quietly closing as the first warm teardrop rolled down her face.

"Coward." She wiped her tears and headed for the bathroom; she had a big day ahead of her tomorrow. Mason Penney could not be on her mind. There were more important things for her to think about.

Abby ran herself a bath and sank into its soothing warmth. Once again she touched her right breast, wondering why she'd never noticed the lump before. Because she rarely performed a breast exam, that's why. She moved her fingers around, familiarizing herself what Dr. Craig had seen on the mammogram. There was a hard mass on the outer side of her right breast. Her fingers hovered over the lump as she considered all the things that could possibly happen. She thought of all the things she had yet to accomplish. If she could not fight this disease, she would never have the chance to do those things. All hope for a loving relationship had just walked out the door, taking with it the dream of having a baby. So what difference did this make now? It made all the difference, she acknowledged. She was too young to have this happening to her.

Exhausted after the whirlwind of emotions she had gone through, she collapsed onto her bed after completing her bath. As she lay on the fluffy peach comforter, all sorts of thoughts whirled through her mind and conspired to keep rest at bay. Rising, she went to the kitchen and fixed a cup of tea. While she waited for it to cool, she looked out the window.

Manchester, by no means a big city, was quiet and still. Lights still shone in from buildings in the distance but most of the population no doubt was asleep. As Abby stood at the window, she saw a car stop for a red light, then go on its way. The traffic lights continued to change at three-minute intervals. All the normal functions still occurred while the citizens slept. What if she chose not to sleep? What if she chose to stay awake? Would that change anything that had happened in the last twenty-four hours or that would happen in the next twenty-four? Would staying awake make anything better? At around midnight, when she could stand it no longer, she called Tammy.

"Jeff? I'm sorry to call so late but I really need to speak to Tammy."

"Is something wrong, Gabby?" he asked.

"No, I just need to talk to Tammy."

Regardless of her answer, she sounded distraught to him so he didn't waste any more time asking questions.

"Gabby, what's wrong?" Tammy asked sleepily.

"I...I just needed to talk to somebody."

"What's wrong? Did Mason do something to you?" It was uncharacteristic of Abby to call in the middle of the night and sound this way.

"No," she managed to say through her tears.

"Okay. Gabby, you hang up this phone and I'll be right there. Do you hear me? Hang up the phone. I'm on my way." Abby did as she was told.

Fifteen minutes later Tammy was at her door and using her key to let herself in. Still in her nightclothes and robe, she rushed into the dark apartment and found her sister lying on the couch crying pitifully. Tammy lifted her so that she could sit beside her. Cradling her, she rocked her gently until the crying ceased.

"What's the matter?"

Abby couldn't bring herself to say. She took Tammy's hand in hers and lifted it to the spot on her breast.

Tammy felt the lump and fear etched her pretty face. "Oh, Gabby." Her sharp intake of breath told that she understood the implications. "Have you seen the doctor?"

"Yes. He suggested a biopsy immediately."

"What's immediately?"

"Tomorrow...I mean today." Abby wiped her eyes and sat up straight. "I'm sorry to get you out of bed but I didn't know who else to call."

"When did you find out?"

"This morning."

"And you waited all day to call me. Damn it, Gabby! I was at the shop, why didn't you tell me? I thought you were upset about Mason. You should have said something." Tammy was visibly aggravated now. "What time do you go? I'll have to find a babysitter. Did you tell Mama and Daddy?"

Abby shook her head no. "I don't want to upset them. The doctor said that it might not even be cancerous." The look on Tammy's face told Abby that she didn't believe her.

"That doesn't matter; they still have a right to know. Does Mason know?" she finally asked.

"No. I didn't see the point of telling him either. It's not like we have a relationship or anything."

Tammy recognized that this was not the time to discuss Mason. "C'mon, get some clothes, you're going home with me. And we'll go to the doctor's together tomorrow...or in a few hours." Tammy looked down at her watch.

Abby didn't argue with her, she was too tired; she simply did as she was told.

They arrived at the hospital early at Tammy's insistence. She had numerous questions for the doctor. When her name was called, Abby hesitated for a second. Tammy took her hand and they walked in together and saw there was another person with Dr. Craig.

"Tamara, it's good to see you up and around. I'm glad you

came with Abigail today." Dr. Craig then turned his attention to Abby and said in a softer tone, "Good morning Abigail. I'd like to introduce you to Dr. Susan Elise. She will be your surgeon this morning. Dr. Elise comes highly recommended by both the staff and patients of Manchester University," Dr. Craig explained.

"Hello, Dr. Elise. This is my sister, Tamara Penney." Abby looked at the tall woman who didn't look much older than she did.

"Mrs. Penney, Abigail, have a seat. We'd like to start this morning with answering before the procedure any questions that you might have," Dr. Elise stated.

"How long will it take before we know if it's cancerous or not?" Tammy asked immediately.

"Because of its size and location, Dr. Craig and I agree that a fine needle biopsy is the best method. It will ensure that we have the results in twenty-four hours. Once we have the results, we will call Ms. Swanson and set up an appointment to discuss our next step."

"Next step? You sound like you already know it's cancerous," Tammy argued.

"We don't know anything for sure, Mrs. Penney. But I've seen lumps like this before and they are almost always cancerous. Although there is a good chance that it has not spread to the lymph nodes yet, the sooner we find out officially, the better." Dr. Elise looked from Tammy to Abby and back again. "Are we ready?" she asked. Abby nodded.

Abby was taken to a room where she put on the all-too-familiar gown and lay on the table. One of the nurses left the room to get Tammy at her request. While she was alone, she said a prayer, asking not for a miracle but for the strength to survive whatever it was they found out.

In moments Tammy was at her side holding her hand. Abby could tell that Tammy had been crying.

"Some support you are, crybaby," Abby teased.

"Oh, shut up." Tammy sniffled and grabbed a tissue from her purse.

"Tammy? I'm scared," Abby admitted.

"I know. I'm scared too. But it'll be okay. Whatever it is, it will be okay." Abby nodded and closed her eyes.

When Dr. Elise returned to the room, Tammy was escorted out and Abby struggled to keep from bawling like a baby. Dr. Elise and two nurses moved around the room, readying their supplies and preparing to begin the next phase of Abby's life.

At each step the procedure was carefully explained. A tumor was a solid mass, thus the need to remove some for testing to be performed by the pathologist. Fluid in the needle was a good sign. Abby silently prayed for fluid. A nurse held Abby's hand as the needle was inserted into her breast to the right of her nipple. She watched the needle going in on the picture displayed via the monitor. It looked like a tiny dot moving into the dark spot in her breast. Abby winced at the pain. Never in her life had she been able to stand pain, and she was not surprised to feel more tears streaming down her cheeks.

The needle came out dry.

As the attending nurse prepared the slides for biopsy, Abby went into the bathroom to get dressed. Tammy was allowed back into the room and immediately questioned the doctor. "It's bad, isn't it?"

"Your sister is going to need your support to get through this, Mrs. Penney. This will not be an easy battle." Dr. Elise left the room. "I will call as soon as I get the official results."

CHAPTER 6

Abby and Tammy went back to Tammy's house. Abby wanted the distraction the girls would provide, at least Melissa would anyway. They stopped at the senior Penney residence to pick them up. Abby moaned as she saw Mason's car in the driveway.

"He was the only babysitter I could get on such short notice," Tammy explained.

"You didn't tell him why you needed a sitter, did you?"

"No," Tammy said.

Abby had a monstrous headache and she was hungry. Mason didn't walk Tammy to the car and the ride home was filled with three-year-old chatter. Melissa recited all the things Uncle Mase let her do. When they arrived at the house, Abby called the store to check her messages. The furniture was in and would be delivered on Friday and her mother was worried about her. She decided she wouldn't call her mother back until she could lie convincingly.

Then there was a call from Mason.

"Just wanted to hear your voice," his voice echoed in her ear. It was amazing how in such a short span of time her life had been turned upside down. What would happen next? she wondered before she fell asleep on the couch.

She awoke to Tammy shaking her vigorously.

"Gabby, Gabby, it's the doctor. She won't talk to me. She'll only speak to you."

"What time is it?" With one eye open, she slowly came awake.

"It's six o'clock. Here, take the phone." Tammy thrust the cordless phone into her hand. She had slept for more than four hours. That was more sleep than she had gotten last night.

"Hello?" Abby said slowly.

"Abigail? This is Dr. Elise. I rushed your tests through and the results are back." Only a moment's hesitation before she went on. "It's as we expected. The biopsy is positive."

Abby heard the words and felt the weight of the world coming down on her. Tammy stood right beside her watching for any clue. Abby held the phone and listened carefully to what the doctor was saying, only nodding her head or mumbling in compliance. When the conversation was finished, she pushed the red button that disconnected the line and set the phone gently in her lap. Her hands were shaking as Tammy grabbed them and held them tightly.

"You will beat this, Gabby. Do you understand? You will beat this...*we* will beat this." Without a word from Abby, Tammy had known. Tears came freely now. The sisters held each other, rocking back and forth, crying and praying. That's how Jeff found them when he came into the house.

"What's the matter? And don't tell me nothing again." He threw his bag down and his voice was demanding as he looked from one sister to the other.

Abby cleared her throat and because Jeff was the closest thing to a brother she would ever have, she told him the truth. He hugged her tightly, a little too tightly, but Abby didn't complain.

"Everything will be okay. You just be strong. You've got our love and support and you can stay here as long as you want." His words were comforting but they just made her cry more.

"I'm going to go home now," Abby said abruptly.

"No!" Jeff and Tammy spoke simultaneously.

"You will stay here with us. This is no time to be alone," Tammy insisted.

"Tammy's right. You need to be with family now." Melissa came into the living room, looked from one adult to the next then burst into tears herself. Abby sat down and scooped her up with her left arm—her right side was still sore. "Don't cry, honey. It's okay."

"Everybody's cryin'," Melissa hiccupped.

"It's happy tears. Happy tears, you know, when you're happy about something."

"Why are we happy?" she asked.

"Because we're all living and we're all family and we love each other." That was the best Abby could do, and with her niece sitting proudly on her lap in her little pink dress trimmed in white eyelet, she made some decisions.

She would read everything, she would learn everything and she would be prepared mentally and emotionally for whatever was handed to her. In the other room Megan gave a wail, signaling that she was hungry. And as she held Melissa and Tammy fed Megan, Abby thanked the Lord for the gift of family.

Despite their insistence that she stay, Abby returned home that evening after dinner. She lay on her bed in her nightgown.

Before slipping the gown on, she'd glanced in the mirror, staring blankly at her now swollen breast. She had decided that she *could* and *would* handle this. She just needed to take one step at a time. Jeff and Tammy would be there for her. That would be a tremendous help.

She needed to tell her parents. But not just yet, she told herself. Not just yet. She needed to get a firm grip on the situation herself first. Then she would tell them.

Abby was thankful that things had ended between her and Mason. He shouldn't have to settle for a sick woman. He deserved better than that. And if it was as bad as they thought, she would not only be sick, but incomplete as well. It just wasn't fair.

Still, she had other things in her life: her nieces, her work, and her family. She would be just fine. She kept telling herself that as another part of her contemplated the emptiness of what she would never have.

There was an urgent knock at the door. She figured it was just Tammy coming to check up on her and wondered why she just hadn't used her key. She didn't bother with putting on a robe but opened the door and was shocked to see Mason standing there.

"Mason! What are you doing here?"

In response, he hugged her tightly, his hands splaying across her back. Moments later he grasped her shoulders and held her away from him. He looked at her intently, as if searching for something. What was wrong with him?

Giving her a little shake, he questioned, "Why didn't you tell me?"

"Tell you what?" She was confused.

"About the tumor."

Abby felt sick just hearing him say it. Damn Jeff and Tammy. They were supposed to keep it quiet.

"Because it's none of your business." Moving out of his arms she walked away, hoping he would take the hint and leave. At the same time she wished he would ignore her and stay.

Closing the door behind him, Mason followed her into the living room. "What do you mean, 'none of my business'?"

"It's my problem, Mason. Not yours. So if you're here out of some misguided sense of guilt, you might as well turn right around and go home."

Mason was looking at her strangely. "You really shouldn't answer your door wearing only…that piece of material." He looked her up and down, desire evident in his face.

She looked down, seeing what he saw. Her nightgown was thin pink satin and she wore no underwear. Beneath his blatant perusal her nipples hardened, straining against the sheer material, giving him a glorious view. She covered her breasts instinctively, wincing slightly as her fingers grazed the bruised breast.

"Will you stop it?" she screeched.

"You've already started it." He walked toward her slowly, giving her enough time to run should she choose to do so. She didn't. She felt a low throbbing between her legs and her breathing hitched.

She wanted him as much as it appeared he wanted her. But more than that, she *needed* him. She needed to feel whole one last time. Mason could give her that, even if he couldn't give her anything else.

She met him halfway. When his hands cupped her face, she

closed her eyes and turned to kiss his palms.

"Gabby, I need you so much. I need to touch you, to taste you." Whispering, he placed kisses along her face, down her neckline. He bent over, scooped her up at the knees and carried her into the bedroom. He laid her gently on the bed, peeling the nightgown from her body slowly.

For long, excruciating moments, he just stared at her. His fingers lightly brushed her stomach, marveling at the creamy caramel tone of her skin; his tongue quickly delved into her navel. Her hands gripped the back of his head, guiding his movements. He laid his head on her body, just listening to her heartbeat.

"Mason…?" Her voice seemed quiet in the stillness of the room.

He rose from the bed and slowly removed his clothes before returning to lie beside her. They didn't speak. They didn't need to. Their need for each other was desperate and unspoken. Their connection was sealed.

Abby took his hand, gently placing it on her left breast. She was eager for him to caress it as he had done so many times before. She wanted him to know that she was still a woman, that his touch was still welcome.

Mason pulled his hand away. His eyes held her gaze as he brought his hand up to touch the right breast instead. He lightly fingered the bruise where the needle had been inserted, carefully applying pressure. He felt the lump.

Abby held her breath against the pain. He dipped his head and kissed that breast, his lips grazing her skin softly, lovingly. "You are so beautiful, Gabby," he murmured. "So beautiful."

That night they made sweet, slow love. Mason was tender and affectionate. Abby was willing and obliging. This was what she needed. Whether or not it lasted didn't matter—it was perfect for now.

She wouldn't think about whether or not he would stay around after tonight. That wasn't her goal this time. Mason had initiated her womanhood and if she were never to experience this type of intimacy again, she wanted her last time to be with him.

Afterwards they lay in the dark remembering childhood events, each ignoring the adult problems they faced. Abby was content. She fell asleep in his arms, her spirit a bit lighter because he was with her.

In the morning as sunlight peeked through the blinds, Abby rolled over to reach for Mason. He wasn't there. She shouldn't have cared. She told herself it didn't matter but nonetheless, she felt the sting of rejection once again. "Stop it, silly girl." Admonishing herself, she slapped her hand against the empty pillow where he had lain only hours before.

He's free to go. That's what you wanted. That's best.

Her appointment with Dr. Elise was at ten and it was already five after nine. She got out of the bed and showered, slipped into a pair of jeans and put on a big sweatshirt. She had become self-conscious of her breasts now, even though through her clothes it was impossible to tell anything was wrong. But on the inside, she knew.

She walked into the living room to get her purse and her jacket and saw his note.

Gabby,

I had to go back to Boston. I'm sorry I didn't say something last night but I didn't want to spoil the moment. Besides, you had enough on your mind without me adding to it. We probably shouldn't have let things get carried away last night, but I felt like we needed it to get out of each other's system. I'm sure everything will be fine with you medically. I've taken the liberty of referring several good surgeons for you and I'll be keeping tabs on your condition. I can't give you what you want but it doesn't stop me from caring. I'll keep in touch.

Mason

She didn't have time to cry or to let the reality of what he had written sink in. Tammy was at the door to pick her up. She crumpled the paper and stuffed it into her purse. In the car they rode in silence, Abby thinking of Mason and their last night together.

"I know you don't want to talk about it, but I didn't tell Jeff that it was a secret. So he inadvertently mentioned it to Mason last night. You should have seen the way he rushed right out of the house to find you when he found out. I think he may be just a little bit in love with you, Gabby," Tammy told her during the drive.

"Tammy, don't. I can't do this right now. Okay?" She couldn't allow herself to dream. She wouldn't fool herself with the fantasy of Mason loving her, no matter how much she wanted to believe it. It would never be and she needed to accept that. She had a lot ahead of her; it was best if she stayed focused.

"Hello, Abigail," Dr. Elise said brightly.

"Hello," Abby responded, not so brightly.

"Let's get right to it. Initially I wanted you to meet Dr. Lewis, an oncologist I've worked with on several occasions. But when I got in this morning I found Dr. St. John, who usually practices in New York, waiting on me. Dr. Sarah St. John, this is Abigail Swanson and her sister Mrs. Penney. Is that correct?" she asked Tammy.

"Tammy is fine. It's nice to meet you, Dr. St. John." Tammy shook the woman's outstretched hand.

"Same here. I received a call early yesterday evening from a friend of mine and a personal friend of yours, Abigail." Before she could say more, Abby knew who it was. "Dr. Mason Penney. We met in med school and we've kept in touch. He explained your situation to me and I was eager to help."

"I'll have to thank him the next time I see him," Abby said blankly.

Dr. St. John asked Abby to undress and put on a gown. The room was silent as they waited for her to begin the physical examination. She was very young and very pretty, Abby noted. She wondered briefly how well she and Mason knew each other and then fought to erase the thought from her mind.

The examination was thorough, with Dr. St. John asking questions while feeling her breast. The mammography film was displayed for the doctor's easy reference. The dark section was clearly visible and Dr. St. John explained that Abby had two options. The tumor was about 4.5 centimeters. Based on the size of her breasts, Abby could have a lumpectomy, which would require removing about half of the breast or a modified mastectomy, removing the entire breast.

One critical factor was the size of the tumor in relation to the size of the breast. A 4.5-centimeter tumor in a large breast, which

Abby had, would almost certainly dictate the lumpectomy. In a lumpectomy the cancerous cells were removed, along with a border of non-cancerous cells, to insure that nothing was left behind that might cause a later recurrence. But the breast would be mutilated on one side.

The other option, a mastectomy, could be followed by immediate breast reconstruction, which was an important factor in Abby's decision. She wanted to remain as whole as she possibly could after this ordeal. While it was apparent what procedure Dr. St. John preferred, the decision was Abby's. Tammy absorbed all of the information given by Dr. St. John. She gave names and numbers of good plastic surgeons as well as the name and number of another oncologist for Abby to obtain a second opinion. Abby felt secure in Dr. St. John's analysis but with Tammy's insistence, she decided that she would get the second opinion.

Two days later they were in yet another doctor's office. This was Dr. Nova, an older man who reminded Abby of a Nazi. His office was located in Trenton, a long forty-five minute drive from Manchester. After a similar examination, Dr. Nova gave the same diagnosis. His only variation was his opinion that the lumpectomy would be best. But that was out of the question for Abby. She did not want her breast to look as if it had been ripped to shreds. Not that it made a difference; in all likelihood no one would be seeing her body again anyway.

Her thoughts shifted to Mason and the fact that he had been gone a couple of days now. What was he doing? And *who* was he doing it with? These questions sat like bricks in her chest. With ferocious strength, she pushed them aside to deal with the matter at hand.

Later that evening, after much prayer and consideration, Abby decided for sure that she would have the mastectomy. The next morning she called Dr. St. John, who had returned to New York, to find out how soon the surgery could be done. There was a risk of the cancer spreading to the lymph nodes so Dr. St. John suggested the following week. Abby reluctantly agreed.

It was only two weeks until Christmas and she still hadn't finished Melissa's room. She would get that out of the way this week; they wanted her to be well rested, as the surgery would likely drain all of her energy. She and Tammy would travel to New York for the surgery to be performed at the City Medical Center where Dr. St. John was the head of the oncology department.

Abby would have the reconstructive surgery done at the same time to cut down on the surgeries. Then they would discuss chemotherapy. It was very overwhelming, but to her credit, Abby was handling it very well. She knew what she had to do and she was going to do it.

She worked throughout the day, stopping only once for lunch. Her afternoon went uneventfully until the door swung open at four o'clock. Pauline made a graceful entrance wearing a chic Versace suit and a brilliant smile. The ice blue color of the suit highlighted the silver streaks in Pauline's hair. Her make-up was flawless. Abby could only assume that she had come to reiterate the fact that Mason had gone back to Boston, just as she had predicted.

"Abigail, I see you're back to working alone," she gloated.

"I don't understand your meaning." Abby's voice was flat as she glanced up from her desk at Pauline.

"It's simple, dear. I don't see anyone in here that shouldn't be." Slipping her matching Coach bag off her shoulder, Pauline eyed the empty chair across from Abby's desk and cleared her throat.

Abby looked at the chair and back to Pauline pursing her lips. With a raised brow, Abby waited for Pauline to say what she wanted.

Pauline rolled her eyes and took a seat, placing her purse on her lap. "Oh, by the way, Mason called this morning. He wanted me to know that he had decided to open his own practice. Isn't that wonderful? It's such a shame that it has to be in Boston, but such is life." Pauline's tone was sarcastic, her smile fake. Her eyes watched Abby carefully, waiting for a response.

"Did you come all the way into town to tell me this or is there something of importance you wish to discuss with me?" Abby asked impatiently.

"Aren't we in a snit today? Be careful, dear, I am paying you, you know," Pauline pointed out. "I'll just get to the real purpose of my visit. Mr. Penney and I will be out of town this weekend and I thought this would be an ideal time for you to finish up. Melissa loved the wallpaper." Removing leather gloves from her hands, she casually placed them in her bag.

"I know, she told me. This weekend is fine. I just spoke to my furniture supplier and he'll have the crib and bed delivered tomorrow. Everything should be finished by Tuesday." Thank the Lord.

"That's wonderful. Just in time for Christmas. I guess I won't expect to see you on Christmas with Mason being gone, although he mentioned that he might come home for Christmas Day. With all the women he knows in Boston, I guess he'll probably bring one of them with him." Pauline rose with poise, staring down at Abby.

Abby thought she was going to say something else. For a moment Pauline had looked at her as if she'd sensed something was not quite right. Not that Abby thought she cared, but her look almost gave the impression that she knew what was going on. As quickly as Abby noted the change, Pauline's features tightened and she moved towards the door.

Abby, already weary from her big decision and the upcoming events, felt a flurry of emotions at the thought of Mason returning to Manchester so soon. Still, she refused to let Pauline have the last word. "You know, Mrs. Penney, I was thinking maybe I could bring a date and come over since I had such a good time on Thanksgiving."

Game and set. Abby almost cheered. Pauline's scowl was ever so rewarding and the sight of her leaving was heaven sent.

Abby's message light was flashing wildly when she entered her apartment. She was almost too afraid to listen to it. She didn't need any more bad news. Reluctantly, she pressed the button while she flipped through the mail.

Tammy checking on her, her mother inviting her to dinner tomorrow night and Dr. St. John's office confirming their arrangements for next week. The last message was brief: *"Hi, I spoke to Sarah today and she told me about the surgery. Everything will be fine. She's very good at what she does. I'll call you afterwards to see how everything went."*

Pressing the button to erase all the messages, Abby thought that Mason certainly was keeping close tabs on her for a person who wasn't ready for an emotional relationship. She tried to ignore the giddy feeling she had gotten from hearing his voice. She missed him terribly but didn't have the nerve to call him. He must have been a little afraid of talking to her personally too, because he could have called the shop if he'd really wanted to speak to her.

The room was lovely. The top portion of the wall was painted dusty rose and a festive ribbon and bow border separated the paint from the rosebud wallpaper. In the far corner was a 'belly-up' chaise lounge chair, representing the ultimate source of total relaxation. A white alabaster crib matched the four-poster white bed, and both were covered in comforters that coordinated with the ribbon and bow border on the wall.

Abby had filled the open spaces with teddy bears and dolls. A large fluffy pink rug and big soft pink and yellow pillows flanked the section off to the east corner. It was simply beautiful. Melissa would be pleased and when Megan was old enough, so would she. But most of all it would impress Pauline, although she was sure Pauline would never admit it.

The drive to her parents' house later that afternoon was filled with nerves and jittery emotions. After a long conversation with Tammy earlier in the day, she had reluctantly agreed to attend tonight's family dinner. Tammy had insisted that she tell her parents about the surgery tonight, going so far as to threaten to tell them herself. Abby had finally given in and called her mother to confirm she would be there.

Abby stepped onto the big porch, stopping just as she reached the door. She had played on this porch as a little girl. Glancing into the east corner, she could picture Tammy and herself playing jacks while the sun beamed down on their backs and freeze cups that they had bought from Mrs. Williams down the road melted in Styrofoam cups.

Turning in the opposite direction, she saw in her mind's eye a rickety baby stroller with one wheel missing and a doll whose hair had been so tangled she couldn't even get the comb through it. She smiled at the memories.

She loved this house, loved her childhood—now those things seemed even more precious to her. Her family seemed more precious to her. She wasn't ready to leave them. She wasn't ready to die. Biting on her knuckle was the only way to stop the tears. *Get it together girl,* she told herself. *You can do this.* Reaching for the doorknob, she turned it and let herself in. The heat hit her as she crossed the threshold, and comfort and serenity took hold. The smell of dinner cooking and the sight of her father sitting in his recliner touched her heart. Loyalty and love swelled in her chest. Jeff sat on the end of the sofa while Melissa wandered around getting into everything. Family. How would she cope if she had to leave them?

Moving into the kitchen, Abby got a grip on her souring emotions and helped with dinner preparations. At the table conversation was casual and lively, with Melissa occasionally offering light banter.

"Tam, you've been awfully quiet this evening, is something wrong?" Jim asked.

"Not with me." Tammy's eyes were on her plate now, but just a second before they had locked with Abby's across the table.

Jim hadn't missed the subtle action. "Abby?"

All eyes were on her. She wanted to bolt.

Jeff didn't miss a beat. "Melissa, honey, why don't you help me check on Megan?" Lifting her from her seat, he carried the little girl into the other room. When they were out of the room, everyone waited expectantly for Abby to speak.

"Abigail Mae, is something the matter? Are you pregnant?" Anna's voice was a cross between elation and distress.

"No, Mama. I'm not pregnant. I have…um…the doctors say that…that…. " Abby couldn't find the words.

"For God's sake, Gabby!" Tammy yelled impatiently. "She has breast cancer."

"Tamara Faye, you will not take the Lord's name in vain in this house again! Do you hear me child?" Anna scorned her daughter.

"Yes, Mama." Tammy rolled her eyes at her sister.

"Pipe down, Anna. Did she say you have breast cancer?" Jim watched Abby, waiting for her answer.

"Yes, Daddy. That's what she said." Taking a deep breath, she continued, "I have to have a mastectomy."

"What? When did this happen? How come you didn't tell somebody, girl?" Jim huffed, throwing his napkin down over his plate.

"I didn't think it was a big deal, until now." Abby spoke softly.

"We'll have to get a second opinion and a third if need be. I don't want them cutting into you without good cause," Anna said.

"We've already gotten a second opinion, Mama. This is the only way. The tumor is very large and they need to be sure they get it all, so she's going to have the mastectomy," Tammy said simply, as if there was no need to question the diagnosis any further.

"How do you know so much?" Jim turned his attention to his elder and more talkative child.

"I went to the doctor with her," Tammy mumbled, never having been able to stand her father's close scrutiny.

"You told her and you didn't tell your parents? What's the matter with you?" Jim shouted.

"I was trying to avoid the scene we're having now." Abby began to cry in earnest. Jim moved quickly to her side, holding her close to his chest.

"I'm sorry, baby. I didn't mean to upset you. I'm just scared. I'm supposed to protect you and here you have this problem and you don't even tell me about it."

"I don't think you could have protected me from this, Daddy."

Anna sat in her chair, crying quietly. She didn't move, didn't blink. She looked as if she were barely breathing.

"Mama?" Tammy reached out to take Anna's hand. "Mama, it's okay. The doctors think that Abby has an excellent chance of making a full recovery once they remove the tumor."

"It's my fault. It's all my fault," Anna repeated.

"How is it your fault, Mama? You didn't put the tumor there."

"No, but I didn't warn you either. Maybe if I had, it could have been caught sooner." Shaking her head, Anna reached for a napkin. She blew her nose and one long, graying lock of hair tumbled from the neat ponytail she wore.

"What are you talking about?" Abby asked.

"My mother had breast cancer. It killed her and her sister. I should have told you sooner. You could have been looking for it and maybe it wouldn't be so big now." This explained a lot. Given the statistics, Dr. Craig had thought it was strange that no one in Abby's family had ever been diagnosed with cancer before. He had explained that though one out of every nine women in America is diagnosed with breast cancer, only one out of 2,525 gets it before age thirty. It was the second deadliest cancer following lung cancer.

"So when is the surgery scheduled?" Jim asked.

"Next Friday. Tammy and I are going to drive to New York on Thursday."

"New York. Why New York? We have hospitals here," Jim persisted.

"I know, Daddy, but I was referred to a really good oncologist in New York. She comes highly recommended. Mason knows her," Abby admitted.

"I knew he was a good boy. Is he going with you too?" Anna asked hopefully.

"No, Mama. Just me and Tammy."

"We'll just have to come along. Jim, you can get off from work, can't you?"

"Of course I can. We'll all go together." Jim's strong hands held Abby close.

"That's not necessary." Abby tried to speak but her face was buried again in the folds of Jim's plaid shirt.

"Shut your mouth. You are my child, Abigail Mae. You don't call the shots around here, I do. I will be right beside you. Do you understand?" Anna came to stand beside her husband and placed a comforting hand on Abby's shoulder.

"Yes, Mama."

"All right, now you eat some more. You need to keep up your strength."

CHAPTER 7

Mason was having the worst week of his life. Since leaving Abby asleep in her bed, he had been miserable. He hadn't meant for this to happen. Somehow she had turned into so much more than a brief distraction.

Her quiet independence and bright personality, so different from that of the little girl he'd known, had captured him from the start. Gabby had definitely grown up.

Their attraction to each other was intense. He credited himself with being very experienced sexually, but what she did to him was beyond words. He was positive it had never been this way with any other woman in his life. He and Gabby were so compatible it scared him. And therein lay the root of his problem—fear.

A man wasn't supposed to be afraid. But Mason was. He had never had a committed relationship before, never even wanted one until Abby. Now he couldn't think of anyone but her.

She was sick now and he couldn't even summon the courage to go to her, to be by her side as she went through this ordeal. He was consoled only by the fact that she had her family and they would surely stay with her. He could keep a close eye on her treatment through Sarah, and Jeff would give him all the personal updates. But was that enough?

She didn't want him. Hadn't she sent him away? *Because you acted like an asshole*, he scolded himself. She hadn't even called.

Well, why should she? You ran out on her. He had been berating himself for that little stunt for days now. He called her house daily, sometimes leaving a message and sometimes just listening to her voice on the answering machine before hanging up. It was simply a joy to hear her voice—he missed her terribly.

Sitting in his living room, he thought about the decisions he'd made in the last few weeks. He had resigned from the hospital with the intention to open up a private practice with his colleagues. Yet he still had not committed to that venture. He had doubts, about himself, about the practice, about how this would affect the other people in his life. Nell, for instance. He thought of her often, even more so now that he would be in a position to spend more time with her.

Lying on the couch, Mason let out a deep breath. He was so unsure about his future. He needed someone to talk to, someone who could reassure him, comfort him. Someone who would yell at him for being stupid would be good right about now. Without another thought he picked up the phone and dialed her number. Expecting her to be out or asleep, he was prepared to leave a message.

"Hello?" she answered, her voice husky and filled with sex appeal.

"Hi," he finally managed.

"Mason?" Surprise evident in her voice, Abby sat upright in her bed.

"Yeah, it's me. I was calling to check on you."

"You don't have to do that."

"I know. I want to." Pleased that she hadn't hung up on him, he continued the conversation. "So how's it going?"

"Fine. I finished Melissa's room today. It looks terrific. The pillows you suggested were an excellent idea."

"That's great. How did she like it? I bet she lit up like a Christmas tree." He smiled at the thought of his niece.

"She hasn't seen it yet. Jeff said he would take her over there tomorrow. I think she might explode with excitement, though."

"I'm sure she will."

Silence.

"Have you told your parents yet?" Mason hated to bring it up, but didn't see a way around it.

"Yeah. I told them tonight. They insist on coming to New York with me."

"That's good." Relief that she was surrounded by family washed over him. "You'll have a lot of support," he added.

But I won't have you, she thought to herself. "How are you? I heard you decided to open the practice with your friends."

"Who told you that? Never mind, I know. Actually I handed in my notice at the hospital but I'm still undecided about the practice." Mason thought of his mother and how pleased she had been at the thought of him opening his own practice.

"What's holding you back?"

You, he wanted to shout. "I'm not sure exactly what I want to do with my life right now."

"You still want to practice, don't you?" she asked.

"That's not the problem. I'm not sure I want to stay in Boston."

Her stomach did flip-flops but her voice remained controlled. "So where do you want to go?" she inquired.

"I don't know," he lied. He knew he wanted to go home.

"You want to know what I think?" Shifting on her pillows, she eagerly offered her opinion.

"What do you think, Ms. Gabby?" Mason smiled at the familiar tone her voice had taken. Sinking back into his sofa he felt pure joy talking to her.

She smiled at the way he insisted on calling her that after she had asked him not to. "I think that you're having a mid-life crisis. You know you need a change but you don't know what that change is. Kind of like you're searching for something and can't find it."

"And what exactly am I searching for?" He was curious now.

"If you don't know, what makes you think I have a clue?" she laughed.

"Since you seem so knowledgeable on the subject I thought you might have some suggestions." Talking to her felt so natural to him, he knew she was the right person to call.

"Maybe you need to try something new. You know, go in a different direction from what you've been doing. Set some new goals for yourself. I don't know, something like that," she explained.

"Yeah, something like that." Silence fell again. "I miss you, Gabby." There, he'd finally said it.

"I miss you, too." The words flowed so easily, so honestly.

"I don't know if that's good or bad," he said.

"I think it just is."

"Yeah."

She could hear his steady breathing on the other end of the phone and wondered what he was doing.

"This thing between us is different. I don't know how to

explain it."

She sighed. "Sometimes in our haste to explain things we end up confusing ourselves even more. Maybe it needs no explanation."

"Is that what you think?" he asked.

"I don't know what to think anymore, Mason. So much has changed for me in such a short amount of time. I'm beginning to believe that nothing is really as it seems." *Except my feelings for you.*

Mason laid his head against the back of his sofa. "I'm sorry to add to your confusion. You have more important things to concern yourself with right now."

"You're important to me, too."

"I'm no good for you, Gabby," he admitted.

"And I'm no good without you," she confessed.

True to form, he clammed up, refusing to admit the depth of his feelings for her. "I'll call you tomorrow," he said quickly.

Abby recognized the change in his tone. "Fine." She placed the receiver into its cradle. How could he make her feel so good one minute and so mad the next? Every time she began to push him from her mind he appeared again.

Sometime in the middle of the night Nell climbed into bed beside Mason. He awakened the next morning to her bushy ponytails tickling his nostrils. He smiled down into the small face of a child, his child. This little person who had come into his life and had stolen his heart instantly. Now, to his astonishment, two females had twined themselves completely and unshakably around his heart.

Mason didn't call before she left. She had been sure that he would, but no matter how many chores she found to keep her in her apartment a little longer, the phone never rang.

The drive to New York took less than four hours with lead-foot Tammy behind the wheel. They arrived at the hotel in early evening, so they decided to go out to dinner.

Jim chose a nice quiet restaurant that sold soul food, of course. "No sense in wasting money on food you can't even pronounce, let alone eat," he explained.

Abby ate quietly, her mind preoccupied with thoughts about the surgery and its outcome. Her family did everything they could to try to keep her mind off it, but it was no use. She couldn't escape the feelings of nervousness, of dread.

When they were back at the hotel, she said goodnight to her parents and went into the room she shared with Tammy, took a shower and climbed right into bed. She knew Tammy wanted to talk, but she didn't feel up to it.

"Are you tired or just worried about tomorrow?" Tammy said from the bed beside her.

"Both," she admitted.

"Have you talked to Mason?"

"Tam, this is not the time."

"This *is* the time. I know there's something between you two. But you're too simple-minded to figure that out. He should be here with you. Why don't you call him?" Tammy propped herself up on her elbow.

"Yes, he should be here with me but he's not! And I will not call him. If he wanted to be here, I'm sure he would be."

"Maybe he doesn't think you need him."

"I don't."

"You do," Tammy persisted.

"Tammy, is it possible that I can get some sleep tonight? I really don't want to hear any more about Mason Penney right now."

"Relationships are about opening up and sharing your feelings with each other. Have you told him how you feel?" Tammy persisted.

"No," Abby said quietly.

"So you're just as silly as he is. Well, I've given all the advice I plan to give on the matter. Where you two go from here is your own business." She fell silent.

Abby lay quietly, thinking about the changes she had ahead of her and how it would feel good to know that Mason was waiting for her on the other side of the operating room doors. But he wouldn't be and she needed to focus on her health and not him. Still, she wondered what he was doing tonight.

CHAPTER 8

She arrived at the hospital at seven o' clock the next morning, just as she had been instructed. Before seeing the nurse, she provided information regarding insurance coverage and answered routine questions. In New York, it was mandatory to file a health care proxy in case a decision needed to be made during surgery, so she signed the necessary documents before heading to the lab for blood work.

After her blood work, she was wheeled to the radiology department for a mandatory chest x-ray. Then she was escorted to the pre-surgical waiting area with a nurse who, once again, asked a host of questions regarding her health history, why she was there (to make sure she knew what was going to happen), allergies, current medications, prior hospitalizations and so on and so on.

The doctor came in for a few minutes to say hello. She advised the Swansons and Tammy that they could expect the mastectomy and the reconstruction to take seven to eight hours. The long length was due to the reconstruction. Then she told Abby that the anesthesiologist and surgeons would be in shortly.

"Okay, honey. This is it. We have to go to the waiting room now." Anna tried unsuccessfully not to cry.

"It's okay, Mama. I'll be fine." Abby knew that it was best if they left her now. They joined hands at her father's direction and bowed for prayer. After the prayer they were all crying, but it was a good cry, a healing cry.

"There is no doctor as good as the Lord," her father whispered in her ear before kissing her cheek and leaving the room.

"We'll be waiting right outside." Tammy kissed her, holding her close for a few seconds. "I love you, Gabigail."

Abby's restrained tears broke free at the sound of her nickname in her sister's voice. "I love you too, Tam," she croaked.

Anna's emotions finally got the best of her and she ran from the room.

When she was alone, Abby dried her eyes and tried to calm her racing heart. In eight hours she would be an entirely different woman and she wasn't sure she was ready for that. Then a quiet calm came over her. She stared at the whiteness of the ceiling, not really seeing it, just staring in that direction. She seemed to hear a voice not really familiar but not strange either. The voice advised her that things would be all right, that whatever hand she was dealt she would handle. It reminded her of what she knew: that the Lord would not give her more than she could handle, that when she could not walk, He would carry her. Her heartbeat subsided and her breathing evened into a comfortable rhythm. The door opened, but she didn't bother turning her head to see who it was, assuming it was another nurse or doctor.

"Hey, Gabby." His voice was quiet. She looked up to see him standing beside the bed looking as good as ever. Although she wanted to jump up and kiss him, too many emotions overwhelmed her and she couldn't even speak. Tears slowly slid from her eyes.

Mason lifted her into his arms. For endless moments he sat on the side of her bed holding her closely, wishing desperately that he could exchange places with her. His decision to come to her had hit him like a ton of bricks on Wednesday morning. He needed to be with her. He had been afraid to trust that she would understand about Nell, but after being with her and seeing her with their nieces, he should have realized that she would be great with Nell. He had realized that the reason he couldn't commit to a practice in Boston was that he needed to be near her. Despite all his denials, he loved this woman. And she needed him, so here he was, sitting with her, waiting for her to endure the hardest task she had ever been given.

Nell was at the hotel with the nanny Mason had hired. He couldn't do anything for Abby except be there, and that's exactly what he intended to do.

"I'm so glad you're here. I was praying for you to come," she told him through her tears.

"I guess He heard your prayer. I couldn't stay away." Kissing her hands, he tried to explain the feelings that were going through him. "Remember you told me that I was searching for something?"

She nodded her head.

"I was searching and searching when what I was looking for was staring me right in the face." His thumbs stroked her hands, his eyes held hers. "I was looking for *you*."

"I'm glad you found me," she answered.

He kissed her tenderly. Then the nurse came in, signaling that it was time.

They let him stay while the IV was started. Then they gave her a Valium. Her high tolerance combined with her emotional state prevented it from working and it had to be repeated. Her last conscious thought was that Mason had been looking for her and, thank God, he'd found her. *Finally.*

Mason sat next to Abby's father in the waiting room. Tammy and Anna occupied another couch in the large area. Everyone was quiet, each with their own thoughts to think and fears to struggle against.

At about one o'clock Dr. St. John came through the swinging doors that led to the operating room. She had finished her part of the procedure, successfully removing the breast and twelve lymph nodes. The family gave a sigh of relief, which was short-lived.

Dr. St. John next informed them that while they had gotten all of the mass, some of the nodes looked malignant. It was not the news they were hoping for. It would be at least four days before the pathology report would be completed, she informed them, but she would do everything in her power to speed up that process.

The doctor left them alone again to wait out the reconstruction portion of the surgery. Tammy wondered how it would look. Anna and Jim wondered how Abby was tolerating the surgeries. And Mason wondered why he had waited so long to admit he loved her.

Tammy had informed him that Abby felt the reconstruction would be important to her psyche. She had elected to have the mastectomy and reconstructive surgery done at the same time in order to minimize procedures. Mason didn't care how she looked when she came through, as long as she came through. With or without the reconstruction, she would hold the key to his heart.

At about four o'clock Mason suggested that the Swansons and Tammy get something to eat. He said would wait there for any word on the surgery. After he pleaded with Jim and Anna and gave them his cell phone, promising to call should he get any word, they agreed.

When he was alone in the waiting room, he called the hotel to check on Nell. She was taking a nap but the nanny said she was fine. Relaxing a little, Mason tried to get some sleep. He'd been up all night thinking about Abby and then he'd gotten Nell up early this morning and prepared her for the trip.

He awoke to Jim shaking his shoulder and holding a white Styrofoam container filled with food. "Anna said for you to eat this," Jim grumbled and pushed the container in Mason's direction. "This contraption you gave me didn't go off so I guess you haven't heard anything." Taking his seat next to Mason, Jim handed him his cell phone.

"No. Nobody's come out yet." Mason looked at his watch to check how long he'd been asleep. It had only been an hour since Dr. St. John had come out.

Another three hours passed and their worry returned in full force. Tammy asked security to call the operating room to see if everything was okay. They advised that the surgeon would come see them once the procedure was finished. "That was helpful," Tammy said sarcastically.

At six o' lock a nurse came out and informed them that the surgery was finished and that the doctor would be out shortly.

True to his word, Dr. Sanzone, the plastic surgeon, came into the waiting area and began explaining the delay but Mason did-n't hear him. He was anxious to see Abby. When the doctor gave permission for them to go in two at a time, the Swansons went first.

When they came out, teary-eyed but visibly relieved, Mason rushed in. She lay there tightly wrapped in blankets on a heated mattress. Her intubation was still present. He watched her slight-ly labored breathing for a few minutes before touching the soft skin of her cheek.

"She's so beautiful," he said to no one in particular.

"She is, isn't she?" Tammy had followed him into the room. She stood on the other side of the bed looking down at her sister. "God is with her. He will keep her safe, Mason." She meant to comfort him but comforted herself in the process.

"I know." He leaned over to place a soft kiss on her forehead. Brushing wisps of her dark brown hair away from her face, he admired her, as if for the first time.

"Let's go. She needs to rest. We can come back in the morn-ing." Tammy gently took hold of Mason's arm in an attempt to lead him out of the room.

"Can I have a moment alone with her?" Tammy nodded, leaving him at Abby's bedside.

He held her hand and closed his eyes to pray. "Dear God, I thank you for giving me the opportunity to be with her, to know her, to fall in love with her. I thank you for making her the woman that she is and giving her the strength to bear this heavy burden. I pray that I may one day be worthy of her. Until then I promise to do everything I can for her…" As if he sensed her joining him, he opened his eyes to see her brown eyes, cloudy with remnants of anesthesia, staring at him. Although she couldn't vocalize what she wanted him to know, he could see it in her eyes.

"I love you, Gabigail, and I'll be right here for you. I'm not going anywhere now or ever." He kissed her again. She blinked and tears streamed down her face.

"No, no. Don't cry. You just rest. I'll be back in the morning." She looked as if she understood. He rose to leave, but could not resist the urge to turn and look upon her one more time. She was staring at the ceiling calmly, as if she were having a private conversation of her own with someone not visible to the human eye but present in her heart.

The next day was a long one. At Mason's insistence, Abby was moved to a private room on the third floor of the hospital. She was slightly more alert, though her breathing was noticeably labored and her lungs a little congested. She was given a tube to exercise her lungs by blowing into it several times a day. After the breathing exercises, she would cough up the phlegm that filled her lungs as a result of the long surgery.

Anna and Jim were worried about what might happen when there was no one in the room with her, so Mason hired a private duty nurse.

Abby's hospital stay followed the same pattern each day. Daily rounds by the physicians would be followed by her family's constant vigil. Between staying with Abby the better portion of the day and spending the evenings at the hotel with Nell, Mason was exhausted. The private duty nurse proved to be excellent and welcomed help. Due to the experimental nature of the breast reconstruction, the plastic surgeon was there frequently, pricking with a pin to see if the blood vessels had connected after the microsurgery. Although most patients were out in two to three days, Abby stayed a full week as a result of the reconstruction and the lengthy surgery.

CHAPTER 9

On Christmas Eve, Abby was released from the hospital and her parents drove her back to Manchester. She had decided to stay with Tammy and Jeff. Her parents had wanted her to stay with them but she thought that would be just a little too stressful. She wasn't sure she could handle recuperating in the same house as her mother and father. They would hover over her until she couldn't breathe. No, staying with Tammy would be better.

Tammy had left New York a few days earlier to prepare Abby's room, which had previously been used as a storage area on the first floor of her house. Tammy figured that would be a good place for her because it was close to the kitchen and the downstairs bathroom.

When Abby arrived at Tammy's, she found a house decorated in Christmas splendor. The tree was so huge Jeff had had to cut about five inches off the top in order to fit it into the living room. And it was still too big. The star had to be stuck in front of the tree instead of on top. Melissa was excited that Aunt Abby was going to stay at her house and that Santa Claus was coming. Abby had gotten her Christmas shopping done before the surgery, anticipating that her condition would most likely stop her from doing it as she usually did on Christmas Eve.

After she was settled in and everyone had gone to bed, she and Mason sat in her room talking.

"Are you comfortable?" He punched and propped her pillows

for the millionth time.

"I'm fine. But I don't think these pillows will survive another day with you hitting them like that." She smiled.

"Sorry." He sat in the chair opposite the bed.

"Can you sit here with me?" Abby carefully slid to the other side of the bed to make room for him.

"I guess I can do that." When he was seated comfortably beside her, one arm draped around her and holding her hand with the other, he asked, "You comfortable?"

"Yeah. I wanted to thank you for staying with me today," she said. She was a little reluctant to say what was really on her mind.

"Thank me? You don't need to thank me, Gabby."

"I just mean you didn't have to stay here all day. Tammy and Jeff are here and my parents are only thirty minutes away."

"But I want to be with you. Is that okay?"

Boy was it! Abby's heart was doing cartwheels in her chest.

"Yeah." With some hesitation she asked, "When are you leaving?"

"I'm not," he answered.

"What?" She couldn't believe what she had just heard. She had braced herself for his answer, hoping for just a day or two more with him.

"I've decided to stay in Manchester. I'm going to open a practice here. Well, not here, probably closer to Trenton. But that won't be such a bad commute. I've put in a few calls to some old colleagues and we're talking it over. I think it might just work. What do you think?"

She was flabbergasted. This couldn't really be happening. Reining in her excitement, she tried to answer him calmly. "I think…um…that's a good idea," she stammered.

"That's all? Just 'that's a good idea'?" He was puzzled. "You, little lady, should be a bit more excited seeing as you instigated the decision."

"Me? What do I have to do with this?"

"I can't very well take care of you from Boston. And while I'm sure you'd like Boston, I don't think your father would go for me taking you so far away from home."

"You don't have to take care of me, Mason." Abby was serious. She didn't want to be a burden to anyone. She fully intended to get back to her life just as soon as her treatment was finished.

"I don't have to, but I want to." Mason had decided that he would wait a few days before announcing Nell's existence to Abby and the rest of his family. The nanny had purchased a small tree and decorated the current hotel room as much as she could. Mason had had all of Nell's gifts shipped from Boston a few days ago so Santa would still visit. This was already a really tough time for Abby so he wanted to make the announcement as smooth as possible. When he saw that she was struggling with what she wanted to say next, he decided to lighten things up. They had plenty of time to discuss their relationship and their future. "Besides, you can't decorate my apartment until you're better, so what better way to protect my investment than to oversee the recuperation personally?"

Abby laughed. "Since you're newly unemployed, I'm not sure you'll be able to afford my services."

"Surely my credit is good with you." Mason was relieved; this was the first time since the surgery he had heard her laugh.

Things were going to be just fine. He believed that with all his being.

"When did all this happen, Mason?" Pauline asked. She watched the toddler playing in her living room.

Mason explained the beginning of his life as a father. "Right after I returned to Boston from Jeff's wedding, Teresa announced that she was pregnant. We had broken up a few weeks before, so initially I didn't believe her. But then she had an amniocentesis done and we did a blood test. It's my child."

"Where is this Teresa now?" Pauline questioned.

"She's still in Boston, working, I presume. Once I confirmed that Nell was mine, I had papers drawn up whereby I would pay Teresa a monthly stipend for Nell's care. I was at the height of my career so I didn't have time to raise a child but I did visit as often as I could. Teresa took the money and I didn't see her or the baby again until about six months ago when she showed up at my door. Apparently she was tired of waiting for me to decide to marry her and single motherhood had become too hard. She wanted me to take Nell. That's when I came home." Mason stared at his daughter who was chasing a bright red ball that her little feet managed to kick ahead of her each time she grabbed for it. "She was going to put her up for adoption. I couldn't let her do that."

Mason watched as his mother tried to absorb what he was telling her. Her hair was drawn into a tight bun, her face lightly made up. Since his last visit, Mason had noticed a slight change in Pauline. She looked tired. Tiny lines, the ones women dreaded, had appeared at the corners of her eyes. His news seemed to deepen the weathered look she now wore. He guessed it was normal; she was getting older.

"This is certainly different." Pauline folded diamond-clad fingers in her lap. She sat, back straight as a rod, in the wingback chair glaring at this unfamiliar person. She was having a hard time believing all this. When Mason had come over this morning, she had been overjoyed to see him, and then she'd seen the child. She had no aversions to children but preferred that they be reared by both a mother and a father.

"Thanks for your support, Mother." Mason wasn't shocked by Pauline's distant reaction but he was disappointed. Rising from his seat on the couch, he crossed the room to collect his daughter. Lifting the little girl high into the air, Mason's face lit with joy as the child giggled and cooed.

Pauline watched them together before deciding to join them. She supposed that she should be proud of her son for taking on the task of being a single father. Even though she hated that he'd had a child out of wedlock, there was nothing she could do to change that now. "How about some ice cream, Nell?" Holding out her arms, she waited expectantly for the child to come to her. When her plump arms stretched toward Pauline, the older woman smiled. "I assume that means yes." She gave Mason a quick wink before whisking her granddaughter off to the kitchen.

Mason enjoyed the view of his daughter and his mother. His happiness showed in the smile on his face. But that smile was quickly erased as he thought of the task that lay ahead of him. He and Abby had grown closer over the past few days and he was hesitant about disturbing their newfound happiness. But this couldn't be put off any longer. If they were going to have any type of future together, he needed to tell her everything. And he needed to do it now.

On the ride to Jeff's house he looked in the rearview mirror at the child in the backseat. Nell had managed to get her rich chocolate complexion and jovial disposition from Teresa. Only her misty gray eyes were Mason's. There was no denying that. She looked as exotic as her mother had when he first met her. He knew that she would grow up to be just as stunning as Teresa was. The gurgling sounds she was making now signaled that she was anxious to get out of the car seat he had buckled her into. As they pulled up in front of Jeff's house, Mason went to the passenger side of the backseat and unfastened her, impulsively kissing her chubby cheeks and nuzzling her neck. "She'll love you. Just like I do." He smiled. Nell giggled and grabbed his nose.

He rang the bell and waited for someone to open the door. It was Jeff, thank goodness.

"Hey, man. Who's this pretty one?" Jeff touched Nell's chubby little cheeks.

"This is my daughter." The look on Jeff's face should have forewarned him of the outcome of the evening, but he foolishly remained optimistic.

"Your what?"

"Do we have to stand outside? It's getting a little chilly." Mason was uncomfortable and wanted to get this over with as quickly as possible.

"Yeah, sorry. I'm just a little shocked." Jeff stood to the side as Mason walked in. "You never said anything…to anyone."

Mason knew that his 'anyone' specifically meant Abby.

"I know. I know. But now's the time. Jeff meet your niece Annell. I call her Nell. Nell, say hi to Uncle Jeff." Nell waved chubby little fingers in Jeff's direction.

"Come here, Nell. It's nice to meet you." Jeff removed the coat from the little girl. "Why don't you come in the kitchen with me. Your daddy has some business to take care of," Jeff said quietly, his eyes moving toward Abby's room.

Mason proceeded in that direction. "Don't remind me." He hoped that Abby would accept Nell as quickly as Jeff had but somehow didn't feel that would happen. The door to her room was slightly open. He had only to push it gently before seeing her sitting amidst an abundance of pillows staring at the screen.

"Hi," he said tentatively.

"Hi! I didn't think you were coming by today." She was obviously happy that she had been wrong. He went to her side, kissing her softly.

"What's the matter?" He didn't look like himself.

"Nothing, why do you ask?"

"Because you look like something's on your mind." She tried to sit up straighter without causing too much pain. She had done her arm stretches as instructed just about an hour ago, so she was more sore than usual.

"Do you need some help?" Mason asked without delay.

"No, I need for you to tell me what's going on," she persisted. She felt an unmistakable stab of alarm. Panic coursed through her.

"Okay." He tried to recall the speech he had rehearsed in the car, but failed. "Remember just before I left for Boston that I came by your apartment to try and explain some things to you?" He didn't expect her to respond. She'd been very angry that day and he doubted she'd heard a word he'd said.

"Yes," she said quietly.

"What I was trying to explain was that back in Boston I had a...um...I had a..." His voice broke off as he struggled to find the right words.

Abby's face depicted the fear she felt. "You had what, Mason?" What did he have? A wife? A girlfriend? As her mind reeled and Mason sat silently trying to figure out the best way to say it, the door to her room was slung open, letting in streams of light from the living room. To Abby's surprise, a dark-haired, gray-eyed cherub with ice cream dripping down her face made her way in. Abby had expected to see Melissa, but this wasn't her niece. Jeff came up behind the child quickly.

"Sorry, she got away for a moment." He attempted to close the door and back away.

"Da-da, Da-da," the child chanted. She pulled away from Jeff and walked towards Mason. Mason reached down and scooped her into his lap. Abby's eyes stayed riveted on the pair.

"Is this...your child, Mason?" Her voice cracked. When he hesitated to answer, she continued, "Is this what you were trying to tell me?" Abby's heart stood still. She wanted him to say no. Oh, how badly she prayed in those precious seconds of silence, that he would say no.

Jeff, recognizing the beginning of trouble, turned and closed the door behind him. They would need to be alone. He'd just wait outside for Mason. To pick up the pieces, for he was sure what Abby's reaction would be and sadly, he couldn't say that he blamed her.

"Yes. This is Nell. She's two years old. Nell, say hello to Gabby," Mason prompted the little girl.

"Yabby!!" Nell repeated. "Yabby!!" Sliding from his lap, she walked towards the bed. Her tiny fingers touched Abby's in exploration. Abby could only stare at the little girl.

Little gray eyes held her stare. She was so pretty, so adorable. And so not hers.

Mason tried to speak. "I imagine that this is a shock to you but…."

"A shock! A shock! Is that what you think this is? A shock?" Abby looked at Mason, then back to Nell's all-too-familiar eyes again. "No, Mason, this is beyond 'a shock.' What are you going to tell me next, that you're married? Or that this is not your only child? Are there more outside?" She was yelling, her anger apparent. Why had he waited so long? She would never forgive him now.

Nell had been startled by Abby's outburst but continued to hold onto her hand, tracing her fingers slowly. The motion distracted Abby from her rage and she focused once again on the child. She was extraordinarily beautiful for a toddler, high cheekbones and intriguing eyes balancing perfectly with her full mouth. The only telltale sign that she was just a toddler was the chubbiness of her cheeks and hands. She had two thick ponytails on each side of her head adorned with colorful ribbons and clips. When she smiled at Abby her eyes twinkled. Abby's heart melted, and tears immediately sprang to her eyes.

This was the child she would forever be denied. And it was *his*, the man she thought she loved. Mason had fathered a child and had never thought to tell her. Why? There was no reason that would explain his deception. Abby was just sorry that she would never get to know this beautiful child. Her father's dishonesty was more than Abby could bear. On top of everything that had happened to her, Mason was the biggest disappointment of all.

That disappointment showed as she raised her head to look at him now. He stood a distance from the bed awaiting her reaction. What had he expected her to say, or do for that matter? Had he assumed that this would all go over well and they would live happily ever after? Abby's fairy tale was floating desperately out of reach. "Could you leave, please?" That was all she could manage before turning away to let her tears fall freely. She could no longer look at him and she certainly couldn't look at his child.

"Gabby, please just let me explain." He moved closer toward her.

Sensing his approach, she held up her hands to ward him off. "Please, I just want you to go."

"Baby, please don't do this. Just let me talk to you." Mason stopped where he stood, pleading with her to listen.

Shaking her head desperately, Abby almost choked on her tears. "Mason, please. I need you to go."

He wouldn't push her. Moving quickly, he scooped Nell into his arms and walked to the door, wanting to scream to her that he was sorry and that he would do anything in his power to make it up to her. Somehow, he knew that those words would not be enough. "I just need you to know that I love you, Gabby. And I'm sorry I didn't tell you sooner," he said before closing the door behind him.

CHAPTER 10

Two weeks after the surgery and Mason's devastating announcement, Abby was sitting in Tammy's living room reading to Megan when the phone rang. It was Dr. St. John calling to check on her. She reminded Abby to schedule an appointment to discuss the chemotherapy treatments she would be receiving and gave her the names of several support groups and seminars to attend. Abby was overwhelmed by the time she hung up the phone.

She was just beginning to get used to the new breast and the way it looked and she wasn't sure how she'd feel in the support groups. The plastic surgeon had done an extraordinary job, nearly matching the remaining breast in size and shape perfectly. There was a four-inch scar beneath her breast but the surgeon had explained it would thin out over the course of time. She was still really bruised, but overall things looked good.

She had, just that morning, become brave enough to allow Tammy to help her dress. Actually, she couldn't get her bra fastened by herself because her arm was still a little stiff with its movements at times, even with the exercises. So she'd really had no choice. Seeing the scar was a bit shocking for Tammy but she wasn't overly grossed out. She even joked about Abby's breasts always being bigger than hers. That had made Abby feel a lot better.

But Mason's reaction would be different entirely. What if he was repulsed and didn't want to touch her intimately anymore? She mentally admonished herself for even thinking about him in that way. What did it matter if he wanted to touch her or not? She didn't want his touches anymore. Since his announcement, she hadn't spoken one word to him. Still, he had been true to his word, he had not left. He was at Tammy's house every day, not all day, but at least a few hours. Most times he brought Nell with him to play with Melissa.

Nell, she thought dismally. The little girl that had come between her and Mason was the same little girl that Abby was inexplicably drawn to.

One day when Abby had come out of her room to use the bathroom, she had run smack into Nell coming out of the kitchen with a handful of cookies. "Yabby!" the child exclaimed, showing her excitement at remembering Abby's name. Abby had looked around quickly before giving Nell a big hug and kiss on her soft cheek. Then she'd gone into the bathroom and cried uncontrollably. She hadn't chanced getting close to Nell again.

"How's my lovely lady today?" Mason asked Melissa, who was sitting at the table concentrating on the picture she was coloring. He'd arrived just before dinner, his usual arrival time.

"Fine." She barely lifted her head from the book.

"Do I get a hug or a kiss?" Mason asked. He was amused, as always, by how much older she seemed than her actual age.

"Not right now, Uncle Mase. I'm busy," she replied.

He decided that it was just as easy to take what he wanted. So he hugged and kissed a very disgruntled three-year-old and received a full-face scowl and outcries for his efforts.

"What's going on in here?" Tammy with Megan in her arms came into the room to investigate the noise. At three months, she was the spitting image of her big sister. Her honey-colored skin and big hazel eyes were to die for. Her hair, however, was still just a fuzzy little patch on top.

"Just hugging my niece. But since she doesn't want to be bothered with me, I'll have to find a more cooperative victim." He lifted Megan from Tammy's arms. Always a happy child, she smiled calmly at him. He nuzzled her neck, inhaling her sweet baby smell. Lately, he had been thinking a lot about children and how he would like to have one with Gabby one day. But that would require her to speak to him, something she hadn't done in days.

"Abby's in the living room. She got a call from the doctor today so she's been a little bummed," Tammy told him.

"What did she say? Is everything okay?" Mason asked. His attention shifted from the baby to Tammy.

"Just reminding her to schedule an appointment about the chemo. She gave her a list of support groups and some seminars to go to. Why don't you try talking to her?" Tammy offered. She understood Abby's anger towards Mason but she also saw the hurt and longing in her sister's eyes every day she continued to stay away from him. She knew they were in love; she just wished they'd both stop being so silly and get on with things.

Mason hesitated. "This probably isn't a good time if she's already upset."

Mason, I know she's mad at you right now, but I also know

she misses you terribly. Your dishonesty really hurt her."

"I know. I was stupid. But I can't seem to figure out how to make it better."

"You just need to talk to her. Convince her that she can still trust you. Try telling her the whole story. Jeff told me and I think you're a pretty admirable guy, raising a daughter all by yourself." Tammy wanted desperately to see her sister happy again, which she hadn't been since Mason's announcement. That wasn't much to ask for, she thought.

"I don't want her to admire me; I just want her to forgive me."

"She will. She just needs a little push." Tammy took the baby from his arms and gave him a gentle nudge in the direction of the living room. "Go ahead in there and push her."

Mason quietly walked into the living room, hoping that his arrival wouldn't be noticed before he had a chance to say anything. On previous occasions when he had tried to approach her, she'd seen him coming and taken cover in her room. He didn't want her to run this time.

"Hey beautiful. What's going on?" He casually took a seat beside her, inhaling the sweet scent of whatever perfume she wore today. He'd missed being close to her and ached to touch her.

Abby looked up at him momentarily before turning away. But she made no attempt to get off the couch; Mason took that as a good sign.

"Tammy said Sarah called. Is everything okay?" he asked.

She didn't answer.

"I'm sure things are just fine. Don't worry about it so much. Just concentrate on getting better." He felt as if he were talking to himself.

She still didn't answer.

He raised his voice when she continued to ignore him. "Damn it! Gabby, you could at least be civil to me. I'm trying to make you feel better."

"You're the last person in this world who could possibly make me feel better," she spat.

"Why can't we just talk about it and get it out of the way?" She looked good, he noted. She wore sweat pants and a blue t-shirt, but her hair had been pulled back into a neat ponytail and she'd even put earrings on. A quick glance at her chest told him that everything there still looked good too. She had been reluctant to let him see the scar even when they'd been speaking to each other. He figured his chances were completely lost now.

"Talk about what? The fact that you lied to me? Or is it the fact that I was good enough to sleep with but not good enough to know about your daughter? By the way, there's no reason to tell her now about me because I have no intention of making any sort of commitment to her." Her voice was raised, and her eyes were flashing with all the hurt and anger that had built up over the last few days.

"You know that's not true." Turning sideways in the chair, he tried to reach for her.

"Isn't it?" Jerking her arm away, she clutched a pillow to her chest, feeling self-conscious now that he was so close.

"Maybe it was at first, but when I realized how much you meant to me, I knew I had to tell you." Dropping his hands into his lap, he settled for the fact that she wasn't going to let him touch her.

"Sorry, but your realization came just a little too late." Although she turned away from him again, she couldn't help noticing that he smelled good. She'd missed being close to him.

"Are you really this upset with me or is something else bothering you?" She seemed extremely agitated by something. He sensed that there was more going on than just the breach of trust, not that dishonesty wasn't enough. "What's really bothering you, Gabby?" Gently, bravely, he placed a hand on her shoulder.

She couldn't hold it in any longer. The sobs came rushing from deep within until she was crying hysterically, her body convulsing violently.

Mason moved closer, pulling her toward him. "Shhh, baby it's okay. It's okay. You don't have to tell me. It's okay." He was truly confused now. What had the doctor said to her? What had *he* done to her? He mentally kicked himself for yelling at her, for pushing her.

"It's not fair, Mason. It's just not fair," she wept into his arms.

"What's not fair, baby? Tell me what's not fair."

"I thought we would be together. You know, like a couple, and that we'd eventually have a family and all that stuff I told you I wanted. But you already have that. You already have a child. And I may never have one. It's just not fair." Her body shook with each bout of tears.

So that was it? It wasn't so much that he had neglected to tell her about Nell, but that she was feeling slighted because she hadn't had a child yet. And now with all the problems with her health, she believed she would miss out on the joy of having and raising a child. He could certainly identify with that. Since taking custody of Nell, his life had changed dramatically. Every day was a new adventure and with each adventure he loved his daughter more. He didn't know what his life would be like without Nell, and he didn't want to find out. He loved Abby, too, with all his heart, and whatever was bothering her he would fix. He had to.

"Gabby, you can still have a child. It's just going to take a little time. I'm so sorry that all of this came at such a bad time for you, but you have to believe me when I tell you it will be okay."

"How? How can I believe you? I have to start chemo in the next two weeks. Do you know what that can do to me? I may be infertile for the rest of my life. I can't be infertile, Mason, I just can't!" Desperation etched her voice and gripped his heart.

"You will have a child, Gabby. Regardless of what we might have to do, you will have a child," he promised her.

She knew she should still be angry with him, but she just couldn't. Here he was promising her something he had no certainty about himself. And the thought of him committing himself to something that he actually had no control over overwhelmed her. Whatever his reasons for not telling her about Nell sooner, she forgave him. If it turned out that she couldn't have a child of her own she would still have Mason's precious gift. That thought brought forth new concerns.

Moving from the comfort of his embrace, she asked, "Where is Nell's mother?"

"That's a long story," he said, not sure if he should go into all of that right now. She was on an emotional roller coaster and he dreaded adding to it. But the look in her eyes told him that keeping secrets belonged to the past—he needed to tell her everything himself and he needed to do it now.

"I've got all day." She snuggled closer to him, ignoring the twinges in her breast.

CHAPTER 11

By the end of January Abby was back at work. She met with her father's construction crew and set the date for construction to begin on the Rubaker house. If she could pull this off, it would expand her business and do wonders for advertising. At Mason's suggestion she had hired an assistant. Because her first chemo session was scheduled for next week, she would need the extra help around the office. Melanie was her name and she would be on hand should there be any questions from the construction crew or the realtors in Abby's absence. This was an important job; she couldn't afford any mistakes due to her illness.

Her intention was to continue working throughout the treatment. Chemo sessions would be scheduled for Friday afternoons to allow the weekend to serve as recuperation time. God willing, those two days would be enough time to get it together before work on Monday.

Last week Tammy had gone to a support group with her. Abby found it to be comforting and very informative. Although most of the women were in remission, their experiences were interesting and kept her encouraged. Abby understood now more than ever the importance of early detection. She would forever encourage the women she knew to have regular mammogram screenings and to perform daily self-examinations.

That evening she and Mason planned to attend a seminar which would discuss the side effects of chemo. It was comforting to have Mason around, although she didn't want to get too used to it. She was still leery about what the future held for them. Mason and Nell had kept up their daily visits, and just last week, Abby and Nell had spent the whole day together while Melissa had gone to pre-school. Abby was falling in love with the little girl, which made her even more anxious about the future.

Mason picked her up at the shop at five. He smelled wonderful and looked scrumptious. She ached to kiss him, for him to touch her, hold her…

"How did things go today?" he asked when she was seated beside him in the car.

She snapped her seatbelt into place. "Great. They're starting the deck on Friday. I'm really excited."

"As you should be, the design is good and once you add your decorating touches, it'll be great. I heard they're thinking about selling it furnished."

"Really? That would be great! I'll have to take extra special care in selecting the furnishings then."

He could see the joy in her eyes. She really loved her work and he was proud of her.

"I think I have two other doctors interested in going into a practice with me. We might be able to get it off the ground by the end of the year if everybody is as serious as I am."

"That's good. What types of medicine do they practice?" His new practice was important to her. She was praying for it to work. This would secure his staying in Manchester. And this new office meant a lot to him, she could tell by the way his face lit up when he talked about it.

"They're both in orthopedics, which works well with my surgical practice. The hospital in Trenton has offered me privileges there, which means I would have my own patients as well as acute surgicals referred through the hospital. I've been looking at office space in Trenton as well. So I want you to start gathering some ideas, floor plans, something workable."

"Sure. Just understand that I work off a retainer," she said.

"So you've told me." He pulled into the parking lot of the hospital.

Memories of the sterile operating room, the doctors in white coats and the strong smell of antiseptic crept into Abby's mind. She had experienced a few nightmares since coming home from the hospital, so she figured it was normal to feel a bit anxious about entering another hospital after what she'd gone through. Her follow-up visits had been in Dr. St. John's office, so this was actually her first time in a hospital since the surgery.

Mason circled the car. He unlocked and held the door open for Abby. "You okay?" he asked.

Abby hesitated. "Yeah, I guess so." Taking the next step was difficult but she managed. Mason held her hand, gave her a quick peck on the cheek and walked with her toward the door.

The speaker's name was Dr. Nancy O'Donnell. She seemed well versed in her field and her remarks were easy to follow. So many times doctors tended to talk so much "doctor talk" that regular everyday people had a hard time following them. Abby had been reading a lot about this disease since her initial diagnosis so she was a little ahead of the game. Some of the terminology and treatments the doctor discussed were already familiar to her.

Dr. O'Donnell spoke about the different types of medicines…an alphabet soup of sorts, from Adriamycin to Cytoxin to Taxol. Abby took notes as the doctor explained options and combinations that could be used and the common side effects of fatigue, nausea, vomiting, blood disorders, psychological symptoms and hair loss. Since each individual was different it would be hard to predict what would be the worst reaction for her.

The doctor also discussed and passed out literature about researchers at the University of California who were conducting clinical trials to study the effectiveness of Chinese herbal medicines in alleviating chemotherapy side effects.

"So, what did you think?" Mason asked as they walked to the car. He noticed that she seemed more relaxed than she had been when they initially arrived.

"It was informative. I think I need to research some of the medicines. I wrote them all down but I want to know the history of each and how well it works. I think I may even call a few of the women I met at the support group to see what combinations they had."

"That sounds like a good idea. I know another oncologist in the D.C. area. I'll give him a call in the morning to find out a little more," Mason added.

"Remember, the first treatment's next Friday, so I'd like to know something by then."

"Yes, ma'am." He gave a quick salute, then turned, stopping in the middle of the parking lot. He took her hand in his. "I'll be right there with you, Gabby. You don't have to be afraid. Whatever happens, I'll be there." He wasn't sure if it would help but he felt the need to remind her of his dedication.

"Thanks," she said solemnly. "I needed to hear that." Abby

stared into his now familiar gray eyes. He'd been like a rock for her these past weeks: standing strong when she thought to crumble, encouraging her decisions, and simply being there when she needed someone. Would she ever be able to repay him for his kindness?

She was still staying with Tammy, figuring it would be best until chemo was finished. Mason pulled into the driveway and escorted her into the house. He waited in her room while she showered and prepared for bed.

When she finished and climbed into bed, he leaned over to fix her blankets. His shirt constricted around his biceps, causing a familiar sensation in the pit of Abby's stomach. Mason hadn't made any sexual overtures toward her at all since the surgery. Dr. St. John had informed her that it would be okay for her to have intercourse as long as she was comfortable, but still he hadn't tried. He had even stopped insisting on seeing her scar.

So she had held her feelings at bay, not wanting to endure his rejection. But now he was so close and she wanted him so badly she just couldn't resist anymore. Nell was asleep in the living room, so she knew he didn't need to rush off to settle her down for the night. She wondered if she should ask him to stay for a while.

He leaned closer to kiss her goodnight as he always did, but when his lips touched hers this time, she reached up, cupping his face in her hands, holding him steady. Running her tongue over his bottom lip she waited for his reaction. He paused for a fraction of a second before his tongue joined hers.

The passion was immediate and intense, fire igniting between them instantly. Its build-up over the past weeks had come to a head. The kiss was hot and urgent, both of them getting more excited by the minute. Mason summoned enough strength to pull away. Resting his forehead against hers, they both fought for air.

"Gabby, what are you trying to do to me?" his ragged voice asked.

Abby sighed. "It's just been so long. And I needed to know that you still want me. I'm sorry." She was embarrassed and frustrated.

"Don't apologize," he said. Taking her hand, he laid her fingers on his rigid arousal. "Does that answer your question?"

Touching him there did wonders for her ego. Boldness taking over, she began to unbutton his pants, an urgent desire to touch him skin to skin encompassing her.

"Gabby...," he gasped. He wanted her, badly. But he hadn't wanted to push. He wanted to wait until he was sure she was ready. Her fumbling fingers confirmed her need.

In seconds she had freed him. She stroked tentatively at first but her ministrations quickly became bolder. His stiff shaft filled her hand. She looked up and saw that his eyes were closed and his jaw clenched. She kissed his eyes, his nose, his cheek.

"Mmmm...Gabby...that feels so good," he whispered in her ear. "Oh, so good." His tongue stroked her earlobe before trailing down her neck.

She moved her hands for only a second to shift the covers, but Mason took that moment to stand up and move away from the bed.

"What's the matter?" she asked. Abby was startled by his retreat. It was obvious that he wanted her, yet he'd pulled away again.

"I don't want to hurt you," he admitted.

"The only way you'll hurt me is if you continue to deny me what I need. Dr. St. John said it would be fine." She got out of the bed and stood in front of him. "Make love to me, Mason? Please."

She was asking him to do what he had wanted to do every night for the past six weeks. After the surgery he had been afraid that she wouldn't want to have sex anymore. As it turned out, it seemed that the opposite was true. She was practically bursting with pent up sexual tension.

Well, he wouldn't let her down. He drew up her nightgown with the intention of removing her underwear. His heart lurched—she wasn't wearing any. "You naughty girl." She smiled mischievously.

Quickly and without further hesitation he pulled the nightgown up over her head and for the first time saw the reconstructed breast. He was stunned. It looked so real, like its counterpart. The only difference was the scar underlying it.

Abby held her breath waiting for him to examine it. Slowly, he reached out to touch it, sliding the pad of his finger over the swollen skin. Abby giggled.

"I'm going to assume you're not laughing *at* me," Mason said.

"No. It just tickles." Bubbling with excitement, Abby was unable to stop the laughter.

"Your nerve endings are still a bit confused. You're feeling a tickling sensation instead of a sensual one. It will go away in time. I guess I better leave this one alone, huh?" They both laughed then. "I'll just have to give all my attention to the other one."

Before she could answer, he moved to the bed and drew her onto his lap. Her legs straddled his waist as he entered her slowly, gritting his teeth against the pleasurable tightness of her walls around him. He eased her down gently until she had accepted his full length. Abby gasped, her eyes half closed, her nails digging into his shoulders.

"Sweet." The word slipped from his lips just as Abby began to move.

Rocked by the sensuous sensations of his engorged penis embedded deeply inside her womb, she pulled her hips back, and his shaft began to slide slowly out of her. Before contact was broken, she thrust her hips forward, drawing him back into her warmth.

A low growl escaped Mason's lips, and his fingers clenched her bottom with ferocious pressure. "Sweet, sweet, Gabby," he moaned, guiding her hips in a repeat of the motion that had just had his eyes crossing.

Abby was in control, riding Mason like an experienced jockey, taking her fill of his powerful manhood, possessing it and making it her own. Lost in her own pleasure, she was taken off guard by the swift waves of pre-orgasmic tension that roared within her. Her thighs shook as her hands tightened on his shoulders.

Mason sensed her release was near and thrust into her harder, quicker. The little sounds that had rhythmically come from her throat became louder, more intense. Mason claimed her mouth, successfully swallowing her screams as she exploded on top of him.

When she was limp in his arms, he maneuvered so that she

was lying on the bed and he hovered above her. "My turn," he murmured, entering her again in one long smooth stroke. Abby's eyes shot open and she moaned in acquiescence. Mason lifted her legs until they locked around his waist. Stroke—pause—stroke—pause. His manhood seemed to swell to the point of bursting. His mind clouded, the friction between them adding fuel to the inferno inside him. When he knew he could hold on no longer, his thrusts quickened, and his release filled her.

Nell was moved into Melissa's room for the night and Mason slept in the bed with Abby that night and the nights that followed.

The room in which the chemo would be administered was small but well equipped. It had twelve patient beds with a chair beside each one, as well as televisions and VCRs at each station and a very friendly nursing staff. The options for treatment were CMF (Cytoxin, Metholtrexate, Five FU) or CA (Cytoxin and Adriamycin) or a third option, which was a blind clinical study offering CA with or without Taxol. Abby had read about it in a medical journal. A random blind study meant that at the time of the first treatment, a random determination was made as to the inclusion or exclusion of Taxol. After Mason's inquiries they had elected the blind study.

On her first visit Abby was greeted by a member of the staff. Her weight, temperature and blood pressure were recorded. Blood was drawn and levels checked before the chemo was ordered from the pharmacy. The session started with the insertion of an IV into one of her veins.

The first fluids administered into her IV were anti-nausea and hydration fluids to be followed by the actual chemo drugs. The treatment lasted for almost six hours. She lay on the comfortable mattress trying not to think about what was going on, instead opting to think about her future with Mason and the children she hoped to have.

Mason took her home and she lay in the bed, completely worn out. Lying against the pillows, she tried to relax enough so that she could fall asleep but that was apparently not meant to be. A few hours later her parents came in to check on her.

"Hi, honey," she heard her father say as he poked his head in the door.

"Hi, Daddy," she answered.

"Are you okay?" Jim moved to Abby's bedside.

"Yeah, I guess. I'm kind of tired, though." Abby hoped that would be a hint, but Anna came in right behind her husband.

"Abigail Mae, I declare you look just wonderful. Who would guess what you just went through?" Her mother was surprisingly cheerful. Abby recognized all the signs. Her mother was going to talk to her about something and Abby had the strangest feeling she wasn't going to like what it was.

"Hi, Mama."

"You look so good. I was talking to your Aunt Hilda yesterday and I told her how good you looked." Smoothing Abby's hair back, Anna continued to talk.

"Thanks, Mama."

"I won't stay long because I know you're tired but I wanted to talk to you about Mason."

Abby took a deep breath before answering. Her father sat in the chair as if to move out of the line of fire.

"What about Mason?"

"I know that he's been staying here," Anna said in a matter-of-fact tone that warned Abby not to attempt denial.

Instead, she decided to take the blasé approach. "And?"

"I know this is not my house but it doesn't look good for a woman...an unmarried woman, to have a man staying with her. It just isn't right. Now if you two need to be together that much, then maybe you should think about getting married. Think about his little girl. How do you think this looks to her?"

"Mama, she's two years old. Furthermore, marriage is not foremost on my mind right now. I would like to overcome this cancer first, if you don't mind." Abby rolled her eyes at the ceiling. Anna would have slapped her had she rolled them at her. But she wanted to.

"Don't get sassy with me, young lady. I want you to beat this disease just as much as the next person but that doesn't give you permission to lay up with this man on a nightly basis while you're not married. Not even engaged, for that matter." Anna's long hair was drawn away from her face by a thin headband and it swung fiercely as she reprimanded her daughter.

"I don't want to discuss this right now, Mama. Can I call you later?" Abby felt sick. She wasn't sure if it was from the chemo or the raging little woman standing at her side.

"I'm going to say my fill before I leave, so you just listen. I don't want him staying with you if you're not married. And if you're going to get married, he still shouldn't stay with you until it's official. After all, that's only proper. And while I'm at it, you better be thinking about some sort of birth control. We don't want any children out of wedlock."

Abby frowned. She hated how her mother referred to the family as "we." This was purely Anna's opinion; she knew that for a fact.

"I don't need birth control. The doctor said that it would be highly unlikely that I would even get a period because of the chemo."

Jim shifted uncomfortably in his chair in the corner.

"That's besides the point…"

"What is your point, Mama?"

"I don't want him staying here with you."

"It's Jeff's house, and I don't think you can tell him not to let his brother stay here."

"Then you'll just come and stay with me and your father."

"I will not!" Abby said defiantly.

"Abigail Mae, you will not disobey me!"

"Mama, I am an adult. It's my choice how I live my life," Abby continued before Anna could get in another word. "I will stay here with Tammy and if Mason wants to stay, he's perfectly welcome. This is all ridiculous. You act like I'm committing a crime."

"You are and you know it. In the eyes of the Lord this is not right, I don't care what the circumstances. I like Mason and I want you two to get married but I do not condone this relationship as it is."

"With all due respect, Mama, I didn't ask your permission. Now, I really need to get some rest."

Anna turned away in a huff. Abby knew that she should have

found a more tactful way of telling her mother to mind her own business but she really didn't have the energy to figure that way out.

Before leaving the room, Anna turned to her daughter one last time. "Then you just get your rest. I won't share my feelings on this matter with you again. But you were raised better and I expect that you will strive not to embarrass your father and me." She was out of the room before Abby could speak. Not that she wanted to comment on that last remark anyway. As if she didn't have enough to deal with already.

CHAPTER 12

Abby awoke one morning three weeks after beginning chemo to a burning sensation in her scalp. Afraid to go into the bathroom to see that the inevitable had begun, she lay in bed, keeping the knowledge to herself. She had been blessed; the nausea was not a dominant effect of her treatment. Mason lay beside her sleeping peacefully. They had decided that they would go to church this morning. She hadn't been since the chemo had begun and she was determined to be there today. She summoned the courage to get up and go over to the mirror. Before she made it out of the bed, she saw strands of hair on her pillow. Carefully she picked them off and dropped them in the trash can.

In front of the mirror she lifted her hand to her head, running her fingers through the brown mass. Without any effort she removed a handful of her hair. She would not cry, this had been expected. Closing her eyes tightly, she whispered, "Lord, please give me the strength to endure what must be."

Going by the trash can again, she discarded more hair. She went into the bathroom to shower. Still a bit weak from Friday's session, she didn't stay in the water as long as usual. Staring in the mirror, she tried to figure out what she was going to do with the hair that was left. She tried to brush it back, so that she could at least braid it. The brush was successful in removing even more of her hair, this time leaving unsightly spots. She would need to wear a hat. Before leaving the bathroom, she let out a little chuckle at the partly bald person staring back at her from the mirror.

Mason sat on the corner of the bed waiting for her to come back into the room. He had seen strands of hair in the bed and more in the trash can. She had begun to lose her hair. He knew that this was one of the things that she had dreaded most. He expected her to be upset, probably not crying in hysteria, but definitely alarmed. He did not expect her smiling brightness as she bounced into the room.

"Good morning, baby. I didn't wake you, did I?" She went to the closet to search for something to wear.

"Ah, no. I didn't feel you next to me and I wondered where you were." He eyed her suspiciously.

"I decided to get an early start. Give myself time to get ready." She searched through her limited selection of clothes. "Is it supposed to be very cold today?"

"What?" Mason was confused. Here he was all ready to console her and she was talking about the weather.

"I wanted to wear the blue suit but if it's going to be cold I'll wear the black. What do you think?" She looked at him, finally noting his confusion. "Is something wrong, Mason?"

"I saw the hair in the trash can. Do you want to talk about it?"

"Not really."

Mason saw the bald patches. He hurt for her. Standing, he walked toward her, holding out his arms. Without a word Abby walked into them and let herself be cradled.

"I thought I would feel much worse but actually it's not that bad."

He held her away from him, twisting her from side to side, analyzing the damage. "I guess I'll get used to it," he smiled.

"It burns though. I wonder how long that will last," she said thoughtfully.

"Why don't we just cut it all off?" Mason suggested.

"You think that'll help?" Giving the thought serious consideration, Abby stared at him.

"It might. I mean, it's bound to happen sooner or later. And there's no sense in you walking around looking like a jigsaw puzzle," he laughed.

"Ha, ha. Very funny. You're not the one who's going to be bald." And then she got an idea. " Unless…"

"Oh, no! Don't even think about it," Mason said adamantly.

"What happened to your undying support? I guess that only applies as long as you don't have to make any personal sacrifices," she pouted playfully.

"Shall I get the shaving cream?" he asked.

It turned into a household project with Jeff coaching Mason as he shaved Abby's head and Tammy, Melissa and Abby laughing hysterically as Jeff shaved Mason's. Before going to church they both thoroughly oiled their newly shaved scalps. Abby wore her black suit and Tammy lent her a black hat trimmed with white satin. Though she had never been a hat person, she decided that she looked rather nice in one. Mason suggested that they go hat shopping after church, as she would need casual ones as well.

Nell, on the other hand, cried for two days after Abby and

Mason shaved their heads. She wouldn't let either one of them come near her for any reason. Jeff thought it was hysterical.

Loving Mason had one drawback. Pauline. She was the proverbial thorn in Abby's side, never once missing an opportunity to put her and her family down. Mason had been good about keeping them away from each other during Abby's treatment; he knew that she had enough to deal with. So when he mentioned that his mother was coming for dinner one night, Abby was astonished.

"What on earth for?" she questioned.

"She says she hasn't seen her grandkids or her sons for weeks. She does get lonely, you know. My father's away a lot," Mason said.

"That's a blessing for him. I would imagine that living with her is hard."

"Gabby, that's not nice," Mason scolded.

"Pauline's not nice, Mason." She rolled her eyes and sighed. "I'm sorry to speak ill of your mother. I guess I'll survive one meal with her. But I'm warning you, if she acts up…" Abby threw him a sly look.

"She won't. I've already talked to her. She was really shocked to hear about your condition."

"I'm sure." Abby rolled her eyes. Pauline, shocked? That was a new one.

"She *is* a woman, Gabby. This is a scary thing for women. You know, you're doing so well, you should really think about speaking at one of those seminars." Abby laughed at the thought. Although she had been doing extremely well with the chemo, who would want to hear her talk?

After ten weeks she was feeling great. Her hair had even begun to grow back, albeit it was yet another color and texture. At first it was a lighter brown and extremely thin, then later lighter still with a stiff bushy texture and now it was dark brown and very thick. She wore it in a low trimmed, boyish style. Mason often teased that they could pass for brothers.

She had to admit that she liked not having to spend so much time in the mornings trying to get her hair to lay the right way or spraying it continuously with oil sheen and holding spray to ensure that it would last throughout the day. She was considering keeping it this length even after her treatment was discontinued.

She had only four more weeks left and she was counting the days. It was such a grueling task, getting poked every week with that large needle. Although she was somewhat immune to the pain, her veins were beginning to give out on her. Just last week they had discussed installing a mediport so that she wouldn't have to get the needles anymore. But with such a short time left, Abby didn't feel that surgery would be advantageous now. So she would stick it out, no pun intended.

"Hello, Abigail. It's so nice to see you again. But what have you done to your hair?" Pauline asked as she studied Abby. "I should say that particular style doesn't suit you." With her nose turned up, she eyed Abby's head disgustedly.

"Well, Mrs. Penney, since I so value your opinion I'll rush out first thing tomorrow morning and have it changed. Is that soon enough for you?" Abby asked cheerfully.

Pauline rolled her eyes, dismissing Abby with a flick of her wrist. "It was just an observation. A bit of constructive criticism, if you will." She shrugged out of her jacket. "If you wish to walk around town like that, then suit yourself."

Abby gave Mason a seething look which told him she wasn't going to take much more from Pauline.

"Mother, you said you would be nice to Gabby tonight," Mason interceded. He guided Pauline into the living room, away from Gabby.

"I am being nice, even though I don't have to. She's such a mouthy little thing." The last sentence was said in the barest of whispers, meant only for Mason to hear.

"Nonetheless, you will be nice to her." Mason's tone indicated he wouldn't discuss this with her anymore and Pauline threw her hands up in despair.

Dinner progressed with Pauline directing all her attention to Tammy's lack of housekeeping skills. Tammy was on her toes tonight; she gave it right back to her mother-in-law, tit for tat. Abby and Jeff found it amusing while Mason simmered like a boiling pot. Abby knew that by the end of the evening he wouldn't be in a good mood.

"Mason, I had the liberty of speaking with one of your colleagues a few days ago," Pauline mentioned while they sat at the table.

"And who might that be?" Mason barely got the words out in a civil manner.

"Teresa Parker. She said that the two of you had gone out a couple of times. She seemed to think it was getting serious before you up and left town. She sounds like such a dear. Tell me, what do you think of her?"

If Abby had been paying attention to the adults and not concentrating on retrieving the spaghetti that Melissa had very cleverly hidden in all the crevices of her shirt and pants, she would have seen the look of absolute horror that crossed Mason's face when he recognized the name.

"She's a good doctor. And that's the end of it," he said through clenched teeth.

Abby was abruptly thrust into the conversation by a swift kick to her knee by Tammy. She looked first at Tammy in question, then, following the insistent nodding of her sister's head, to Mason, who was now quite visibly outraged. *What had just happened?*

"I was just inquiring. Didn't mean to ruffle any feathers." Pauline's cold, mocking stare rested on Abby. Abby stared back in confusion.

Whatever had just transpired must have been a doozy because the dinning room was uncommonly quiet. Abby was pretty confident that the feathers that had meant to be ruffled were hers, so to get on with the evening she simply remarked, "Never fear. My feathers don't ruffle that easily, Mrs. Penney."

"I think I'll be leaving now. I have been disrespected enough. I trust that my sons will bring my grandchildren to visit me so that my presence in the company of you people will no longer be necessary." Pauline threw her napkin into the plate of uneaten spaghetti and stood to leave.

UNCONDITIONAL

"I will be sure to remind your sons of your specifications where visitation is concerned, Mrs. Penney. We wouldn't want to cause you any displeasure." Tammy gave Pauline her brightest smile. She was tired of this witch causing a ruckus in her house and the fact that she was leaving was a blessing in her eyes. She'd be perfectly content if she didn't have to see her again until Christmas.

Jeff, noticing that Mason was about to explode, rushed to get his mother out of the line of fire. "Come, Mother, I'll walk you out." No matter how rude and obnoxious she could be, she was still his mother and he would protect her as much he could from impending disaster. Once in the living room, Jeff hurried to get her jacket, throwing it over her shoulders and almost pushing her out the door.

"Lord, Jeffrey you don't have to push. I know your wife and that sister of hers want me out of here but I didn't think my own son would feel the same," Pauline snorted.

"It's not like that, Mother. It's just that you have gone out of your way to be rude to Tammy and Abby tonight and they've endured enough. I think it's best for all if you go home now." Jeff stood by the door, hoping he hadn't hurt his mother's feelings too much. But then, he thought, she hadn't cared how much she had hurt his wife's feelings in her own house.

"This is not the first time you've chosen them over your own mother. I raised you. You should treat me better. Show a little respect." Pauline pulled her mink coat around her chest and clasped it at the top before reaching for her purse that Jeff had unceremoniously dropped on the couch.

"Mother, respect is a two-way street. If you can't respect my wife in her own home, then you have to leave. It doesn't mean that I don't love you; it just means that I love my wife as well." Jeff kissed his mother on her cheek, hoping this would be the end of the conversation.

"I guess that's as it should be with husband and wife. I just wish you had made a better choice. But that's all done now. Can't fix it, no matter how hard I try. Your brother, on the other hand…" Her eyes traveled in the direction of the dining room. "I won't lose another son, Jeffrey. I just won't."

"If you're not careful, Mother, you may very well lose us both." Those were his last words before Pauline stalked out of the house.

After everyone had gone to bed Abby waited patiently for Mason to come to the room they still shared. He and Jeff had been sitting in the living room talking while she and Tammy cleaned the kitchen. That was well over an hour ago. She knew that he was upset but she couldn't tell if it was with her or his mother. If it was her, she had no idea what she had done. Actually the same went for his mother. She was still clueless as to what had happened at dinner.

She had started to doze when she heard the door open. He didn't turn on the light to undress but she could hear him moving around. She felt his weight on the bed. She wanted to turn and say something to him but she didn't know what. They lay in silence. It seemed painfully clear that he wasn't going to share what he was upset about with her.

But try as she might, sleep evaded her. She never could go to sleep with something unsettled in her mind. It would have been different if they had an argument or disagreement but that wasn't the case. And for that reason she turned to him. "Do you want to talk about it?" she asked quietly.

"No," he snapped.

"Well, I do." Raising herself on one elbow, she looked at him. The bright red numbers on the clock/radio cast a faint illumination across his face. Still, he fought to keep his eyes closed.

"You've got a bug up your butt and I want to know why. Did I do something?"

"No."

"Did Jeff or Tammy?"

"No." Good, that narrowed it down to just one person.

"What did Pauline do to *you*?" She was surprised that he could get this angry with his mother. She knew that she could be pretty pissed off with her, but Mason usually defended her, so this attitude baffled her. And besides, as far as she knew, Pauline had directed all her insults to either her or Tammy, never once attacking her sons.

"I didn't say she did anything to me. Just go to sleep."

"If she didn't, then who did?" Just then it hit her like a ton of bricks. Tammy had told her about the conversation. Was it this Teresa person? Why would that upset him?

"Is it Dr. Parker?" She held her breath waiting for the answer, not sure if she wanted to accept that this woman could cause this reaction in him.

He let out a deep breath, but didn't turn to face her. "Teresa Parker is Nell's mother."

Abby fell back against her pillows. "Oh."

"What I'm really upset about is that my mother continues to harbor such ill feelings toward you and Tammy. It's an old battle that's gone on too long. Jeff has always dealt with her with more finesse than I ever could. I love my mother, but I don't like her very much sometimes."

Abby fought to bite her tongue. Now was not the time for her comments about Pauline. Mason was clearly disturbed.

"Am I the reason she's turned on you now? Of course I am. That was a silly question," she quipped. When he didn't answer, she continued, resting her chin on his upturned shoulder. "Mason, I never meant to come between you and your mother and I understand if you want to make things right with her. You're right, this feud has gone on a long time but that's because your mother keeps it brewing between us. In a million years I would have never guessed that you and I would be together and I know that upsets her.

"It shouldn't upset her. She should be happy that I've found someone to build a future with. Someone to help me raise Nell."

"I agree. But baby, she doesn't see it that way." Abby touched her hand lightly to his cheek. "I'll try to be a little more tolerant of her if you think that'll make it easier." Abby doubted it would but for Mason, she was willing to try.

"I am a thirty-six-year-old man, Gabby. She can't choose who I can or can't love. I would appreciate any efforts you make but she's the one who is going to have to accept us and change her attitude."

"I don't think that's likely to happen," Abby sighed.

"You never know, people change all the time. Just a few weeks ago I noticed something different about her but I can't put my finger on what it is," he said thoughtfully.

"It certainly isn't her feelings towards me." Abby rolled her eyes. "But that's fine. I can't make her like me but I'll do my best to ignore her. For your sake."

Mason smiled, then leaned to drop a quick kiss on her lips. "Can we go to sleep now?"

"I guess so."

Mason turned her so that her backside was spooned against him.

Abby snuggled close against the warmth of his body. "Goodnight," she said airily.

"Goodnight." He kissed her ear.

Mason's heart swelled with love for this woman who never ceased to amaze him. Her strength and character were a true testament to his idea of an ideal wife.

CHAPTER 13

Abby walked slowly across the wood beams that served as the floor of the soon-to-be study/office in the old Rubaker house. Her father's crew was doing a fabulous job. They were actually ahead of schedule, which pleased the real estate brokers. In her last meeting with them they had informed her that they were indeed going to sell the house furnished. They believed that it would enhance their profit, which with Abby's eye for design, was sure to happen.

During the weeks that the crew had been diligently building the addition, she had taken advantage of her access to the house. She had to admit that she was beginning to get too close to this project, which was not a good thing. It was neither healthy nor ethical to form a personal bond with a job. She hadn't meant to fall in love with the house. After all, it wasn't like this was the first time she had seen it.

But it was the first time she had been allowed unlimited access, giving her ample time to walk from room to room by herself, imaging all the things she would do to each room were she to live there. Where she would put a giant hanging fern, where the antique dining room set she had always wanted would sit in the large dining area, how it would look beneath the glittering chandelier hanging gracefully from the ceiling. There were so many different things she could do and she had been given the chance to do them. This was definitely going to put her business on the map.

Melanie had already taken calls from companies, other prominent citizens of Manchester, and persons as far away as Trenton who wanted to retain her services. And just this past week she had been featured in *The Room Dresser*, Manchester's version of *Good Housekeeping*. Her business was definitely booming, which made her very happy.

But this house was almost consuming her every thought. During her chemo sessions she would envision plans for the kitchen or the guest bathroom. At night she sketched ideas for the living room and the yard. It was becoming an obsession. Luckily, Mason had embraced the house with the same passion she did. The cathedral ceilings and large rooms had hooked him immediately. The emotion the house evoked in her was surreal, and most nights she would talk abut the house to Mason.

The previous night she'd even dreamed about it. In the dream she'd gone up the stairs headed for one particular bedroom. It was next to the master bedroom and had a large bay window with a window seat. She'd walked across a creaking hardwood floor and opened the walk-in closet. To her astonishment, tiny little dresses hung on white plastic hangers. Then, in the way of dreams, she suddenly saw a handcrafted crib with a white comforter splashed with blue, green, red and yellow and she caught the scent of baby powder.

Abby remembered other bits and pieces—teddy bears, the tinkle of a lullaby, and most of all, a powerful wanting that had coursed through her body, a yearning she'd never known before. She'd awakened from the dream in a terrible sweat, her heart hammering in her chest.

Even now, as she locked the house and prepared to go home, the dream seemed all too real. After taking a few steps, Abby turned to look at the house once again. Sighing, she admitted to herself that she understood the dream all too well.

Abby's cell phone rang as she drove home from the Rubaker property. Reaching over to the passenger seat to retrieve her purse she tried to clear her mind of the emotions triggered by going into the Rubaker house. She needed some rest or a really good drink, she told herself. Numbers flashed across the neon blue screen. Mason. She pulled into a gas station and dialed the number back. He answered immediately. "Hi!"

He sounded winded when he answered, "Hey, baby. Where are you?"

"About fifteen minutes from the house. Where are you?" She could hear a lot of commotion in the background.

"We found an office. I want you to drive up and see it."

"Now?"

"Yeah. It won't take you that long and besides, I rode with Margaret so I need a ride back."

"Who has Nell?"

"She's visiting my mother."

Abby sifted through her purse for a pen and paper. "Okay, give me the directions." She wrote them down hastily. The last thing she wanted to do was get on the highway going to who knew where to look at some building. But Mason had sounded pretty excited, so she figured she should boost her spirits and join in his celebratory mood. After all, he had been working hard with his attorney and his two colleagues to get the practice on the way. He was adamant that it be opened by the end of the year.

An hour later she pulled into a business park. A tall silver building towered above everything else. Abby craned her neck to look out the window. This was fabulous and clearly did not look like the average doctor's office. Maybe she'd gone to the wrong address. The parking lot was fairly empty as she got out of her car and crossed to the double doors of the building. A black and gray marble foyer with expertly maintained potted plants and sparkling chrome molding made the entrance intviting.

At the sound of a bell Abby stepped onto a luxurious elevator and stared at herself in the mirrored enclosure. Getting off the elevator, she was enveloped by walls of hunter green and dark wood moldings. Plush carpeting cushioned her feet as she followed the sound of voices down a long, winding hall.

Mason stood amidst a group of people who were as noticeably excited as he was. They were sipping champagne and laughing merrily. "You made it!" he exclaimed when he noticed her standing in the doorway. Crossing the room, he hugged her enthusiastically before leading her towards the small group.

"Mason, this is absolutely gorgeous." Abby surveyed the granite-slated desk in the reception area, visualizing what wonders she could perform in this large room.

"I know. We love it!" Mason was bursting with joy. "Baby, meet Larry Carter and Daniel Spellman, my new partners. Gentlemen, this is Abigail, the love of my life." If Abby had not already been so overwhelmed by the fancy office, she would have been stunned at his introduction of her, but as it was, she was still trying to get a grip on her surroundings.

"Hello, gentlemen. It's nice to finally meet you. I've heard a lot about you. Shall I also say congratulations?" she added with a smile. Extending her hand, she politely greeted Mason's partners. She felt like one of those corporate wives, smiling and being congenial with her spouse's business associates. But she wasn't Mason's wife.

"Thanks. We've heard a lot about you too." This was Larry, a tall thin man who looked to be about thirty or so.

"It's nice to finally meet the woman who tamed Mason Penney." Daniel shook her hand earnestly. Abby blushed as if on cue.

"Abby, this is Martha Bohan. She's from Beston Realty. She helped us find this place." Mason introduced her to a tall, very pretty woman in her late fifties. Abby felt a little embarrassed by her appearance. Since she had known she'd be working in the house, she'd dressed in jeans and a button-down cotton shirt. Her short hair wasn't sprayed and groomed; instead, it looked like a curly bush framing her make-up free face.

"Hello, Ms. Bohan. I must say this is a wonderful building." She glanced around the office again, patterns and fabric swatches soaring through her mind as she pictured all the wonderful things she could do with the space.

"Ms. Swanson, it's very nice to finally meet you. Mason speaks very highly of you. I saw the recent story on you in *Room Dresser*. I understand that you will be lending your talents to this project," she smiled.

"I haven't been formally commissioned, but I could definitely do some great things in here," Abby said.

Mason put an arm around Abby's shoulders, pulling her close to him. "I know you can. So when do you want to start? We've already signed a three-year lease, so you can get started right away."

"I'm kind of engrossed in another project right now but I guess I could squeeze you in," she smiled.

"I'm sure you can." They smiled at each other conspiratorially.

"Mason, we're going to get going now. I'll call you in the morning so we can talk more about dates and advertising," Daniel said. "It was nice meeting you, Abby."

"Same here," Larry chimed in as they walked out the door.

"I think I'll be leaving too. My husband won't be pleased that I've spent all day with three attractive young men." Margaret grinned. "Mason, it's been nice working with you and Ms. Swanson, I will definitely keep you in mind if and when I decide to do a little room dressing," she said as she slipped into her very expensive cashmere coat.

"Yes, I would be delighted to work with you, Mrs. Bohan." Abby smiled, feeling a bit better to find out that the woman was indeed married. If she were a man, she would surely have been tempted, even though Ms. Bohan was an older woman. Alone in the office, she walked around getting a better view of the place.

Mason followed behind her, not saying a word. She came to the corner office at the far end of the long winding hall. It was huge. One wall was almost completely windows. The light would be good in here.

"Whose office is this?" she inquired.

"Mine. Would you like to join me in christening it?" Mason

pulled her close to him, covering her lips with a smoldering kiss as his hand eagerly explored the body he had become very familiar with.

"Well, well, well. Now we uncover the true motive in getting me to come all the way up here tonight." She smiled, enjoying their intimacy.

Mason held his hands up in mock surrender. "You caught me. Now, how does my suggestion sound?" Dropping his hands to her waist, he leaned forward to nuzzle her neck.

Her senses were responding in rapid measure. "Mason, this is an office building."

"And?"

"And there's no bed."

"Baby, we don't need a bed." He lowered her to the soft carpeted floor. He was under her shirt in mere seconds, suckling her breast through the thin material of her bra. She was gradually getting normal sensation back in the reconstructed breast, so Mason tended to shift a lot of his attention there. He called it "physical therapy." It didn't make her giggle this time.

No, the sounds that managed to escape her throat were far from giggles. And Mason was far from finished. His sweet torture went on for quite a while longer. It was almost midnight before they left the office, glowing with satisfaction and filled with love.

CHAPTER 14

The time had come for Abby to go home. She'd continued to pay the rent on her apartment, knowing that she would not stay with Tammy and Jeff forever. After six months, though, she felt it was time to leave. Although she loved seeing her nieces on a daily basis, she wanted to return to her own apartment. It was time for things to get back to normal.

She was going to tell Tammy and Jeff that night. Summer was here and the weather was pleasant. It would be easier to move her stuff in nice weather. Just the other night she realized she had accumulated quite a number of things there in six months.

"Hey. Whatcha doin'?" Tammy sauntered into the room and sat on the bed.

"Packing." Abby waited as Tammy digested her words.

"Are you and Mason going away?"

"No. I'm going home." Abby looked at Tammy closely. Tammy stared at her blankly.

"Come on now, don't get all upset. You knew that I wouldn't be staying forever and besides, you should be tired of me by now."

"I am, actually. Jeff and I can't run around naked anymore. We're afraid you and Mason might decide to switch partners." Tammy laughed, even though she really didn't want Abby to go. "I might as well help you pack."

"I'm glad you're taking this so well." Abby was a little surprised that the announcement had been accepted so easily.

"You know I'll miss you. You're my built-in babysitter." Tammy stood to hug her tightly. "What did Mason have to say about this? Is he leaving too?"

"I don't know, I haven't said anything to him yet. Now that the practice is almost on its way, I assume he'll find an apartment. I doubt that he'll stay with Pauline again."

"How anybody could live with that woman is beyond me." Rolling her eyes, Tammy sat back on the bed, grabbed one of Abby's sweaters and tossed it inside the open suitcase.

"She only dislikes the Swansons. She loves her own kids," Abby noted. "You know, Tam, I've been thinking." Abby dropped to the bed beside her sister. She retrieved the sweater Tammy had neglected to fold and carefully creased the garment before placing it back into the suitcase.

"Oh goodness, you're back to thinking again," Tammy sighed. She picked up another sweater.

"Hush." Abby rolled her eyes. "I've been thinking that maybe you should lighten up on Pauline. Maybe invite her over more often or just go and spend time with her, just you and the girls."

"Is insanity a side effect of chemo?" Tammy stared at her sister incredulously.

"No, silly. And I'm finished with chemo, remember?" Abby sighed. "I just think she's lonely. And terribly unhappy." Abby picked up another sweater and folded it.

"Both of which are her own doing." Tammy shrugged. "Look, Abby, I married her son, not her. And I didn't do anything to cause her dislike except be born. I'm not going to kiss her butt just because she's unhappy. That's her problem."

Abby sighed. Deciding she really didn't feel like an argument, especially since Tammy was right, she grinned. "No, you're right. Being lonely and unhappy is Pauline's problem. Your problem, on the other hand, is you've always been lazy. Now, if you're not going to neatly fold my clothes and pack them, then I'd rather you not help at all. You're just making a mess for me to clean up." She smiled in Tammy's direction.

Tammy giggled. "Whatever. They're just a bunch of sweaters; they won't get wrinkled." For good measure Tammy tossed another sweater into the suitcase.

"Stop it!" Abby laughed as she retrieved the garment. "I think I hear Meagan crying. Isn't it her feeding time?"

"Yeah, yeah. I get your point." Tammy stood and left the room.

When Tammy left to feed Megan, Abby thought about what Mason's reaction would be to her leaving. She didn't foresee a problem, but then, she'd been wrong about Mason before. Tammy had mentioned that he could stay in the room if he wanted to. She figured that was what he would probably do.

In the end, it seemed she was more like her mother than she had been willing to admit. The thought of continuing to sleep with a man that she wasn't married to every night didn't seem to sit well with her any longer.

She hadn't taken the time to consider how she would feel not sleeping with Mason every night. The thought of it was a bit distressing since she had come to rely on him so much in the past months. She used to pride herself on her independence, but lately she had been completely absorbed with Mason and their relationship. Although she hadn't really lost any of the independence in the process, it just didn't dominate her life anymore.

Mason had meetings with his attorney and his partners for the bulk of the afternoon, so he didn't get a chance to go home early and speak with Gabby as he had originally planned. With the practice preparing for its opening in early December, God willing, he was anxious to find an apartment for them to live in. They needed their privacy and now that Gabby was finished with chemo, he wouldn't feel bad about her being home alone while he worked. Nell needed to be enrolled in a preschool and she too needed her own space. The first couple of months with the practice were bound to be hectic; hence the need for some sort of routine. He and his partners had finally agreed to join an HMO so that their work hours would be set and the number of patients controlled. In addition, the bulk of their salaries would be guaranteed. He wanted to maintain the amount of time he and Gabby spent together, his goal being to make her as happy as she had managed to make him.

But as luck would have it, the meetings took longer than expected and then the partners had suggested dinner. So here he was, just putting his key in the door at eleven o'clock. She was probably asleep and he would have to wait another day to give her the news. The house was quiet, as it tended to be at this time. Tammy was a stickler for Melissa's eight o'clock bedtime, and Megan had begun to fall right into step with her sister's schedule.

After checking on Nell, he tiptoed into the bedroom, not wanting to wake Abby. Switching on the lamp beside the bed, he looked down on her sleeping face. Her hair had grown at a rapid pace this time and was now permed and almost at her shoulders. He watched the constant rise and fall of her breasts. Breasts, he noted with a burning hunger, that were both absolutely gorgeous. He had never imagined he would love a woman so completely. But Abby had walked into his world and taken charge. She had invaded his heart and soul and he loved it. He remembered her saying that he had been looking for something when he found her. He was so thankful that she'd allowed herself to be found. She stirred briefly, murmuring something inaudible before slipping back into slumber. He decided that there was nothing he'd rather do right now than lie beside her, feel her warmth and enjoy the comfort they had discovered in each other's arms.

The morning dawned bright and clear. The Penney household was a bumble of activity on Saturday mornings and this one was no different. Jeff had gone into the yard to survey the work that needed to be done this year while Tammy had dressed the kids and was heading to the grocery store. Mason was even up and dressed. This surprised Abby because he usually lingered in bed with her on Saturdays. It didn't matter, she had a lot to do anyway so she showered and dressed. The bags she'd packed the night before she now retrieved from the closet. Mason hadn't been home when she went to bed and she hadn't wanted him to walk in and see them, so she had hidden them like a child hiding a test that had received a bad grade. She finished removing her clothing and personal items from the dresser. She wanted to be in her apartment tonight. Abby noted that the room looked a little strange now that it had been stripped of her belongings. Mason's things looked a little lonesome and she felt a twinge of sadness. She sat on the bed contemplating how she would approach this subject with him.

Mason came into the room smiling happily. "Hey sleepy-head. I was beginning to think you'd never wake up." He looked as if he were about to say something else when he noticed the suitcases. "Are you going somewhere?"

Abby stood and took a step towards the suitcases. "I'm moving back to my apartment. I figured I'd leave voluntarily before they kicked me out." She tried to sound lighthearted.

"I wanted to talk to you about that but I got in pretty late last night." He sat on the bed, patting the spot next to him. "Come, sit with me." When she was close to him, he looked at her for a long moment. "I don't know how to go about this. Um, I was thinking about getting an apartment," he started.

"That's a good idea. Not that your mother wouldn't be delighted to have you back home with her, but I think your own place is even better." She watched the shocked expression on his face. "What's the matter?"

"I was thinking of getting an apartment for all three of us. I want us to live together," he said.

"Live together? Are you serious?" Of course he was serious she told herself as she stared at him. He was so handsome with his strong jaw and charismatic smile. His hair, which he'd shaved to empathize with her, was fully grown in again.

"Yes. I'm quite serious. Is there a problem with that? I mean, you and Nell are getting along great and I kind of like having both my girls under the same roof." He reached out, taking her hands in his.

"For one thing we're not married and for another, I already have an apartment."

"What does that have to do with anything? We've been practically living together for the past few months. What's the difference if we do it officially?"

"That's the difference; it isn't official. And the only reason we've been 'practically living together,' as you put it, is because of extenuating circumstances. Now those circumstances are all but resolved and I don't want to be just shacked up with you." To her own ears, Abby sounded just like her mother.

"Are you saying you don't want to be with me anymore?" His voice was a hoarse whisper and pain etched the fine features of his face.

"No. That's not what I'm saying. I'm saying that we should continue as we are, but not living together."

"And how is that? What would you call what we're doing now?"

"I thought we were in a relationship, you know, like dating."

"I believe it's a little more serious than just dating, Gabby. I thought we were in love." His eyes searched hers for some sort of explanation. He didn't quite understand what she was saying. He'd been all excited about their sharing an apartment, sharing a life, only to have her toss those dreams back in his face.

"I thought so, too. I mean, we are." Abby struggled to find the right words. "Mason, I can't just live with you. At the risk of sounding hypocritical, I want to be married before I live with a man. Can you understand that?"

Of course he could. Hadn't that been one of the things that he'd warned himself against, the fact that she was a woman with morals? He both admired and hated that particular trait she possessed. He could feel her slipping away from him. This was not what he had envisioned for them.

Throwing up his hands, he shrugged. "Okay, then let's get married," he said seriously.

"What?" she screeched before taking a few steps back.

"Let's get married," he repeated.

"Just like that?"

"Gabby, what is it that you want? You say you don't want to shack up, that you won't live with me without getting married. Fine, I can understand that. Then I suggest marriage and you question that. I don't understand what you want." His forehead knotted in frustration.

"I don't understand what *you* want! One second you're content with us just living together and in the next breath we're getting married. Marriage is a big commitment, one that we've never discussed before this morning. I don't think that's a feasible proposition at this moment." Her words hit him like bullets, tearing at his flesh and leaving him crippled.

"Are you saying you won't marry me?" He stood to face her. This was definitely not turning out the way he had planned.

"I'm saying that rushing into marriage is not the way to remedy a disagreement." Abby fidgeted, nervous about where this conversation was headed.

"That's saying you won't marry me, Gabby."

"I won't make a rushed decision about something that important. And you shouldn't have suggested it under such obvious duress."

"Duress? What are you talking about? If we love each other, then we should get married. That's simple." Mason smoothed his hands over his close-cut hair, trying to get a grip on the situation.

"Then why didn't you come in here and ask me to marry you instead of asking me to live with you?" He didn't have an answer to that. And she didn't have the strength to continue the conversation, afraid of where it would lead on its present course. She picked up two of her suitcases and left the room. A few minutes later when she returned for the others, Mason was gone.

She didn't know where in the house he had gone and figured it was best if she didn't seek him out. She finished loading her bags into the car and said her thank yous and goodbyes to Tammy and Jeff. She drove home in a daze, not fully understanding what had just taken place. Feeling as if her heart had been torn from her chest, she walked into her apartment and sank to the floor. Tears came freely. Was it over? Would he come to her? She didn't know. And uncertainty was the worst feeling of all.

Abby sat in the familiar waiting room of the City Health Center. Her appointment wasn't for another twenty minutes so she settled into the chair with a magazine. Her last chemo session had been three weeks ago and now she was getting a follow-up mammogram for good measure. While absently flipping through the magazine, she replayed the argument she and Mason had had about their living arrangements. His anger over her decision had been a constant source of distress over the last few days. His cold concern for her now was even worse. But what could she do? Their situation had been different at Tammy's; now things were more serious and she needed to approach them in a serious manner.

She had to admit that she *had* allowed herself to dream of marriage to Mason. Of making a family with him and Nell. But honestly, she'd thought that dream unreachable. Their relationship had begun with much uncertainty, and then her medical condition had surfaced, turning her world on its axis.

Mason had decided to commit himself to her then, but was that based more on his natural compassion for the sick or his true feelings for her?

If he were sincere about his feelings for her, was it fair to saddle both him and Nell with the fact that her cancer could return? And there was still the possibility of infertility.

Of course Anna and Tammy had been elated when she'd told them of the marriage proposal. But they were sorely biased and didn't consider all the elements to the equation. Jeff had wisely kept his opinions to himself, while Mason seemed to have tacitly accepted her decision since he was keeping his distance.

The last week had been terribly lonely without him, and now she sat in the doctor's office with a mind full of uncertainties and confusion.

Down the hall a door slammed, snapping Abby out of her reverie. She slightly altered the angle of the magazine so she could discreetly see what was going on. To her surprise, she saw Pauline walking defiantly out of the office. What on earth was she doing here? Abby rose to follow her out, but the nurse called her name, signaling it was time for her appointment. For a moment Abby stood undecided, looking from the door Pauline had just exited to the nurse holding her chart and waiting for her to follow. She sighed, deciding she needed to deal with her own health first. Then she'd find out what was going on with Pauline.

Abby walked into a room which was familiar except for the bed-like machine in the middle of the floor. The nurse explained that instead of the normal x-ray mammogram, she would be getting an MRI breast screen today. The MRI would examine the breast tissue for abnormal function, not just for abnormal appearance, which was key to this follow-up visit. Dr. St. John wanted to make sure that the chemo had killed any remaining cancer cells before declaring that Abby was in remission. Abby undressed and waited impatiently to get this over with. The machine was intimidating and she was nervous.

After the screening was complete, the technician led her into another examining room where she was instructed to wait for the doctor. She had wisely chosen not to question the technician this time, remembering the advice of the last one she'd encountered. Dr. St. John came into the room smiling brightly.

"Hi, Abigail. How are you?" Leaning over the table that doubled as a desk she scribbled notes in Abby's chart.

"Nervous," Abby answered honestly.

"Then let's get right to it. Lie back for me." Dr. St. John began the exam, kneading Abby's breast softly but thoroughly. At one point she hesitated and checked a particular area in her right breast twice. Her smile silently reassured Abby that it was okay. To Abby's surprise, her left breast was examined just as thoroughly.

"Okay, let me first begin by explaining to you again the dangers of recurrence following treatment. There are reports that women under the age of forty are at increased risk of cancer recurrence and spread following breast-conserving and radiation. But as I told you before, in your case I don't think we'll have to worry about metastasis. Everything looks fine today. The mammogram is clear and you feel fine. If you feel any changes, you call in immediately. Otherwise, I'll see you in six months." She smiled at Abby with that warm, understanding smile that Abby had become accustomed to over the last few months.

"I don't mind telling you that's a relief." Abby was elated. She couldn't wait to tell Mason. He would be just as pleased as she was. They could move on with their lives without this threat hovering over them for a while. They could...they could what? she wondered.

"What about kids? Can I have kids?" she asked hesitantly, almost afraid of the answer.

"I would suggest you give your body more time to filter out the last of the chemo before you start trying. Your period should return in a few weeks. Wait a while and then see your gynecologist and have him examine you again," she suggested.

"How long?" Abby needed to know.

"Maybe six to nine months." Dr. St. John could see that Abby didn't like that answer. "I'm sorry, Abigail, but I think it's for the best."

"Thank you. You've been a great help and I appreciate all you've done." Abby rose to leave.

"Tell Mason I said hello," Sandra told Abby as she left the office.

On the drive home Abby realized that her hesitation in marrying Mason was that she wanted to be sure that she was coming to him a completely healthy woman. Dr. St. John couldn't have given her better news. She knew there was still a possibility that the cancer would return but there was also a possibility that she could get run over by a truck. Sitting in that office had made her realize that life was full of uncertainties.

Initially, her health had been her reason for not marrying Mason. Now that she'd been given a clean bill of health, well, as clean as a woman recovering from a bout with breast cancer could get, did that mean that her answer to Mason's proposal would change? Did she love him enough to marry him? Did she love his daughter enough to raise her as her own? Even if she could never conceive on her own? Was she ready to abandon her old way of living to start a new life? A life with a family of her own?

Mason was still staying with Tammy and Jeff, so that was her first stop upon her return from Dr. St. John's office. Her spirits immediately plummeted when she didn't see his car in the driveway. She went into the house anyway.

"Hey girl! Why aren't you at work?" Tammy was out of breath when she answered the door. Abby had interrupted her aerobic time. Music and the voice of an instructor blared loudly from the television in the living room. Tammy, her streaked hair pulled on top of her head in a sloppy ponytail, was dressed in a vibrant yellow and blue leotard and matching spandex. She walked stiffly away from the door.

"I see I've interrupted your gym time." Abby closed the door behind her and followed Tammy.

"Don't worry about it, I was almost finished anyway. So what's going on?"

"Nothing really. Just looking for Mason. Is he at the office?" Abby tried to be nonchalant but her excitement threatened to bubble over at any moment.

"I don't know." Tammy glanced at her sister before switching the television off. He doesn't tell me his comings and goings. Especially not since my kid sister broke his heart by refusing to marry him."

"I did not refuse. Anyway, I don't want to talk about that. Not with you anyway."

"You're ready to answer him? Is that why you're looking for him?" Tammy's voice perked up.

"I would like to see him and that's that. Where's Nell?"

"Jeff took her and Melissa to the park."

Abby looked at her watch and considered going to Mason's office but decided against it. "I'll just get going. I have some errands to run." She turned to leave.

"I'll bet you do," Tammy mumbled.

"What?" Abby asked.

"If I hear from him I'll tell him you stopped by," Tammy offered.

"Thanks a lot, Tam," Abby said sarcastically.

"Don't mention it." Tammy smiled. She had a funny feeling things were about to happen for Mason and Abby.

CHAPTER 15

Mason's heart was about to somersault out of his chest. He stared blankly at the pages on the table before him, quietly praying that this would be the answer.

"You will see that all is in order, Mr. Penney. And as I informed you earlier, should you marry, it would be no problem to add your wife's name to the deed," Mr. Stewart assured him. Mason read over the description of the property again and smiled to himself. He remembered how much Abby loved that house. And here he was buying it for her–for them. She hadn't turned down his proposal but she had hesitated, for a week to be exact. He had tried to give her space, not stopping by her apartment as much as he wanted to and only calling each a day to see if she was feeling okay.

The idea about the house had come to him after he had stormed out of his brother's house angry as a raging bull because she hadn't given him the answer he had wanted to hear. Once he calmed down, he realized he had driven to the very spot on the Rubaker property where they had decided to take their relationship to the next level. The house stood there steadfast and unmoving, like a symbol of the commitment they had unknowingly made on that night. He knew they ought to be together, in that house, for the rest of their lives. There was no doubt in his mind. The next morning he had walked into Stewart Realty and submitted a contract for the house.

Now he was about to sign the papers taking ownership of this property she loved so much. He didn't think of it as a bribe because he was sure she loved him as much as he loved her. It was meant to be a nudge in the right direction, the direction of their future. After affixing his signature in the designated space, he left his attorney's office and headed for his new home.

Abby's nerves were frazzled. She had called Mason's office and paged him numerous times; still, she hadn't heard from him. She briefly wondered if something were wrong. He wouldn't willing-ly ignore her pages. After all, he'd finally told her he wasn't angry and that he understood her needing time to think. Although she had known that the last was a lie, she had believed that he wasn't upset with her. This might be proving otherwise.

She put her keys in the door to her apartment and stepped inside. With summer eagerly approaching, the sun sat high in the sky in all its glory well into the early evening hours. Light spilled through her open blinds. While turning to lock the door, she noticed a slip of pink, frilly-edged paper lying on the floor. She picked it up and fingered it absently, trying to figure out what it could be. It was folded in half and sealed with an adhesive red heart. Her heart fluttered and a smile tickled her lips as she unfolded the paper.

What would I be without your love to guide me? How would I make it through the day? I can't imagine my life without you. My only wish is that you love me and that our love will lead the way.

29 Old Seminole Road 7:30 p.m.

She re-read the note and then read it once more for good measure. With her heart brimming with love for the man she knew she'd spend the rest of her life with, she closed her eyes and sent up a silent thanks. It was already quarter of seven. She needed to hurry and change. She showered quickly, then changed first into a breezy pink sundress. Unfortunately, the spaghetti straps would not allow for the thick straps of the stiff cotton bras she had been wearing, and with her size she had never been able to go braless. She rummaged through her lingerie drawer to find a solution. In her hurry, a few pieces fell to the floor, and she bent to retrieve them.

Looking down at what had fallen, she blushed. She held in her hand a lacy strapless bra and panties in almost the same shade of pink as her dress. Maybe she could still wear the bra. Nervously, she slipped it on, not sure how comfortable it would be. After a few moments of adjustment, she found that it felt fine and donned the matching bikini panties. She stared at herself in the mirror, bursting with excitement.

She noted too, that her stomach was still smooth and flat. A small edge of disappointment tried to pry its way into her mind but she kept it at bay. Dr. St. John hadn't said she could never have children; she'd just told her to wait. She slipped the dress over her head and stood to the side to admire herself. Her butt had always been a source of agitation to her. Like the butts of all the women in her family, it sat out, kind of like a basketball protruding from her backside. Sucking it in didn't work, so she had learned to live with it. Tammy said it was a blessing. "All men love a big booty." Tammy was insane, Abby had always known this, but unlike Abby, she did have a proven track record with men.

Abby hunched her shoulders, deciding that she was what she was and there was no changing it. From the tight fit at her waist to her ankles, the voluminous material swirled around her. She slid her feet into white sandals with sexy three-inch heels. Checking the mirror once again, she caught sight of the clock on her night-stand. It was seven-thirty. She was late, but she didn't panic for she knew that he would wait for her. They had both waited so long that another few minutes wouldn't hurt. That was her mind talking; her heart couldn't wait. She spritzed herself with body spray and ran out of the house.

Abby drove like a mad woman through Manchester's back-roads. As she crossed the bridge that led to the house she caught sight of candlelight through the screening of the newly finished deck. At the last minute she had decided to enclose it so that the new owners could enjoy the lake even in the winter months. She skipped the front door entrance in favor of the door that led directly onto the deck.

She was greeted by scented candles—vanilla, she guessed—and the smooth, sultry sounds of Anita Baker serenading her from a CD player in the corner. A furry blue blanket had been laid on the wood floor, along with three very large pillows in turquoise, Mason's favorite color. A gleeful giggle escaped her lips.

"Not only is she late but she laughs at my meager attempt at romance." Hearing Mason's deep voice behind her, she turned quickly to face him. She was not prepared for the sensual assault the sight of him caused. He wore cream-colored slacks with a matching silk shirt that was left unbuttoned to mid chest, allow-ing for a tantalizing view of his taut muscles and smooth mocha skin. His eyes sparkled in the candlelight. Her mouth watered as her eyes combed the length of him.

"Sorry. I got your note a little late." Standing awkwardly, she continued to stare. "I didn't mean to make you wait."

"Yes, you did. But I would wait a lifetime for you, Abigail." Closing the distance between them, he cupped her face and kissed her tenderly, with all the love he felt at that very moment.

"I've missed you," she willingly admitted when he held her close to him, her cheek against his muscled chest.

"I missed you too, baby." His feet began moving to the beat of the music. Abby obediently followed suit. As his body molded itself to hers, her skin became alive, incredibly sensitive to his touch. She hummed along with Anita Baker as he held her closely, one hand holding hers tightly, the other resting comfortably on her butt.

"I won't let you go, Gabby," he stated sternly.

"I don't want you to," she whispered.

"We will be together always."

"I can promise you that."

"You are the love of my life."

"Without your love I have no life." They ceased moving, the music fading in the background, as his gray eyes held her hazel ones.

"All you have to do is say when," Mason prompted.

"September," she said without hesitation. "The month we found each other."

"And the day was…"

"The fifteenth. Megan's birth," she said.

Mason seemed to contemplate that day. "I'll be there."

"You'd better be," she smiled.

Somewhere around two that morning as they lay in each other's arms on the thick blanket in the light of the dwindling candles and the moon hanging low in the sky, it occurred to Abby that they were trespassing.

"Mason, we could be arrested. I'm not supposed to be on this property when I'm not working. I could lose this job or worse…wait a minute." Abby propped herself up on one arm so that she could look into his face. "How did you get in here?"

"Usually when you buy a house they give you a key." He waited for his words to register.

"You didn't?" she whispered.

Mason grinned. "I did. And since you've finally agreed to be my wife I guess I'll let you live here with me."

"I can't believe it! Why?" she asked.

Mason folded his arms behind his head, staring at the amazed expression on her face. "Because you love this house. And I love you. I thought we could make a fair trade," he teased.

"You thought this would convince me to marry you? You were going to bribe me?" she asked seriously.

"I sure as hell was gonna use it but then things just sort of fell into place. Why is that?"

Abby looked away from him. Mixed emotions paraded through her at a rapid pace. "I couldn't accept your proposal before because I wasn't sure about my condition. You deserve a whole woman and I wasn't sure of that then," she explained.

"And now you are?" he said.

She smiled weakly. "I went to the doctor's this morning and was given a clean bill of health."

UNCONDITIONAL

Mason sat up. "You know, for a woman as intelligent as you are, you come up with the silliest notions sometimes." He pulled her against his broad chest. "When I asked you to marry me, I wanted *you* to marry me. That meant that I wanted you, just you. It didn't matter what you were or what you weren't. I just wanted you," he told her.

Abby sighed, his words comforting her. "I just wanted to be able to be everything I could for you—physically. The doctor even said that in a few months I would get my period back," she announced happily.

"I didn't know you were looking forward to that," Mason chuckled.

Abby swatted his bare arm playfully. "I want to have a baby. Our baby. I mean, Nell is great, I love her like she was my own. But she's not and I'd just like the experience of having one myself. What do you think about that?" She held herself stiffly as he seemed to be digesting the announcement.

"I would love for you to have our baby."

CHAPTER 16

"We must have a party. It's been too long since we've had something to celebrate in this family," Tammy suggested, eyeing Abby and Mason.

"What's worth celebrating?" Jeff questioned when he walked into the house, dropping his suitcase in the middle of the floor.

"Oh hi, honey. I thought you were coming in this evening." Tammy kissed her husband whom she hadn't seen since yesterday.

"I finished the bid early and rushed home. I missed my girls."

"Did you get the contract?" Abby asked.

"I get the feeling that we have more exciting news to discuss than my job." Jeff's gaze examined Abby.

"Well, Abby got a clean bill of health for one thing," Tammy started.

"That's great, Abby!" Jeff hugged his sister-in-law.

"And…Mason bought the Rubaker house. I guess we'll have to call it the Penney house now, though. Wouldn't that make sense?" Tammy pondered her own questions.

"Really?" Jeff began.

"And…they're getting married!" Tammy screeched.

"What? Can't a man go out of town for a moment without his family making a bunch of changes on him?" Jeff said. "Congratulations! Or should I say it's about time?" He embraced Mason. "I have to agree with my wife. I think we need a party."

"See, I tried to tell them." Tammy was all smiles.

"I don't want a big fuss. Maybe we could just have a small dinner," Abby suggested.

"How about a barbeque? The Fourth's coming up. We could do it then," Mason prompted. He was in the mood for a big celebration.

Tammy agreed wholeheartedly. She loved a good party.

"Like a housewarming/engagement party," Jeff added.

"I like that idea. What about you, baby?" Mason asked Abby.

Abby shrugged. "It doesn't look like I have much choice. The majority rules in this case." Throwing her hands up hopelessly, she agreed.

"I guess it does. You seem to be completely outnumbered." Jeff smiled in her direction "Now, if you'll excuse me, I have two little ladies to surprise." Jeff headed out of the room but halted suddenly. "Mase, have you told Mom?" The silence that fell over the room was deafening. All eyes rested on Mason, whose expression had gone from complete bliss to utter distress.

Mason groaned. "Can't we just invite her to the barbeque and surprise her?"

"I say we conveniently forget to invite her," Tammy mumbled.

Abby remained quiet, letting the decision be Mason's alone.

"No. Somebody in town is bound to mention it to her. I'll go see her this afternoon," Mason said.

"I'll go with you." Abby surprised herself by volunteering to go into the lion's den. But she figured if God could save Daniel, he'd surely be with her while she braved Pauline Penney.

"First, I need to get to the office and pick up some papers. You girls start the party planning." Mason stood to leave.

"Great! This is going to be great," Tammy exclaimed.

"I'll walk you out," Abby volunteered. When they were alone, Mason hugged her closely.

"What was that for?" she asked, "not that I'm complaining. A few of these a day will do wonders for my self-esteem, not to mention our sex life," she joked as she cuddled against him.

"I just wanted you to know that I appreciate your support. I know going to see my mother is the last thing you want to do."

"Actually, I'd like to start my relationship with my mother-in-law on the right foot. Besides, I need to be there to defend myself. She's bound to try to talk you out of marrying me and I can't let that happen, now can I?" She smiled up at him.

"There's no way she could do that." He kissed her soundly on the lips. "I'll come by and pick you up in a little while. Now go plan our party." His hands on her shoulders, he turned her toward the kitchen, giving her behind a soft pat as he sent her on her way.

Anna rushed right over after speaking to Abby on the phone. The excitement of her last daughter getting married was more than she could stand in her house all by herself. She couldn't wait to see her daughter walk down the aisle.

"Abigail Mae, I am so happy for you. You don't know how many nights I've prayed for this. And Mason is such a good man. The Lord sure is good," she exclaimed as she hugged her daughter for the hundredth time since entering Tammy's kitchen.

"Yes, He is. I'm glad you're happy, Mama." Abby kissed her

mother's weathered cheek.

"Your father is going to be so happy. I tried to call him but he was in the field. I'll have to tell him tonight. Now, I have a missionary meeting at the church later, so let's get started." Anna pulled out a notepad and pen. Tammy grinned and Abby rolled her eyes.

Four hours and half a pineapple upside down cake later, they had decided that the barbeque would be on the Fourth of July. They wouldn't send out invitations because they would be repeating the task in another four weeks for the wedding. Instead, Tammy and Anna had agreed to call the members of their family that would be invited and Abby would call Mason's colleagues. They were at a loss as to who to invite from the Penney family, so Abby opted to discuss it with Pauline on her visit that afternoon.

Abby hadn't been to the Penney estate since last Thanksgiving. That alone added to her apprehensiveness. When she and Mason walked into the house, they were greeted by a strange silence.

"Did you call to tell her you were coming?" Abby asked.

"Yeah. She said she'd be here all day. Hello?" Mason yelled.

"I'll be right down, dear." Pauline's voice echoed through the halls. They took a seat in the living room while they waited for her. As she descended the stairs in her usual regal manner, Abby saw the disappointment mask Pauline's well-kept features. She knew that she alone was responsible for the change.

Abby spoke first. "Hello, Mrs. Penney. You're looking lovely today."

Pauline ignored her, moving directly to her son. "Hello, darling." She hugged Mason as he kissed her cheek. "It's so wonderful to see you. I've missed you since you moved in with your brother."

"Mother, Gabby and I wanted to tell you our news personally." Mason began by taking Abby's hand. When Pauline witnessed that show of affection, her back stiffened her and her face grew cold.

Abby attempted again to break the ice. "Mason has purchased the Rubaker property. Isn't that wonderful?"

"That's an awful lot of space for you and Nell," Pauline replied.

"Nell and I won't be alone. Gabby has agreed to be my wife."

A chilly silence filled the room. Pauline stilled, her eyes fiercely glaring at her son as her jewel-clad fingers gripped the arms of the chair with fierce intensity.

"You cannot be serious," she said in a low voice, emphasizing each syllable.

"We are very serious and I would appreciate it if you could put aside any hostile feelings you have for Gabby and her family and come to our engagement party. It's on the Fourth of July, at our new house," he stated firmly.

Pauline looked from Mason to Abby, then back to Mason again. "I don't think I'll be able to attend any sort of engagement party."

"Mother," Mason began.

Abby stood and held her hand up to stop Mason mid-sentence. "Mrs. Penney, I know that you don't particularly care for me or my family. But I would ask that you put those feelings aside to support your son. I *am* going to marry Mason and we will be forced to spend time together as a family at some point. I would hope that you can be woman enough to deal with this in a mature manner."

Pauline stared up at Abby, her cold dark eyes assessing her thoroughly. "So you think you've done something by convincing my son to marry you?" She chuckled. "Just know that I *am* woman enough to deal with whatever situation is thrown my way. My son knows that I love him and would do anything for him. But I will not attend another wedding of Anna Swanson's children." Standing finally, she eyed Abby again before walking from the room.

Mason dropped his head into his hands.

Abby sat back down beside him, rubbing her hand over his back. "She'll come around, baby."

"You think so?"

"I'm sure. We just caught her off guard." Abby wanted desperately to believe her own words. She wanted to believe that no mother could be that selfish. Yet she wasn't quite convinced.

The Fourth of July barbeque arrived and Abby still hadn't found any house furniture that suited her taste. Since Mason had purchased the house before she could decorate it, all the rooms except the kitchen were still empty. Because they still hadn't moved in, she suggested canceling but Mason wouldn't hear of it.

The deck was furnished with a huge gas grill, chairs and two tables with umbrellas. He was really excited about the whole party despite his mother's refusal to attend.

They hadn't heard from Pauline since their last encounter, so when she suddenly called the shop two days before the party to say she was coming to the barbeque, Abby was astonished. Their conversation was brief. No apologies, no truce, just, "I'll be at the party, please let Mason know." Then she abruptly hung up. Abby only had the chance to say hello. She stared at the phone for a few minutes after placing it back on its stand.

The phone call jarred her memory to the day she had seen Pauline at the doctor's office. With the flurry of activity going on in her life since that day, she hadn't gotten the chance to tell Mason about it. But now it worried her.

Why would Pauline go to a clinic all the way in New York? Manchester had a wealth of good doctors and even Trenton was closer than New York. Abby hadn't seen what office she had come out of, so she had no idea which doctor she had seen. Of course she could have investigated the matter further, but after the exciting news she had received, Pauline's reasons for being there had immediately taken a backseat in her mind. She made a mental note to mention it to Mason this evening.

By the afternoon of the party, Abby was a bundle of emotion operating purely on adrenaline. She'd been up since six making deviled eggs and dicing fruit for the summer salad. She hummed cheerfully as she went from one chore to the next before driving to her parents' home to pick up her mother, who waddled to the car with a load of food trays.

"Mama, what did you cook?" Abby asked as she got out of

the car to help her load the food into the back of her car.

"Oh just a little of this and that." "This and that" added up to fried chicken, potato salad, seafood salad and baked beans, as well as spare ribs to be barbequed on the grill. Anna was filled with joy, as was her daughter. This was a good time for the Swansons.

"I'm so happy for you, Abigail Mae. This will be a blessed union, I can tell," Anna said as they drove to the house.

"I hope so. I mean, it feels right and I've waited so long. I can hardly believe it. A few months ago I was faced with the likelihood of dying and now I have a fiancé and I'm looking forward to moving into my new house. Who would have thought?" Abby fairly squealed.

"God never gives you more than you can handle. And when you put your trust in Him, He blesses you continuously. You deserve to be happy, and you will be," Anna confirmed.

"I hope Mason's as excited as I am," she said.

"He is. He came over to borrow some tools to put together that fancy grill he bought and he was grinnin' from ear to ear." That made Abby blush. "Has he heard from his mother?" Anna asked.

"No. She hasn't talked to him personally but she called me a couple of days ago to say she was coming to the cookout."

"She called you? Mmph, I'm surprised," Anna clucked. "What else did she say?"

"Nothing. Just that she was coming," Abby said dismally.

"Don't let it worry you, child. She's very unhappy. An unsettling spirit is what she has. Just leave her be. She's not worth your worry."

"I know, but I feel kind of responsible. I mean, I don't want Mason to resent me later for the loss of his relationship with his mother." Abby turned onto the road that led to her new home.

"Don't. She causes her own unhappiness. She's done so for so long I don't think she even knows any other way to be. Stanford's been stepping out on her for as long as I can remember. He never wanted to marry her in the first place but he couldn't stand up to his parents." Anna's eyes glazed as she remembered so long ago when she had been in love with Stanford Penney.

Abby listened intently. It was quite a shock to hear her mother speaking this way. She'd never talked openly about Mr. or Mrs. Penney aside from the obvious.

"Parents have to let their children make their own decisions." Anna shook her head at the thought of history repeating itself. "The only responsibility you have is to love her as God has loved you." Anna noticed the grimace on Abby's face and chuckled. "I didn't say you had to *like* her, Abigail Mae." Anna chatted incessantly throughout the rest of their ride.

Mason and Jeff were already in the front yard setting up tarps to shade the guests. It was a typical summer day in Manchester, hot and muggy. The lake water glistened and sparkled, offering a cool reprieve. Abby momentarily entertained thoughts of jumping in. Her mother's voice yelling directions to her brought her back into the real world, and she abandoned her idea.

Finally the food was ready and guests began to arrive with hugs and sincere congratulations. Abby had decided not to tell

UNCONDITIONAL

Mason about Pauline's message, just in case she didn't show. But while guests were dancing to old favorites from the Four Tops and the Temptations, Pauline and her guest made their entrance.

Apparently Tammy witnessed Pauline's arrival as well and was at Abby's side in minutes.

"Who the hell is that with her?" Tammy asked Abby as they both watched the two women approach.

"I guess it's too much to hope it's a relative." Abby was experiencing some very bad vibes.

"Hello, Abigail. Tamara." The smile on Pauline's face and the pleasant way she greeted them was definitely not a good sign. "I'd like you to meet Dr. Teresa Parker."

Abby froze where she stood, staring at the adult image of Nell. Pauline noted the recognition and smiled pleasantly.

"It's nice to meet you, Dr. Parker." Abby extended her hand to shake Dr. Parker's but Pauline grabbed it instead.

"Why don't you run along and find Mason and Nell for us, Abigail. Teresa is most anxious to see them," Pauline said with a chilling smile on her face.

"I'm sure she is," Tammy mumbled. When they were well out of Pauline's hearing range, Tammy abruptly pulled Abby to the side.

"I can't believe she's done this," Tammy said.

"I can," Abby said. "Let's just find Mason."

"What!" Tammy exclaimed.

Abby yelled to Tammy over her shoulder, "What would you suggest I do, Tammy?"

"I suggest you trot your little butt right back over there and tell them to get the hell out of your house. You know they're only here to start trouble," Tammy said vehemently, grabbing Abby's arm to stop her from walking away.

Abby yanked her arm free of her sister's grip. "Tammy, that's rude and I won't do that. She has a right to see her daughter."

"And does she have the same right to crash your engagement party to see your fiancé?" Tammy questioned.

"I will not be rude, Tammy," Abby insisted. So many questions were going through her mind. Would Mason be glad to see Teresa? Would this cause the problems Tammy was so sure it would? Would Nell be happy to see her mother?

"Rude is showing up at your son's engagement party with his ex-girlfriend in tow. *That's* rude! And I'm telling you, if you let her run over you in the beginning she'll do it for the rest of your lives. You have to put her in her place now," Tammy said adamantly.

Abby had earlier thought she had, but apparently it would take more to intimidate Pauline.

"Look at her over there gloating. And Dr. Parker didn't even want Nell. She was going to put her up for adoption. What kind of mother is that? If you ask me, Nell's better off without her." Tammy was noticeably in a rage at this point.

Mason interrupted the scene, grabbing Abby by the waist. "Who's gloating?"

"Nobody," Abby said quickly, then sighed when she heard Tammy suck her teeth. "Your mother's here."

"And look who's with her," Tammy added, directing Mason's gaze in Pauline's direction.

"Did you know she was coming?" Mason asked Abby without looking at her.

"Yeah, we invited her and Dr. Parker," Tammy said snidely.

Mason ignored her, focusing all his attention on Abby and how she was handling this turn of events.

Tired of Tammy's comments, Abby yelled, "Hush!" She took a deep breath. "I knew your mother said she was coming. She called to tell me the other day. I didn't say anything because I wasn't sure she really would. But she didn't say she was bringing a guest." Abby's stomach churned at the way Mason seemed to be entranced by the sight of Teresa.

"We will be hospitable. Shall we?" With his upturned hand, he waited for Abby to respond. When she hesitated, he looked at her and smiled. "Trust me."

She did trust him, so she took his hand and silently prayed that things would turn out all right.

He led her toward the spot where Pauline and Dr. Parker stood. They were about two feet away when Teresa turned to face them. Abby felt the tension rise in Mason. She wished she hadn't. This woman had been an important part of his life.

"Hello, darling." Pauline hugged her son, watching Abby with a self-satisfied look.

"Hello, Mother. I'm glad you changed your mind."

"You knew I wouldn't miss it. This is a lovely house. Tell me, was it very expensive? Not that you can't afford it since you are opening your own practice." Pauline practically beamed.

Abby had never seen her this way and couldn't decide which Pauline she disliked the most.

"It was reasonable." Mason barely masked his anger.

"Don't be rude, dear. I'm sure you remember Teresa." Pauline nudged the woman who stood next to her. She was very tall for a woman and very confident. Her skin was like melted dark chocolate and her body looked perfect in the miniskirt and fitted blouse she wore. Her hair was piled high atop her head in a cascade of micro-mini braids. She was beautiful. Abby felt suffocated.

"Yes. I remember Teresa. But I have to admit I'm very surprised to see her here."

"Mason, she's not deaf or mute. I'm sure if you at least looked at her she could tell you why she's here," Pauline insisted.

"I'm really not interested, Mother."

Abby felt as if she were sinking. She remembered her loneliness from a year before. She would not feel that way again. All she needed to do was convince this woman that Mason was unavailable.

"Dr. Parker, I'm Abby, Mason's fiancée. I'm delighted you could join us in our celebration." Her smile was bright, her eyes focused. She meant business and she wanted Dr. Parker to know it.

"Thank you. I was a bit surprised to hear that Mason was getting married."

Damn it, she had an accent too. It sounded Caribbean. Abby couldn't compete with that.

"When I last saw him he was quite against even discussing the possibility of marriage. I wonder what changed his mind." She stared at Mason.

"I have to credit that to Abby," he said stiffly. " Now if you'll excuse us, we have other guests to tend to." Mason stalked away, practically dragging Abby behind him.

"Mason?" Abby said. He continued walking. "Mason?" she

said a little louder. When she still got no response, she stopped walking, realizing a little too late that wasn't a good idea because he almost pulled her arm out of its socket before he even noticed.

"Damn it, Mason! I would like to keep my limbs intact if you don't mind," she yelled.

"What?" he yelled back.

"What are you running from?"

"I'm not running from anything."

"Well, you sure as hell could have fooled me," Abby said.

"Gabby, I don't want to do this now."

"Fine," she said quietly and walked in the opposite direction.

They managed to get through the rest of the day and at the end of the evening they presented a united front, seeming to be the epitome of happiness as they bade goodnight to their family and friends.

Abby had expected she and Mason would linger in the house after all their guests had gone and talk about what had happened. Instead, he offered to take her aunt and uncle home. So Abby went back to her apartment alone.

She was home by midnight. After undressing, she fixed a cup of tea. She told herself it was for relaxation, but deep down she knew she was stalling in case Mason called or stopped by.

The next morning she awoke to a throbbing headache but managed to fall out of bed and make her way to the answering machine. No calls. Not sure what she should be feeling, Abby sat in the living room contemplating the previous night's events.

Mason had put on a good show for their guests but she'd known he was angry.

As the party had gone on, she'd seen him talking to Teresa and wondered what was being said. Surely Mason could not still have feelings for a woman who had lied to him and then threatened to give his child up for adoption. And what about Nell? Abby had kept Nell close to her for the duration of the evening, hoping to talk to Theresa alone when she decided to visit with her daughter. But that didn't happen.

Abby told herself that Mason loved *her* and he was going to marry *her*. He had brought her a house and was making plans for their future. She had nothing to be afraid of.

The phone rang and Abby almost fell off the edge of the chair where she had been perched. She stumbled over the lamp cord and dove onto the couch, landing with her body half on and half off the sofa, and snatched the phone from its cradle.

"Good morning," Tammy's voice said.

"Mornin'," Abby mumbled, noticeably disappointed that it wasn't Mason.

"He came in about one this morning, climbed into the bed with Nell and slept for a few hours. Woke up about an hour ago, showered, changed clothes and stormed out ten minutes ago. Which means that he should be at your door in about ten to fifteen minutes, give or take a few." Tammy spoke matter-of-factly.

"Thanks for the update." Abby appreciated the rundown of Mason's actions. But it didn't put her at ease.

"Just thought you'd be wondering right about now. And from the way you answered the phone, my guess was right."

"Does Jeff know anything about her?"

"Nope. I asked him after we left. He said Pauline introduced them last night. He thought she was innocent in this, but I don't know. What do you think?"

"Maybe she is. I mean, what kind of woman would want to come to her ex-lover's engagement party?" Abby wondered aloud. "She didn't even ask to see Nell."

"The kind who had intentions on getting her ex-lover back. There's no telling what Pauline led her to believe. I'm sure the old woman didn't bother telling her Mason was engaged, let alone that it was his engagement party they were crashing. And as for Nell, I told you she didn't give a rat's ass about that poor baby."

"Yeah. Right." Abby's heart stopped when she heard the knock at the door. Her silence allowed Tammy to hear it as well.

"Damn, I'm good. Fifteen minutes exactly. Go answer it," she said.

"I'm not sure I want to. I mean, maybe if I just ignore it it'll go away." She'd wished for Mason to call or stop by last night but now that it was probably him at the door, she was nervous.

"Abby, this is your future you're talking about. Do you want to lose him?"

"No. But I'm not desperate either."

"No, you're not but if you want something you should fight for it. What happened to my sister the rebel? The one who argued the price of a worthless lamp because it had sentimental value? The one who bloodied Johnny Cassidy's nose because he called her a wimp?"

"I don't know," Abby shrugged.

"I know. She fell in love and now her mind is all filled with romance and happiness. Get over it 'cause if you don't fight this battle to win, Dr. Parker will have your man and you'll have nothing but a lot of bitter feelings. And I don't want you to turn into some man-hating old maid," Tammy said seriously.

Abby laughed at her sister's assessment of the situation, realizing that she was probably right. In any other situation Abby would not have backed down. So what was so different about this time? She wasn't sure, but the thought of not doing anything was suddenly not so appealing.

"All right. I'll call you when he leaves."

"Oh no you won't. I'll just stay on the phone and listen," Tammy suggested.

"No!" Abby screeched.

"Come on, all you have to do is place the phone gently in the cradle, you know, off to the side just a bit so it doesn't disconnect me."

"You are insane." The knock sounded again.

"Think about it."

"No!" Abby hesitated before hanging up. "You've done this before haven't you?"

"Bye, girl." Tammy hung up the phone and Abby ran to open the door. Mason stood on the other side. He looked tired and irritated.

"Hi."

"Hi." He stepped into the apartment, grabbing her in a fierce embrace. Abby didn't know what to say or what to do, for that matter.

"Are you okay?" she asked.

"I'm all right. Now." He led them to the sofa to sit down. When she would have sat beside him, he shifted her so that she sat in his lap. "Teresa wants to take Nell."

"Are you serious? How can she suggest such a thing?"

"It seems that my mother has convinced her it would be in Nell's best interest. You aren't exactly her choice for stepmom of the year."

"So once again, it boils down to me." Abby shook her head at the irony. "Mason, you have to do what's best for Nell. You know Teresa doesn't really want her. So you have to decide whether or not you're ready to fight for your daughter," Abby said earnestly.

"There's no question that I'm going to fight for her. I just need to know how you feel about that."

Abby was momentarily taken aback. "Me? What difference does it make what I say?"

"Gabby, you are the love of my life. My future is with you. I need to know that you're behind me on this. That this is what you want too."

Abby smiled, her heart filling with love for this man who'd made her a part of his life. "Of course it's what I want. You and Nell are going to be my family in a couple of months. We belong together."

"That's what I wanted to hear." He sighed, then let his head loll back on the chair.

He'd had a rough night talking, or rather, arguing with Teresa for hours, then storming out of his mother's house in such a rage he couldn't see straight. He'd fallen into bed in an emotional stupor when he finally arrived at Jeff's house.

"Mason," Abby said. "Why would she come back now?"

Mason opened his eyes. "Oh, that was entirely my mother's

doing. You see, she came up with the brilliant idea that if Teresa came back claiming to want Nell, I would drop everything to deal with her. Even the wedding."

His raised his head then, looking at her intently. Her hair came to her shoulders now and was tousled and her eyes were still a bit sleepy. But she was beautiful and she was his. That was all that mattered. He knew she was thinking that all this had happened because Pauline didn't like her. And that was probably true, but he didn't plan to let that get in the way of his and his daughter's happiness. And that happiness hinged on Abby.

He lifted his hand to her chin and tilted her head so that they were eye to eye. "Don't blame yourself. You didn't do anything to her. In fact, I'm really proud of the way you've dealt with her these past weeks."

Abby blinked furiously to keep from crying. Pauline was pulling out all the stops. And, yes, she blamed herself. But she was going to fight for her happiness as well as the happiness of her new family. "We're going to be so good together," she told him.

Mason smiled. "Tell me something I don't know." Pulling her face closer to his, he let his lips lightly graze hers.

Abby leaned into his warm embrace, inhaling his intoxicating scent.

CHAPTER 17

It was September before Abby could turn around. The day before the wedding, she found herself in the bridal shop with arms outstretched. The seamstress was talking around the pins dangling from her lips, demanding that Abby move this way and that. Her mother and Tammy sat in the chairs across from the mirror, making their own comments on the dress. It seemed that with the completion of chemo Abby had picked up a few pounds, and those pounds had landed everywhere. Not that she looked fat or sloppy but it was a change from her usual petite size. Mason insisted that he loved it, but Abby wasn't too sure. Fortunately, the dress didn't emphasize any unsightly bulges; in fact, it was actually very flattering to her.

Her dress was made of the brightest white satin she had ever seen and had iridescent beads and sequins lining the hemline. The sleeves were sheer with tiny roses around the wrists. As she swayed this way and that, sunbeams caught the iridescent beads and cast tiny rainbows onto the floor and the walls. Her mother was crying again but Tammy was giddy with excitement.

Abby, however, was strangely calm.

After their sessions with Bishop Miles, she felt that she and Mason were already married—mentally and emotionally at least. They had established a strong commitment to each other and to God, the combination Bishop Miles said was the groundwork for a good marriage. Everything else to do with the marriage just seemed like a formality. But tomorrow morning those formalities would be taken care of and she would be spending the night in her new home with her new husband. She could hardly wait. From somewhere she suddenly caught the scent of baby powder and lotion and wobbled on her feet, woozy. She couldn't help remembering her dream. A lump formed in her throat.

"Abigail Mae? Are you all right?" she heard her mother saying.

"She's gonna be stuck in her behind if she doesn't keep still and let me finish," Natty complained.

"I'm...I'm okay, Mama. Just thinking," she stammered. She hadn't shared her dream with anyone else and she doubted if she ever would. She was afraid that if she talked about it, it would jinx her, and as silly as it sounded, she felt that she was getting a wonderful glimpse into the future...her future.

Finally, two hours later, the threesome left the bridal shop. That gave them just enough time to get to the church for rehearsal. The wedding party was small, consisting of only Mason, Abby, Tammy and Jeff. So things went smoothly, with Tammy and Jeff being veterans at this wedding thing. They had dinner at Abby's parents' house, where she was spending the night. After dinner, everyone left to get a good night's sleep but Mason and Abby lingered on the front porch.

"In just a few hours you'll be Mrs. Mason Penney. Are you excited?" Mason asked.

"Not really. I already know what I'm getting into." They laughed before falling into a comfortable silence, each lost within their own thoughts.

"I'm going to stop by my mother's to see if she's changed her

mind about coming," he said out of the blue. They hadn't discussed Pauline since the day after the barbeque.

"That's a good idea," Abby honestly agreed. It was easy to
love people who loved you back or who were easy to love. The
true test was loving someone who didn't want to be loved. She
had made a vow that she would try to love Pauline despite the
way she treated her. "Maybe after the wedding we could invite
her over for dinner," Abby offered.

Mason shrugged. "If she'll come."

"We'll keep inviting her until she does. We can't have our
children not knowing their grandmother, now can we?" Abby
said, realizing belatedly that she had mentioned children. They
hadn't talked about this subject much. But Abby was ready to.
She wasn't so sure about Mason, though.

"We have a while to work on her before she becomes a grandmother again," he replied. Abby didn't let that deter her.

"I got my period a few days ago." She noted a flicker of
understanding in his eyes.

"Is that why you came up with that 'let's not have sex for a
week before the wedding' idea?" he smiled. Abby had forgotten
all about that. Actually she had come up with that idea a few days
before she had gotten her period; it had just worked out that way.

"No, but that was a coincidence, wasn't it? Anyway, Sandra
said I could start trying after I got my period." She let the words
hang in the air.

"Sandra said six to nine months, Gabby. Let's not rush it,"
Mason said slowly. He didn't want to discourage her but he did-
n't want to endanger her either.

"I know, but I don't think it'll hurt. I feel fine," she said.

"I know you do, sweetie, but what about the baby. What if the baby can't survive inside of you right now?"

"Mason, don't think that way."

"Gabby, I'm just trying to make you see the benefit in waiting until the doctor says it's okay. Have you even seen your gynecologist yet?" Mason asked. She frowned in response. "I didn't think so. Look, I want a baby as much as you do, but I want you to be able to handle this, okay? Nothing is more important to me than you. And if we can't have a baby we'll be fine," he offered.

"Don't say that! We will have a baby, I know we will." She was convinced they would. She had to be.

Mason didn't want to argue; instead, he took her into his arms. "After the wedding, call the doctor. We'll see what he says and then we'll go from there. Deal?" Holding her back slightly so that he could see her face, he raised a brow in question.

"Deal." She kissed him hungrily.

When he reluctantly pulled away, he rested his forehead against hers.

"I see this week has been as hard on you as it has on me."

Abby giggled. "Yeah, so you'd better get out of here before I attack you."

"I'm going." He began to walk down the steps but he turned suddenly. "I love you so much, Abigail. I can't wait until you're mine forever." He stood in the middle of the walkway beneath the pitch black sky.

Abby warmed all over, and her heart filled with happiness. "Just a little while longer and you'll never get rid of me."

She lay in her childhood bed that night staring out the window, amazed at the dull darkness that was the sky. There were no stars in sight, no moon, nothing. Just a quiet blackness blanketing Manchester.

She couldn't sleep; she couldn't think; she just lay there, waiting patiently. The clock in the hallway struck twelve and Abby closed her eyes to capture the moment. It had finally come. Her wedding day. She would have a husband, finally. Her happiness was almost complete. She felt a sudden wariness, but quickly pushed it aside. The Lord had brought her from loneliness to happiness, from illness to good health; she would not doubt Him now or ever. He'd told her that she would have a baby, so she knew it would be. When would not matter. Still, she hoped it was soon.

Nell and Melissa were the cutest flower girls anyone could ask for. They were quite a hit in their flowing white dresses and the halos of baby's breath circling their little heads. Mason came in a close second in Abby's mind. He was gorgeous on a daily basis but dressed in white tails, he was the best looking man she had ever seen. And after today he would be her husband. That thought had butterflies dancing gleefully in her stomach.

She barely remembered walking down the aisle, let alone repeating her vows. It wasn't until after they had walked back up the aisle hand in hand that she regained her composure and began to function with a semblance of normalcy.

The reception was lovely. The church fellowship hall had

been decorated in shades of pink and white, Abby's favorite colors. Tables were filled with family members, friends and business colleagues of both herself and Mason. Nell and Melissa ran around in their pretty little dresses, falling and laughing and thoroughly enjoying themselves.

Abby had noticed that Pauline was not at the ceremony and she waited for Mason to comment, but he never did. However, at one point during the reception, when it was almost time for her and Mason to leave, Abby caught a glimpse of Pauline leaving a gift on the table before making a hasty exit. She wondered if she had even stopped to say hello to her son.

CHAPTER 18

After the honeymoon, Abby arrived at her office and was greeted by a stack of messages and catalogues piled high on her desk. The realization that she had to get down to business hit her as she sat down at her desk. Just before the wedding she had been commissioned to decorate a new hotel they were building downtown. She had also been sounded out about decorating a vacation home for Manchester's mayor and his family.

"Welcome back!" Melanie breezed in from the stockroom.

"Thanks. I see things have been moving right along without me." Abby flipped through the messages.

"Oh, I wouldn't say without you. No one wants to talk to me; they have to speak to you personally, the mayor included. All I can do is take a message." Abby laughed at Melanie, who was in her last year of college studying interior design, just as she had.

"I guess I'd better get started. By the way, did Mayor Benton happen to say who recommended me?" Abby questioned as she read the message Melanie had written.

"He said Pauline Penney." Melanie eyed Abby cautiously.

"Are you serious?"

"Yep. That's why I didn't write it down. I knew you wouldn't believe it." Melanie knew that Abby was not one of Pauline's favorite people; the whole city probably knew that. If they didn't before the wedding, they surely did now. Pauline had skipped the ceremony and showed up at the reception for all of five minutes, long enough to give her son a gift that was clearly for him alone, a plaque with some silly saying about doctors.

"This should be interesting." Abby picked up the phone to return the mayor's call. After speaking with him for a few minutes, she talked with his wife for almost an hour. They definitely wanted Abby to decorate a cabin that was being built for them. Although it wouldn't be ready until the next summer, they wanted to make sure that she'd be available. In the meantime, the Bentons wanted a new look for the master bedroom of their Manchester estate. The commission would be impressive. Abby felt she needed to call Pauline to thank her.

The rest of the day went by quickly with Abby accepting two other commissions. It felt good to be back to work. Although she didn't know how she would have time to decorate her own home while she was so busy decorating everyone else's, she would manage. Since officially moving into the new house with a minimum of furniture, she and Mason had already discussed ideas for the living room and their bedroom. Ready to call it a day, she placed the order for the lobby furniture of Mason's office. As she prepared to leave, she noticed a big black, expensive-looking car pulling up in the driveway. To her amazement Stanford Penney, her father-in-law, got out of the car. He had been out of town when she and Mason got married and it looked as if he were bringing them a wedding present now. Then he turned to help a woman out. It wasn't Pauline.

He walked into the shop, holding the door open for his lady friend. "Hello, Abigail. I hope I'm not disturbing you." Abby recognized the woman as Carolyn Booker, a widow. It certainly looked as if she were out of mourning. "You know Carolyn, don't you?" he asked.

"Yes. Hello, Mrs. Booker. What brings you by tonight, Mr. Penney?" Abby tried to appear at ease. Mrs. Booker, apparently uncomfortable herself, made a small mumbling sound that Abby accepted as a greeting.

"It's all right, dear. I'm sure this is a bit difficult for you. Pauline and I have separated, I'm sure she didn't tell you since she refuses to speak to you but I thought it was time. We've been unhappy for a while now."

"There's no need to explain anything to me, Mr. Penney." Mason, was another story. Abby was sure he didn't know about this and she frankly didn't want to have to be the one to tell him.

"I just stopped by to bring you kids a gift and to wish you all the best." He handed Abby a large, festively-wrapped box.

"Thank you. I'll open it with Mason tonight. Why don't you stop by the house this evening. I'm sure he'd love to see you," Abby suggested.

"I don't think so. But I'll call him as soon as I get a chance. You take care now." Stanford left as quickly as he had come in. This was the strangest family, Abby thought. She questioned what she had gotten herself into when she married Mason.

Mason came home to mouth-watering aromas coming from the kitchen. He and Abby had eaten take-out or leftovers from her mother and sister since returning from their honeymoon so this was a welcome surprise. He spied his lovely wife leaning over the island that graced the center of their kitchen. She was flipping through what else, a furniture magazine. He could swear that woman woke up with decorating on her mind and allowed it to put her to sleep at night. But he conceded that the bare walls and echoing sound of their voices in this huge house was reason enough for her to be so dedicated. He walked up behind her, grabbing her at the waist before gently slipping one hand inside her blouse to cup one plump breast. He could barely tell her breasts apart now except for when his fingers stroked the skin just beneath each breast. The scar was thinning and in another year he'd have to really concentrate on identifying it. His lips found the spot beneath her ear that held remnants of the body spray she had worn today.

"Hello to you too." Abby tilted her head, allowing her husband greater access.

"Where's Nell?"

"She's at Tammy's playing with Melissa. Jeff said he'd bring her by later," she told him.

"I missed you today," he murmured.

"I can see that." She turned to face him, entwining her arms around his neck. Her period had come again when they returned from their honeymoon so it had been almost two weeks since he had been able to enjoy her. His lips found hers, and their tongues danced together with familiarity. Their passions were very soon ablaze.

Before long they were both naked on the kitchen floor working towards a very pleasurable climax.

"I love you, Gabby." He held her atop him, not wanting to sever their connection.

"I love you too, sweetie." She smiled, placing feather light kisses on his shoulder. "Do I get this type of greeting on a daily basis?" she asked.

"Hell, no. I'd never get to work the next day if you did." Mason stroked her bottom adoringly. "Speaking of which, baby, we've got to get some furniture in this place. We can't do it on the floor all the time."

Abby grinned. "We do have a bed, if somebody weren't in such a hurry. And I've ordered some things for Nell's room. I put a rush on them so they should be in by the end of the week."

"You looked so irresistible. Just leaning over waiting for me. It *was* me you were waiting for, wasn't it?" His forehead crinkled, his brow arching in question.

"No. Actually my husband should be home any minute now." She lifted off him so she could stand up.

Mason groaned. "Where're you going?"

"Mason, we're on the kitchen floor, or didn't you notice." He watched her gather their clothes.

"You know, I've never seen a backside quite as pretty as yours," Mason mentioned before standing to help her.

"I think I'll take that as a compliment," she said.

"You should." He put his hands on her bottom to knead and caress. "It's perfectly round and plump, and it sort of bounces in my hand."

She pulled away from him, embarrassed by his bold perusal of her body. "Mason, I don't need an assessment of my personal parts."

"It's mine now, so I can assess it as often as I like, and as freely." He dropped a quick kiss on her lips before pinching her bottom and making a dash for the bedroom.

"Mason!" Abby yelped, then took off behind him.

Two hours later, when Nell arrived, they ate dinner.

Two months after their wedding, Abby missed her period. Needless to say she was very excited. She held off mentioning anything to Mason, not wanting to spoil the surprise. But she couldn't keep the secret either, so she went to Tammy. Mistake—big mistake.

"I have a pregnancy test right upstairs. Let's take it and see," she suggested about ten minutes after Abby had walked in and told her of her suspicions.

"Tam, I was thinking of going to the doctor," she said.

"They're just going to tell you to do a home test first, before they spend the money on a blood test. I keep one on hand all the time. You know how fertile I am." Before Abby could respond, Tammy darted out of the room and returned momentarily with a blue and white box. "Here, go in the bathroom and take the test." She thrust the box into Abby's hand.

"I don't know. I think I'd like to talk to Mason first. I'll just take this with me until I decide what to do." Abby turned the box around and read the instructions.

"Oh, come on, just pee on the stick and wait for the plus sign," Tammy instructed, pushing her toward the bathroom.

"Gee, thanks. You're so helpful. But I'd like my husband to be the first to know." Abby dropped the box into her purse.

"Hurry up. You know I can't stand suspense," Tammy yelped.

"Hurry up and what?" Abby lifted her glass and took a sip of the water she'd been given when she came into the house.

"Go find your husband and do the test. And you call me as soon as you know the result." Tammy picked up Abby's purse and handed it to her. She then proceeded to guide her to the front door.

"Aren't we being pushy?" Abby laughed. "But I do have to go to Mason's office. His furniture came and I have some pictures to hang. That was where I was on my way to until I foolishly stopped by to see you." She paused to slip on her jacket. "By the way, what time does the preschool you enlisted the girls in let out?" Abby was now a stepmom and had the duty of picking Nell up from preschool. Mason dropped her off in the morning.

"Three. But I'll pick her up today since you're going to see Mason. This is a very important trip for you. Just stop by on your way home and get her unless you want me to have Jeff bring her home," she said.

"I'll come and get her. I have to get used to my parenting role, you know." Abby felt quite proud to be considering herself a parent.

As Abby drove to Mason's office she thought of how she would tell him. Smiling to herself, she decided to act as if she'd come only to hang the pictures.

In front of Mason's building she parked her car and began to unload the oil paintings that would hang on the walls of his office. In the elevator, she propped the pictures against the door and turned to the side to check for physical signs of pregnancy in the mirrored wall. She saw none. Still not sure of how she was going to tell Mason, she stepped off the elevator and walked calmly through the glass doors. The leather executive chairs in the lobby were as beautiful in the office as they had been in the catalog, though they needed to be arranged differently. The burgundy color accented the green marble and complemented the cherrywood end tables. She was pleased.

She lined the paintings up on the opposite wall and searched for just the right one to go over the couch. She selected one of a family reunion in a park, which she thought beautifully symbolized unity in families and their communities. She had liked the painting immediately upon seeing it. The others to be hung were representative of African American experiences as well. She was pleased with her selection as the pictures were elegant and very evocative of African American culture.

"That's pretty," Mary said from her desk in the corner.

"Oh, thanks, Mary. You weren't at your desk when I came in, so I decided to just get to work." Abby smiled at the nice woman Mason had hired as secretary for all three doctors, a job Abby did not envy.

"Dr. Penney's going to like that."

"I think so too. I haven't shown him any of them but I think he'll agree that they bring a pleasing ambiance to the office." Standing back, Abby admired the way the worked with the furniture in the room.

"All right, who's messing with the ambiance out here?" she heard Larry say as he peeked out of his office.

"It's just me. Trying to add some culture to your lives. How do you like this one?" Abby asked.

"Let me think about it." Larry stared at the picture on the wall, tapping a finger to his chin. Then he looked down at the ones on the floor.

Abby ignored his silence. "I know your taste usually runs to skeletons and nervous systems but I thought they were nice."

Larry frowned. "I guess they'll do. I was sort of thinking about dogs playing poker."

"You were sort of thinking about your basement and not our office," Mason commented as he came to see what all the commotion was about. "Hi, baby. I didn't know you were coming today." He kissed his wife in front of his co-workers, not ashamed to show how in love he was.

"I can't believe how whipped you've got him, Abby," Larry laughed.

"I wouldn't call it whipped," Mason added.

"No? What would you call it?" Abby asked playfully.

"I'll let you know what I'd call it later. For now, I don't wish to give Larry any more ammunition. He rides my back enough as it is." Mason looked at the pictures. Abby could tell instantly that he liked them. "These are great, baby. Where'd you find them?"

"You'll never guess. They were at a flea market. You know, the one Tammy and I went to last weekend. They were in cheap little frames, but I took them to the antique shop downtown and they re-framed them for me," Abby said proudly.

"The flea market, huh? We should go there more often. This is just what I had in mind," Mason stated, absently caressing the small of Abby's back.

She leaned closer to him. "I'm glad I could please you."

"You always please me." He watched her with passion in his eyes.

"Please! Not in the office. Mary, let's get away from them before they start makin' out right here in the lobby," Larry joked. "Geesh, newlyweds!"

"Jealousy is an unpleasant characteristic," Mason admonished. "Let's go in my office, Gabby. I believe we're disturbing people."

"Okay, but first pick out the pictures you want in your office. If you don't like any of these, I have some more at the shop." Mason surveyed the pictures again and scooped up one entitled *The Classroom*, another of Abby's favorites. The other two he picked up were of children. Abby wondered if this was a sign of his eagerness to become a parent again. The thought brought her attention right back to her pregnancy and how to tell him.

She followed him into his office, watching his broad back as he walked. He was an extremely well built man, she had to admit, and an excellent lover. Not that she had anyone to compare him to, but she knew a good thing when she had it all the same. She closed the door behind them and looked to the empty walls, searching for the perfect spot for the paintings he'd chosen.

Mason watched her small form as she walked from one part of the office to another. He noted the sway of her hips and the curve of her butt in the trim fitting slacks she wore. The swell of her breasts in the turtleneck had him adjusting certain parts that admired the sight as well. It was hard to believe that just a year ago she had been in danger of dying from a deadly disease. They rarely talked about it now, but it was always there in the back of their minds. She had been blessed to survive and he had been blessed to wed her. He wondered briefly how she would look carrying their child. Though he had said nothing, he was really looking forward to expanding their family. Despite the fact that they had to be extra cautious, lots of women who had cancer went on to have children after recovery. He hoped that Abby would be one of them.

When she turned to pick up a picture, she noticed him watching her. "What are you staring at?"

"Just admiring my woman." He sat on the end of his desk and extended his arms to her.

Stepping into his arms, she felt cocooned with love and adoration. Her heart swelled, her spirits soared. The moment seemed so right, so perfect. "Mason, I think I might be pregnant."

Mason pulled back slightly, keeping his hands clasped behind her. "You're kidding."

Abby thought she saw a hint of laughter in his eyes. "No, I'm late and I haven't been feeling quite myself lately. Tammy gave me one of those home tests but I kind of want to see the doctor first."

"How late are you?"

Abby toyed with the buttons on his shirt. "About two weeks. I haven't really been on any type of schedule, so it's kind of hard to tell."

Mason grinned. "I was just sitting here thinking of you carrying our child and you tell me that you're pregnant," he said.

She still couldn't quite tell if he was happy or mad. The yell he let out before lifting her into the air answered that question. "I take it you're not mad." She smiled into twinkling gray eyes.

"Hell no! I'm thrilled. This is so good. Nell will be so excited to have a little sister or brother. I can't believe it! This is so wonderful. Thank you! Thank you! Thank you!" He showered her with reverent kisses that landed everywhere but her lips. "I have to call Jeff, he's been hounding me about not knockin' you up sooner. He's gonna eat his words now." Abby smiled as she watched Mason walk over and dial Jeff's number.

CHAPTER 19

Her appointment with Dr. Craig was for nine o'clock; she was there at eight-fifteen, anxiousness written all over her face. The nurse quickly took her back and administered the blood test. Abby, having not had a needle in months, almost fainted at the slight pain and the unwanted memories that coursed through her. She got undressed and put on the gown that was left on the table for her.

"Abigail. How are you?" Dr. Craig spoke to her in his usual jovial voice.

"I'm fine. Just a little nervous."

He slipped on the latex gloves. "Oh, don't be. It's just a little pelvic exam. Lie back and relax for me."

Abby did as she was told.

"When was your last cycle?"

"The twelfth of last month was the first day," she recalled.

"Okay, so then you would be around six weeks."

Abby nodded her head.

"And you didn't perform any other tests? "

"No, I wanted to be perfectly sure. I mean, if I am pregnant I don't want there to be any mistake about it." Abby winced slightly as he inserted his fingers and pressed on her belly with his free hand. He was quiet for a few minutes. Then he stared solemnly at her. "What's the matter?" she asked.

"Nothing. I'm going to go and check with the lab. Get

dressed, I'll be right back."

Once the door closed behind him, Abby dressed quickly and sat in the chair, trying not to panic. Dr. Craig returned in moments.

"Abigail, I know how much you want a baby but the test is negative."

"How can that be? I'm late and I'm fatigued. I haven't been nauseous but not all women get nauseous. I don't understand." Abby's eyes frantically searched Dr. Craig's face for an answer.

"I know, that happens from time to time. Especially if something else is going on in the woman's body. Have you been sick lately?"

Abby was devastated. She struggled for some sense of control. "I ah... ah...I had a little cold," she managed.

"Which would have caused your body to undergo certain changes. Not to mention the fact that your system is still pretty messed up right now. That's why you haven't gotten your period."

"So what now? I mean, how long does it take for my system to get itself together?" Abby was pretty ticked off at her system right now.

"Each woman is different. But everything seems to be okay. It'll happen soon enough."

She drove home in a daze and went straight to her room. She hesitated momentarily at the door of the room next to the master bedroom. When she smelled the familiar aroma of baby powder, the tears came freely.

"Mason, there's a Ms. Parker on the line for you." Mary's voice interrupted Mason's review of the latest medical journal.

"Thank you, Mary." Mason had left a message for Teresa when he didn't hear anything more about the custody dispute. Picking up the receiver, he was prepared to offer her whatever she wanted to keep her out of his family's life.

"Hello, Teresa."

"Mason. I got your message," she answered. "I wanted to contact you sooner. There were some things I thought you should know.

Ignoring her words, Mason proceeded with his already pre-pared speech. "First of all, I want you to know that Nell is happy. She's never been happier." He paused. "And I don't think it's fair for you to want to disrupt the first real home she's had. She and Gabby have a terrific relationship..."

"Mason," Teresa stopped him. "I'm sure that Nell is fine. And believe me, I have no intention of interrupting her life."

Mason was confused. "What? What about suing me for cus-tody?"

"That was all your mother's doing. She called me one night when I was down and out and offered me a huge amount of money to come there and tell you I was going to take Nell." Teresa paused a moment, waiting for Mason's reaction. When she got none, she continued. "I don't want Nell. I told you already I'm not cut out to be a mother. If we had stayed together, maybe things would have been different but I don't want to be a single parent. Besides, Abigail seems like a nice woman. I'm sure you two will do a good job raising Nell."

Mason was still reeling from what Teresa had said about his

mother. "My mother paid you to lie to me?" He was flabbergasted. He shouldn't have been; after all, he knew his mother. Still, the realization that she could hate Gabby so intensely that she would pay someone to break them up cut him like a knife.

"I couldn't believe it when she first suggested it but then I needed the money. So I said I'd do it."

"How much did she give you?" Any amount would be disgusting, but he was curious to know just how much it had been worth to his mother.

"She offered me thirty thousand, five to come to the party and tell you that I was going to take Nell, and the other twenty-five thousand when I actually got you to come back to Boston with me. You see, I was never really supposed to take her. I was just supposed to tell you that and then when you fought it, I was supposed to say that I just wanted Nell near me. Your mother was convinced that you would come back to Boston if that was the only way you could keep Nell." Teresa's voice was strained, tired.

Mason took a deep breath. "But you've changed your mind. Why?"

"I found a job for one thing. And I knew deep down in my heart that it was wrong. Just because I don't want to be Nell's mother doesn't mean that I don't care about her. I want her to be happy, and she's happy with you and Abigail. So I gave your mother her money back."

Mason frowned in disgust. "You held up the first end of the bargain. You didn't have to pay her back."

"Guilt's a witch, Mason. You told me that before, remember?" She spoke in a quiet voice as she brought both their memories back to when she'd first given up her child.

"Yeah, I remember," he said solemnly. "I'd like to get something in writing. You know, something legal, so this kind of thing can't happen again."

After a brief hesitation Teresa asked, "You think Abigail would want to adopt Nell?"

"I know she loves Nell and she was willing to stand by me in my fight for her. I haven't really talked to her about adoption but I guess that would probably be best."

"That would be nice. A real family for Nell."

"I'll talk to her and have some preliminary papers drawn up. I'll send them to you when they're done," Mason told her.

"That sounds good."

"Teresa, thanks for telling me the truth." He felt as if he should say more but wasn't sure what more to say.

"Don't thank me, Mason. It should never have happened in the first place. That was my fault and I apologize."

When Mason hung up the phone, he thought of his mother and the measures she had taken to end his relationship with Abby.

Two months after the ominous "false alarm," Christmas had come and gone and Abby still had not conceived. Although the doctors assured her she was perfectly healthy, she was not yet pregnant. Distressed and disappointed, Abby was tempted to give up. But in the end she knew that she needed to keep the faith. Maybe it wasn't meant for her to become pregnant the old-fashioned way. Although she had jokingly harassed her mother with the idea of a test tube baby, it was increasingly apparent to her that this might be her only option. Hadn't she prayed for insight into this situation? Perhaps this was it.

The nurse in Dr. Craig's office had been good enough to forward her some literature about a fertility clinic in Florida, but she hadn't yet approached Mason with the idea. She wanted to be knowledgeable about the pros and cons before she presented it to him, knowing that his first instinct would be to resist the suggestion. She spent the day reading and taking notes, sorting through the massive pile of papers and brochures. Enthused by the idea that this might work for her, she closed the shop at five and hurried home.

She saw Mason's jeep in the driveway. Earlier she had been uncertain about discussing this with him, but now she was looking forward to it, convinced she could make him understand.

"Hey baby, you're home early," he said as she walked into the room he'd claimed as his office. The moment she saw him her doubts resurfaced and she re-thought her approach.

"I know. I finished up a little earlier today. Having an assistant really takes some of the load off. I figured I'd come home, cook some dinner and lie around."

He noted her nonchalant attitude and was concerned.

"Da-da, see. Pretty." Nell bounced on the chair, showing Mason a drawing she had done in school that day. He looked at it and commented on it quickly, more concerned with the mood his wife was in than Nell's rendition of a sunny day.

A few minutes later he found Abby in their bedroom getting undressed. "You want some company?" His voice had lowered at the sight of her partially naked body and he smiled. They had never had a problem in that area. Almost two years after their first intimate encounter, they still shared the same hunger for each other. If it hadn't been for her illness, they would probably have had a couple of kids by now.

"You know you're always welcome. But I have to warn you, I probably won't be good company tonight." Abby tossed her clothes into the hamper and retrieved her robe from the closet.

"Are you all right?"

"Yeah, why?"

"I don't know, you look a little funny. Like you're hiding something." Closing the distance between them, he placed his hands on her cheeks, lifting her face to meet his. He stared into the deep brown eyes that still captivated him, searching for a sign that would explain her mood.

Abby swatted at his hand. "I'm not hiding anything, so stop staring at me like that. I just wanted to come home," she lied unconvincingly.

"Okay." He dropped a quick kiss on her forehead. "So what's for dinner?"

Abby shrugged. "Why don't we order out? Cooking doesn't appeal to me."

"Fine. Chinese or pizza? What's your pleasure, madam?" Mason headed out of the room. He wasn't going to get anything out of her right now. He'd wait until after dinner.

"Chinese. Oh, and…"

Pausing at the door, he yelled over his shoulder, "I know, no MSG."

The food was delivered by the time Abby had finished with her soothing bubble bath, which Nell had readily interrupted three or four times to insist that she needed a bath as well. Since Mason was reading some medical digest, she transferred the food from the small white boxes it had been delivered in onto paper plates. She hated washing dishes with a passion and was convinced it was because she and Tammy had alternated days clearing the kitchen as she was growing up. Mason didn't like the idea much but he learned early on that she would not compromise in this area. As they ate, they chatted about this and that, nothing too serious. When Nell had eaten her fill, she was released from the high chair to play on the floor.

Abby thought the time was as good as it was going to get. Either she was going to tell him now or she was chucking the whole idea. She sat back in the chair and adjusted the belt on her robe before she began.

"I was reading about this infertility clinic today. It was pretty interesting," she mentioned calmly.

Mason stopped chewing and stared at her. This was it; he had known that she had something on her mind but he hadn't dreamed it was anything like this. He wanted a baby as badly as she did, but he was willing to be patient, to wait until it happened in God's time. Abby was ready for it to happen now, it appeared.

"What was so interesting about it?" His tone was stiff.

Abby felt mild waves of panic but held strong. "There are procedures that can be taken to become pregnant."

"Methods other than the one we try so frequently?" he said with a grim smile.

"Yes, other than that. I mean, if we really concentrated on getting pregnant we probably could."

Mason struggled to stay calm. "Concentrate on getting pregnant. Gabby, do you hear yourself? Who in the world concentrates on getting pregnant?"

"Someone who wants a baby." Mason's attitude was not encouraging and she was becoming irritated.

Mason took a deep breath, willing himself to calm down. She wanted a baby, and for that matter, so did he. But he was willing to wait in order to insure that she was well enough to carry one. It was apparent that Abby did not possess that type of patience. "Honey, I know you want a baby but I think we should just relax and let it happen naturally."

"Damn it, Mason! It isn't happening naturally." She slapped her hands down on the table. "We have sex about ten times a month and I'm still not pregnant. I think it's time we took more assertive measures."

"What other steps do you suggest? Test tubes?"

"You know, for a doctor you're pretty narrow-minded. There are several different things we could try besides test tubes."

Mason was quiet.

Abby's voice softened. "Can't you just try to understand? I thought you wanted a baby too."

Reaching across the table, he grabbed her hands. "I do. But this whole thing is making you crazy. You've had a difficult year, Gabby. I want to make sure you're okay before I can worry about a baby."

"The doctors said I'm fine. I can do this." She stared down at her plate, her appetite lost.

She looked so disappointed, he felt the need to do something. Besides, what harm would it do to hear her out. "What do you suggest?"

Her face brightened considerably. "We could start tracking my most fertile days. I called a counselor at the clinic and she told me some methods I think are worth a try. You don't even have to do anything. I mean, you do but only when I tell you it's time."

He couldn't help chuckling. "All right, Gabby. If this is really what you want. So what is it that you have to do before I do what I do?"

"Chart my cervical mucus," she said.

"What?" he laughed.

"Come on, Mason, you're a doctor. You know what I'm talking about."

"Yeah, I know. You need to chart the changes in your body to pick the most fertile times. They're doing a bunch of new studies on this. Are you sure this is what you want?"

"This is still natural. It's just planned. I think we should give it a try."

"Does this mean we can only have sex on specific days of the week?" he teased.

"No, it just means that we should be *sure* to have sex on those days." She smiled seductively. "We can still have sex sporadically since I know how you enjoy it so much."

After months of charting her cervical mucus and taking her temperature and endless sexual trysts, Dr. Craig cheerfully informed Abby that she was definitely pregnant. In light of her earlier disappointment, Dr. Craig opted to perform a pelvic sonogram. She and Mason watched a small white spot on the screen flash continuously. She cried as she realized the white spot was her baby's heartbeat.

CHAPTER 20

Mason sat placidly in his office thinking of the brightness he'd seen in his wife's eyes when she focused on the crib he had put into the nursery. In four months they would be parents again. He could hardly wait. He knew they would do a good job because they were good people.

That thought had him thinking about his mother. She had turned down the last two dinner invitations Abby had extended and was less than thrilled about the baby. He had spoken to her personally several times, but had not brought up the subject of Teresa and the payoff, not wanting to further complicate things. However, Pauline just refused to warm up to Abby. The fact that Teresa had sent Mason a notarized affidavit relinquishing her rights to Nell, thereby opening the door for Abby to legally adopt her, had not gone over well with her either.

"Dr. Penney, there's a Dr. St. John on line four. She says it's urgent." Mary's voice echoed through the office.

"Thanks, Mary." He hoped there was nothing wrong with Gabby. He hadn't seen Sandra recently and he was almost positive that Gabby hadn't gone to see her.

"Sandra, how are you?" he said.

"I'm fine. I heard about the baby. Congratulations," she began.

"Thanks." Silence filled the line "I know you didn't call me just to say congratulations. So what's going on?" he asked seriously.

"It's about your mother, Mason."

Mason was shocked. "My mother? How do you know my mother?"

"She's my patient." Sandra waited for a response, but when Mason said nothing, she continued, "About a year ago she came to see me. She had large tumors in both breasts. By the time she consented to the biopsy the cancer had spread significantly."

The realization of what Sandra was saying hit him hard. He sank back in his chair as his mind reeled from her words. "I don't believe this! Why didn't she tell me?" Mason felt torn between anger at his mother and anger at this disease that had crept back into his life.

"She said she didn't want to bother you, now that you have a new wife and a family of your own."

"So she changed her mind about me knowing and asked you to tell me?" He was confused at why Sandra was calling him.

"Not exactly. She doesn't know that I'm calling. For the last year I have abided by doctor/patient confidentiality but I couldn't keep this to myself anymore," she explained. "I know she hasn't told Jeff and she rarely ever speaks of your father. So I don't believe anyone knows about this."

"Thank you for calling, Sandra. I'll call her right now," Mason said.

"Mason, wait. There's more."

"More?" He let out a deep breath.

"She's dying, Mason. There is nothing medically that we can do now. Maybe if we had detected it earlier or if we had performed surgery. But Pauline refused. She didn't want to consider any form of surgery or medication. And I couldn't force her; she's a grown woman. I just wanted you to know. I know you haven't seen her much since you and Abigail became involved and I don't want to stick my nose in your business. But I think you need to see her, make amends, do something."

"You're telling me that my mother will die regardless of anything we do from this point on?" he asked, not sure he wanted to hear the answer.

Sandra didn't hesitate. "That's exactly what I'm telling you."

Silence filled the line.

"Thanks for calling, Sandra," Mason said before hanging up the phone.

How could this have happened? How could she have walked around for the past year ignoring this, not telling him, not telling Jeff? And his father, he was off running after some rich widow, so he didn't have the time or inclination to deal with his wife's health.

He should call her. No, he should go and see her. He didn't know what he should do. As he sat there in confusion, Mary buzzed his office to let him know that Gabby was on the phone. It was as if Gabby had sensed that he needed her.

"Hello?" he spoke slowly.

"Hi, baby. I was just thinking about you and I wanted to call to tell you how much I love you." When she didn't hear any response on the other end, Gabby became concerned. "Mason? Mason?" she repeated.

"I'm here," he mumbled.

"What's the matter?"

"It's my mother."

Good Lord, what had Pauline done now? "Is something wrong? Has she done something?" Gabby hoped the latter wasn't the case.

"She's dying."

"What?" Surely she hadn't heard him correctly.

"Sandra called. She's been her patient for the last year. She refused treatment for breast cancer until it was too late. There's nothing they can do for her."

The memory of Pauline storming out of the medical center in New York flashed in Abby's memory and she felt the sting of guilt course through her veins. Should she tell him about seeing her there or should she wait until he got home tonight to tell him?

"I'm leaving here. I need to see her. I'll call you when I'm on my way home."

"No, wait. Do you want me to meet you there?" Abby asked, silently hoping he would say no.

"No. I want to see her alone first."

"Okay," she said softly.

"Gabby?"

"Yes?"

"I love you, and I appreciate your wanting to help. I'll see you later."

"I'll wait for you. We can go out or order some dinner when you get home. Or I can cook something." She hated the thought of cooking but she'd do it if that was what Mason wanted.

"No, I won't be long. Just pick up Nell and go home and rest. I'll get something on my way."

"Okay. Give her my love, Mason." Abby was shocked to discover she really meant it.

Mason must have been shocked too, but he didn't comment. "I will."

At home, Abby stood on the deck watching the sunset. As streaks of crimson and dusty grays faded from the sky, the city lit up like a Christmas tree and twinkled across the skyline. It was so peaceful, so comforting. How could a world so beautiful be filled with such a horrible thing as cancer?

It was a known killer and yet when it struck home no one was ever prepared. While many people did not survive, she had. And for that she would be forever grateful. She wanted Pauline to have the chance to live, the same chance that she had been given. Realizing that this was not in her power, she decided to do whatever she could to ease her situation.

She would be there for her in any capacity that she could. Although the woman that had done nothing but cause her distress, she would do all she could. She began with prayer. She prayed for Pauline's spirit, for it to be healed before she took her last breath. As she prayed, she felt the now familiar movements of her baby kicking inside her womb. She prayed that Pauline would live to see her newest grandchild.

It was another hour before Mason came home. In that time Abby had managed to fix Nell dinner, ravioli from a can and milk, and bathe her.

Nell had demanded a bubble bath and it had been quite an event. On her knees, her protruding stomach pressed against the side of the tub, she and Nell had washed her baby doll's hair, then Nell's. Abby had started out with the intention of washing Nell's hair but she'd soon learned that if Nell's hair needed washing, so did Thumbelina's.

Abby was at last lying in her bed when the security system beeped, signaling that Mason had come into the house. She sat up in bed, knowing that once he'd checked on Nell he would come straight to her. A few minutes later he walked into their bedroom, undoing his tie and the first button on his dress shirt.

"Hi, how is she?" Abby asked, anxious for the news.

"She wasn't there. I waited for a while, and then I decided to come home." He looked as if he were suddenly eighty years old as he came to the bed and sat beside her. His shoulders sagged and his face drooped with the hurt of a child. Abby's heart ached for him and what he must be going through. Unsure of what to say, she simply held her arms out to him. With a tired sigh, he went willingly into her embrace, holding on to her as if his life depended on it. They both shed silent tears, knowing deep inside what would be the outcome of this situation. As if on cue, movement erupted in her stomach.

Mason's arm had been draped casually over his wife's belly. Initially the movement startled him; then it warmed him. Splaying his hand across the middle of Abby's girth, he let the rampant movements of his unborn child relieve some of his tension.

The stomach that used to be as flat as a pancake was now round and protruding largely from his petite wife. Each day she seemed to look more beautiful, with the brightness only a pregnant woman could radiate. How in the midst of all his newfound happiness had devastation seeped back into his life? The devil was always busy, he reminded himself.

"We get to see him tomorrow, right?" he asked without lifting his gaze from her stomach.

"Yes," she said, remembering the sonogram that had been scheduled weeks ago. "Do you want me to postpone it?"

"No. I've been looking forward to this for a while now. I need to see who's been kickin' me at night," he laughed softly.

"You're sure? Because Dr. Craig said that everything looks fine so if we postpone it until maybe next week it should be okay."

Mason shook his head adamantly. "No. I want to do it tomorrow. I'll deal with my mother. There's no need for you to get all stressed out over it. You just concentrate on bringing our baby into this world as healthy as possible." Dragging his eyes away from her stomach, Mason looked up to his wife's worried face. Gently he brushed his knuckles over her cheek. Abby leaned in to his touch. "Don't worry, everything will be fine. I'll deal with my mother." Rising from the bed, he dropped a quick kiss on her lips and headed toward the bathroom.

Abby stared after him. Mason was a strong man and as it often was with strong black men, expressing emotion was hard for him. She could just imagine all the feelings that had to be going through him today. Abby, on the other hand, now allowed herself a moment to grieve openly. Tears for Pauline and her sons streamed down her face.

Unable to turn off his thoughts about his mother and her idiotic decision, Mason didn't sleep much. He left the bed just before dawn, finally giving up all hope of sleep and not wanting to disturb Abby, who seemed to be in a deep slumber. The pregnancy had taken away most of her vibrant energy and now the moment she hit the bed she was usually fast asleep. Their appointment was at nine so he would go in and wake her soon.

For now, he was content to sit on the deck and watch the sun rise. Beginning with deep shades of crimson and pink dramatically streaked with gold, the sky gradually grew brighter. Toward the east he could see some cloud formation. A storm was coming. In more ways than one, he thought to himself.

His solitary time passed quickly. Nell awoke and had to be fed and dressed, which lately had become a chore. After chasing her around her room, Mason finally managed to get her into the pants and shirt Abby had laid out the previous night. Then her exuberant three-year-old legs carried her into the kitchen, where she attempted a solo climb into her high chair. Just as her chubby body was about to crash to the floor, Mason scooped her up and secured her in the seat. Intending to give Abby a break this morning, he prepared Nell a breakfast of Cheerios, milk and bananas.

When Abby walked into the kitchen, Mason was on his knees picking discarded Cheerios off the floor while Nell eagerly smashed bananas through her little fingers. Giggling, Abby moved closer to Nell.

Mason looked up from his place on the floor. "Hey, honey, we're having breakfast."

"I see. Come here, sweetie. We'll get you all cleaned up." She lifted Nell out of the high chair. "A word of advice, Daddy," she said to Mason just before leaving the kitchen with Nell. "Breakfast before getting dressed." Her gaze went to Nell's shirt which was covered with milk and fruit.

Mason grinned. "Right, I'll remember that next time."

In another twenty minutes they had dropped Nell off at school and were on their way to the doctor's office. Mason had been to other doctor's appointments with her early on in the pregnancy, but since things had started to look all right, she had gone alone. The nurse escorted them into the room and as Abby changed in the small bathroom, Mason looked at the machinery and felt a familiar chill go through his body. He couldn't help remembering all the machines in Abby's room when she had her surgery. Would there be machines surrounding his mother as well? He dropped into the chair beside the examining table and tried to will away his negative thoughts. He'd think about his mother and what lay ahead later.

"Mrs. Penney, how much water did you drink this morning?" the nurse questioned when Abby came back into the room.

"All eight glasses, just like you told me. I think if I laugh too hard or take a deep breath I'm going to make a mess right here on this table." She and the nurse laughed. Abby noticed Mason's pensive look but decided not to comment on it. They needed to get through the procedure, then talk. She knew he had to be tired from lack of sleep last night but guessed that was not even the main source of his problem.

Dr. Craig entered the room. "Good morning. Are we all set?"

"Yes, I think we'd better hurry up," Abby said, rubbing the bottom of her stomach. Dr. Craig chuckled as he put the chilled jelly on the transducer and lifted her gown so that he could slide it easily across her stomach. All eyes were riveted on the image on the ultra sound machine. Dr. Craig took measurements and his assistant recorded them in Abby's chart. Mason and Abby stared at the screen, trying to figure out just what they were seeing.

"There's one leg." Dr. Craig pointed to the screen. "And there's the other leg."

Mason began to recognize formation of a tiny body.

"This flashing white spot here is the baby's heart."

"Oh, Mason, look at his heart beating." Abby fought back the tears she knew would eventually come.

"That's the head right there." Mason got out of the chair and moved closer to the screen, amazed at what he was seeing. "Look, Gabby that's his head!" he exclaimed.

"Yup, you've got yourself a good-sized baby there," Dr. Craig confirmed. "Would you like to know the sex?" Abby and Mason looked at each other questioningly. They had discussed this before and Abby wanted to know but Mason wanted to be surprised. In the end she had let him make the decision.

"I don't think so. We want to be surprised." He looked at his wife for conformation and was relieved by her nod.

"Everybody says that and then two days later they call and ask me anyway. I'll write it down on a piece of paper and put it in a sealed envelope. That way when you call I can just mail you the envelope. Does that sound all right with you?" he asked.

"That's fine," Abby said, knowing that her curiosity would eventually get the best of her and that her nagging would eventually get the best of Mason. Dr. Craig moved the transducer from side to side, stopping to apply more jelly to Abby's stomach. Pausing his movements, he stared at the screen so intensely Abby became alarmed.

"Is there something wrong?" she asked, immediately alerting

Mason. Both their eyes rested on Dr. Craig.

"I don't believe it," he whispered.

"You don't believe what?" Mason stared from Dr. Craig to the screen and back again.

"There seems to be another one," the doctor said.

"Another what?" Abby's eyes bulged as she tried to see what he was commenting about on the screen.

"Another baby." He smiled.

"What!" Abby and Mason said in unison. The nurse came closer to the screen as well, and she turned, giving them a big smile.

"You're having twins, Abigail." Dr. Craig's smile broadened.

"What? How could I be having twins?" she asked in disbelief.

"Why didn't you tell us this before?" Mason continued to stare at the screen, still unable to see a second child.

"Well, at each of Abigail's visits we measured her growth, took her weight, took blood samples and listened to the heartbeat. Somehow we missed it," he said.

"Missed it? How do you miss another baby?" Mason asked.

"Look here, Dr. Penney." Dr. Craig pointed to the monitor. "The babies are lying directly alongside one another; hence, the measurements of her stomach would not have been significantly affected. Since there was no history of twins, we didn't look for them." Dr. Craig pointed to the screen again. "It also looks as if they share one placenta and one umbilical cord," he continued.

Mason couldn't believe what he was hearing. "Is that a good thing or a bad thing?"

"It means that they are identical."

"Identical?" Mason had to sit down. He looked over at his

wife, who had been unusually quiet throughout this discovery. Tears streamed silently from her closed eyes. He lifted his hands and wiped them away, kissing her dampened cheeks.

Once the doctor left the room with heartfelt congratulations and more instructions for Abby, Mason helped her dress. As she stepped into the dress she had worn to the office, a baby moved. With her hands on her stomach she laughed. "No wonder you kick so much. You're probably in there wrestling."

"Can you believe it?" Mason asked as he buttoned her dress.

"No. But I'm so happy I could just burst," she said.

"You look like you are about to burst," he said playfully.

She jabbed him in the stomach and was about to walk out the door when another thought occurred to her.

"What is it?"

"With the mention of bursting, my bladder has made it perfectly clear that that's what it intends to do right this very moment." She walked quickly into the bathroom.

CHAPTER 21

Abby still couldn't believe it. She had prayed for one child, one baby, one miracle to add to the special angel Mason had already given her. The Lord had given her two. It seemed now to be almost too coincidental; Mason's mother would be taken away, she would be blessed with twins. God never did anything in vain.

Abby and Tammy accompanied their husbands to visit Pauline. When Mason confronted her, Pauline did not deny what she'd done. He and Jeff questioned her endlessly and Pauline, as was her nature, sat calmly, regally, and watched her sons fall apart before her eyes.

"This is why I chose not to get treatment. Nothing pains me more than to see my children hurt," she said slowly.

"What did you think it would do to us if you died and we had no idea why? If when the doctor came back with the autopsy report, he told us you had died of breast cancer? Breast cancer can be treated. Your life could have been prolonged. Don't you understand that?" Jeff said sadly.

Pauline folded and unfolded her hands in her lap. "Maybe. But for how long?"

"Look at Gabby. She's been cancer free for almost a year now and she's having a baby. There's no telling how much longer you could have lived." Mason understood all too well the repercussions of not receiving treatment and it pained him to watch his mother so at ease with this decision.

"But at what price? I am not as young as Abigail is. In fact, on my next birthday, if I live to see it, I will be fifty-seven. I have lived a fulfilling life. I have no regrets. I also have no desire to be poked at and prodded on, or take experimental drugs that make me sick all the time, and maybe even die in shame because I can't even go to the bathroom on my own. I won't live out my remaining time that way. I hope you can understand." Pauline stared down at her hands.

"But what about us? What about how we feel?" Jeff struggled to keep his composure. Tammy held his hand and solemnly stared at Pauline.

Abby couldn't stand it, the arguing, the pleading, the misery of the moment, any longer. "I think what we're all missing here is that it wasn't our decision to make and it's selfish of us to sit here and judge Mrs. Penney for doing what she wants to do with her own life. While we may ultimately be affected, it is still *her* life." Abby spoke softly but in the quietness that had fallen over the room, her voice echoed off the walls. Mason and Jeff stared at her disbelievingly and Tammy wept quietly into her hands. Pauline's eyes met Abby's and they exchanged a mutual feeling of understanding.

Of all the people in that room, Pauline had known that Abby would be the one to understand just as she knew that she would be the one to make her sons understand in time. It was a shame, Pauline thought to herself, that she had not taken the time to get to know her daughter-in-law better. She'd let the past dictate her life for far too long. Abigail was a very strong woman. And after much soul-searching, Pauline had found that she actually admired her.

It was probably too late for her to make that declaration now. Her treatment of Abigail and Tamara would be a permanent blotch on her record as she reached the Pearly Gates.

"There's no explanation for her allowing herself to die. There's medication out there that can save her." Jeff stood, his emotions apparently getting the better of him.

"Medications won't help her now, Jeff. All we can do is accept it," Abby said.

Mason sat quietly staring at his mother. Had this been the change he'd sensed in her? Had she been struggling with this decision all along while they thought she was just being selfish and unreasonable? He'd been so involved in his personal life that he hadn't really paid attention to what was happening to his own mother.

"She could at least try," Jeff sobbed. Tammy held him as she fought to stop tears of her own.

"At this stage there is no point. The medications that are available will only make her suffering more unbearable. Do you want that for her?" Abby asked.

"None of us want her to suffer unnecessarily," Mason began. "But we would have liked to know before things got to this point." He stared pointedly at Pauline.

She lifted her head, searching the four faces in the room. "Maybe I should have told you sooner." She took a deep breath. "I should have done a lot of things sooner." Her gaze rested on Abby.

They drove home in silence, Nell in the backseat fast asleep and Mason not wanting to talk about their visit or about anything else for that matter. They had chosen not to announce the news of the twins because it was not the right time. Abby went straight to her room when she arrived home and lay on the bed. The day's events had exhausted her. She was asleep instantly and soon began to dream.

She walked slowly into the bright room that belonged to the babies. When she saw that the cribs were empty, her heart skipped a beat and she began searching. She ran down the hall and still couldn't find them. As tears streamed from her eyes she heard someone humming and followed the sound to the deck. As Abby approached, she recognized the tune as "Jesus Loves the Little Children," and saw that Pauline was holding in her lap two baby girls dressed in frilly pink dresses. The big brown eyes of each baby were focused on the face above as they listened. Her heart slowing to a normal rhythm, Abby sat at Pauline's feet and listened along with the babies.

"Such pretty little girls, don't you think, Abigail?" Abby opened her mouth to speak but nothing came out. "I never had any daughters, and now I have five granddaughters. I love them above all else. You know why?" When Abby didn't respond, Pauline continued, "Because their love is unconditional. It's the most rewarding and the hardest love to come by."

Pauline began to hum again. This time Abby sang the words with her. She felt as though she were rocking back and forth as she inhaled the all too familiar scent of babies in the air. Suddenly it

*was Abby sitting in the lawn chair holding her daughters in their
frilly dresses and they were watching her wide-eyed with absolute
adoration.*

Abby awoke with the scent still fresh in her memory, and discovered Mason had already left for work. She managed to shower and dress and got into her car to go to work. She was in the
car for a half an hour before she realized that she was on her way
to Pauline's house instead of downtown. She pulled into the
driveway and rang the doorbell. A tall white woman dressed in a
nurse's uniform answered the door.

"Hi, I'm Abigail Penney. I'm here to see Mrs. Penney," she
said.

"Oh, yes, you must be her daughter-in-law."

"Yes. I am. Well, one of them anyway," Abby said quickly.

"I'm Donna. I visit Mrs. Penney in the mornings and again
in the evening to check her vital signs and things of that nature."

Abby extended her hand to the woman. "It's nice to meet
you, Donna. How is she this morning?" Donna shook Abby's
hand and began walking up the steps. Abby followed.

"She's tired. She had a pretty painful night but her vitals are
good."

"Do you know how serious her condition is at this moment?"

"As you probably know, the cancer has spread progressively.
She won't have any more testing done. It's like she's given up."
Donna folded her hands in front of her as she stopped at the door
of Pauline's bedroom.

"No, she hasn't given up. She's just resigned herself to death," Abby said solemnly. Donna opened the door and stood to the side as Abby entered.

This was the first time she had ever had the pleasure of entering Pauline's bedroom. Spectacular was the only word to describe its cathedral ceilings, huge windows covered with heavy velvet drapes and lovely Victorian furniture. Pauline lay in the huge oak bed covered in pink satin sheets. Her face looked just a little pale and her eyes were tired. Abby felt a pang of familiarity at the sight of the pink sheets. She approached the bed slowly, not wanting to alarm her.

"Hello, Mrs. Penney," she said quietly.

"Abigail?" Pauline's voice creaked. "What are you doing here?"

Abby didn't know the answer to that herself but she was glad that Pauline hadn't immediately sent her away. "I don't know actually. I just ended up here instead of at work. How are you feeling?"

"I'm okay," Pauline lied.

"The pain's pretty bad, huh?" Abby noticed the slight wince Pauline made when she spoke.

"It's worse than usual today. I think I may have over-exhausted myself yesterday," she said.

Abby moved closer to the bed. "Yeah, you should probably take it easy for the next couple of days."

"'Come to me, all you that are weary and are carrying heavy burdens, and I will give you rest.' That's what He said."

Abby nodded in understanding.

Refusing to dwell on Pauline's decision any longer, Abby

changed the subject. "Donna seems pretty nice."

"She's competent."

Abby smiled at Pauline's comment. They were quiet for a while. Abby didn't know what else to say. She just felt she needed to be there, so that's what she was doing, being there. She sat in the chair next to her bed.

"I'm glad you survived, Abigail." The simple statement almost had Abby falling out of the chair. "Don't look so shocked. It's true. I am glad. Mason has been happy with you and you've been good for him."

Abby decided that she would not mention the fact that Pauline had never seemed to approve of them before. Instead, she just listened as she sensed Pauline needed to get this off her chest.

"You know, Mason was a funny little boy, always so serious. Never taking much time to smell the roses, so to speak. When he left for school, I hoped that he would fall in love but he didn't. He was always so focused on his career. And when he came back for Jeff's wedding, I could see that he wasn't happy. But he was so far away there wasn't much I could do. Then he came home and I just wanted to spend time with him, help him see what life was really about, help him find his happiness." Pauline grasped the sheets in pain.

Abby rubbed her hand until she released her grip on the blanket.

"Then you came along. You were that happiness. I saw that Thanksgiving that you were the one for him. By making him happy you did what I couldn't do. That's a hard pill for a mother to swallow. The son that was always so far away from me was back but you managed to take him before I had the chance to get to know him. I blamed you. I was wrong." She closed her eyes again in pain. Abby rose and sat on the side of the bed. She held Pauline's hand and smoothed the sheets. When she was sure the pain had passed, she kissed her weathered cheek.

"You love your son, Mrs. Penney. Mason knows this and he loves you very much. That's all that counts." Forgiveness was hard for some people but for others, like Abby, it came as easily as the air to breathe.

Abby spent the whole day with Pauline. She fixed her lunch, they watched the soaps and then they both took a well-deserved nap.

Mason stormed into the house slamming the door behind him. "I called the shop all day. Where the hell were you?"

Abby looked up from the pot of water she'd just added salt to. "I was with your mother."

"With my mother? Is she okay?" He looked confused as he peeled his jacket off.

"Yeah, she's fine. She was in a lot of pain today so I sat with her. We had a nice day. I learned a lot about you and your brother." She dropped spaghetti into the pot.

Mason paused. "You spent the day with my mother?"

"Mason, please stop asking the same questions over and over again. I said your mother and I spent a glorious day together. You know, she's a really nice woman once you get to know her," Abby said.

"Yeah, she is. Gabby, at the risk of starting an argument, I have to say this," he continued.

"What?"

"*You* are the last person I would expect to spend the day with *my* mother."

Abby sighed. "I know, it's weird. But I feel this connection with her now. And she's very lonely with your father leaving the way he did."

Mason frowned. The thought of what his father had done disturbed him and he hadn't yet figured out how to handle it. "Did she tell you that?"

"No, but I can tell she's hurt. She dedicated her whole life to him and he just left. He knows about her condition yet he doesn't really seem concerned." Abby shook her head in dismay.

"I know. That's what I told Jeff when I talked to him earlier." Mason took a seat at the table, pulling out a chair for Abby and signaling her to sit down.

Abby moved across the room to the chair, thankful to sit down. Standing for long periods wreaked havoc on her back nowadays. "How's Jeff holding up?"

"He's doing his best." He lifted her hand in his.

She smiled. "And how are you?"

"I'm much better now that I'm home with you." He leaned over to kiss her.

In the next three months Abby spent at least two hours each day with Pauline. They came to be very good friends. After she'd convinced Mason it would be a good idea, he spent a day alone with his mother as well. He'd come home with a lighter spirit and a new handle on his mother's situation. They shared their feelings and made peace with the past. Abby was glad she'd suggested it.

Tonight Abby awkwardly dressed in her bedroom, determined not to be late for Pauline's party. She had been planning it for two weeks now, trying to invite all of Pauline's friends and close family. She knew that Pauline would love it. One more time in the spotlight for her. The doctor had told Abby on his last visit that Pauline's condition was deteriorating. Abby had decided not to share that piece of information with the rest of the family. She'd insisted that they all gather and talk about Pauline's arrangements as Pauline had run down her requests to Abby at lunch one day.

"You look like you could use some help." Mason stepped behind her.

"I can't reach the zipper," she said as her too short arms strained to catch the material.

"I'll do it," he said. But when his fingertips brushed against her bare skin, he had to catch his breath. It had been weeks since they had been able to enjoy each other. She had been busy seeing after Pauline and he had been busy at the office or spending time with Nell. Their gazes met in the mirror, their desire apparent. Mason turned Abby to face him and kissed her thoroughly.

"I've missed you so much," she breathed between kisses.

"I've missed you, too." He placed her hands between his legs. "Can't you tell?" He fingered her breast until her nipple hardened.

Abby giggled. Still weakened by his sexuality, she gave in to the cravings of her own body.

The material fell to the floor and she stood in her underwear and stockings. A quick glance in the mirror had her groaning loudly.

"What?"

"I look like a penguin," she moaned.

"You do not." Mason rubbed her stomach slowly. "You look like my beautiful wife who is carrying my beautiful babies." His hands moved under the protruding girth, slipping ever so delicately into her stockings and beneath her underwear to lightly graze the mound that rested beneath ebony curls. He felt her wetness and lost all focus.

Her sharp intake of breath signaled that she needed this as much as he did. He moved her slowly to the bed, removing the few clothing articles she wore. Quickly undoing his pants and freeing himself, he entered her slowly, taking extra care not to hurt her. Because of her stomach he could no longer lay his full weight on her while they made love. Instead, he rested on his knees and grasped her breasts as he watched her reach her peak. Her release came in quick waves of glory, causing the taut muscles to contract around him and bring his own furious release.

They arrived at the party thirty minutes late, but no one noticed. Pauline celebrated her fifty-seventh birthday with a bang. Donna had helped her dress in a gorgeous silver gown and had done her hair and makeup. She looked lovely. Abby had wanted the party to be small and intimate but glamorous enough for Pauline to feel in her element. She and Mason still had not mentioned the twins and it was an ongoing discussion between her and Pauline about how big she was. Pauline had even laughingly compared her to a walking circus tent. It was wonderful to see her so happy. Although her body would eventually fail her, her spirit had been healed.

Three days after her birthday Pauline succumbed. The arrangements had long since been made so there was no need for anyone to have to bear that burden. The church was filled with solemn citizens of Manchester who had known Pauline. As the family was ushered to the front pews, Abby's eyes searched the sanctuary for Mason's father. She didn't see him anywhere.

They sat in the front of the church with Pauline laid out peacefully in front of them. They had jointly agreed on a deep burgundy coffin that had been specially lined, at Abby's insistence, with pink satin. Pauline wore a pink Chanel suit and pink gloves. Her diamond earrings sparkled like cool chips of ice, signifying all the class that was the woman.

"She's still elegant," Tammy said to Abby.

"She wouldn't have it any other way," Abby answered.

The minister proceeded with the service as Mason and his brother openly mourned the woman who had raised them.

Later, they stood at the burial site and prayed over the grave that would house the remains of Pauline Elizabeth Spectrum Penney. As they turned and prepared to leave the cemetery, Abby felt a sharp pain course through her lower abdomen. Her knees buckled and she grabbed hold of Mason.

"What is it? Are you okay?" he asked.

"No, I think my water just broke," she said through clenched teeth as she braced herself for another pain.

After hours of intense pain and endless cups of ice chips, Kayla Pauline and Kiya Elizabeth Penney came into the world at 11:54 p.m. When her family left the hospital, Abby finally had a private moment. "Don't think I didn't notice how you took Pauline and gave us Kayla and Kiya at the same time," she spoke quietly. "Thanks. Thanks for giving me the chance to know her, finally. And for giving me parts of her to keep." Her precious moment was interrupted by the wail of one of her daughters. Abby lifted the crying Kiya into her arms. As she fed her daughter, Abby looked into eyes that so resembled those of the woman they had laid to rest. They had a hint of fierceness in them and pools of warmth.

EPILOGUE

When the will was read two weeks later at Pauline's home, Mr. Penney mysteriously reappeared. Mason and his brother calmly ignored him and the new woman that clung to him like a wet blanket.

"Five million dollars is to be divided evenly between Melissa, Megan and Annell Penney, along with the two unborn children of Abigail and Mason Penney," the attorney read, passing a brief glance in Mason and Abby's direction. Abby smiled as Mason stared at her blankly.

"You told her?"

"No, I didn't. But she knew." Abby smiled.

"My business and stock holdings are to be run and owned jointly by my two sons, Mason and Jeffrey. My house and its surrounding property I leave to my daughter, Abigail Swanson Penney," the lawyer read on. The room filled with silence as all eyes turned on Abby.

"I don't believe it," she said more to herself than anyone in particular. But then she remembered a conversation she and Pauline had had on one of those days she had spent with her. Pauline had expressed the desire that for other women with cancer to have the proper treatment and the best chance at life. She had talked first of donating money for research, but then decided that was not personal enough. Two days before her death she'd said to Abby, "I wish every woman who faced dying from this dreadful disease had a daughter like you to be with them through their last days."

In the months that followed, Abby worked at transforming Pauline's lavish mansion into a home for women who had received as much treatment as possible and who didn't have a home or family to live out their last days with.

When the work was finished, Abby walked through the halls of the new Pauline Penney Resting Place and gave herself a pat on the back for a job well done. She had successfully turned the upstairs into a ten-bedroom hospice complete with full-sized beds with lots of pillows and pink satin sheets. The downstairs sported a large dining area, as well as a game room and a roomy kitchen where the women could prepare their own meals if they so chose. The living room remained exactly the same as Pauline had left it, and her elegant picture still hung in the downstairs hallway.

Abby stood in front of that picture before receiving her first two residents. Who would have ever thought she'd be where she was today? But here she was, standing in the foyer of the home that had belonged to Pauline Penney. Life was funny that way, she thought to herself. You never really knew what hand you were going to be dealt.

More than two years ago Abby had thought she had all she'd ever wanted: her career and her independence. Now all that seemed distant and shallow in the wake of what she'd gone through to get to this point.

Abby smiled at the fingers of the woman in the portrait. "We came a long way, didn't we?" From hostile glares at the hospital when Megan was born to tender embraces half a year ago when Pauline lay dying. She was grateful for the time they had shared. Grateful for the insight into the woman who had given birth to the man she loved. A feeling of warmth coursed through her as she remembered the dream where Pauline had sung to the children and given Abby advice about unconditional love. Abby felt that love each time she looked at her girls, all three of them and each time she fell asleep at night with Mason beside her. Pauline had been right. There was nothing more rewarding than unconditional love.

An estimated 215,990 new cases of invasive breast cancer are expected to occur among women in the United States during 2004. An estimated 40,580 deaths (40,110 women, 470 men) are anticipated from breast cancer in 2004.

-American Cancer Society

Early detection is key. Mammography is especially valuable as an early detection tool. Get tested early... get tested regularly.

ABOUT THE AUTHOR

Artist C. Arthur was born and raised in Baltimore, Maryland where she currently resides with her husband and three children. An active imagination and a love for reading encouraged her to begin writing in high school and she hasn't stopped since.

Working in the legal field for almost thirteen years now she's seen lots of horrific things and longs for the safe haven reading a romance novel brings.

Her debut novel *Object of His Desire* was written almost six years ago when a picture of an Italian villa sparked the idea of an African-American/Italian hero. Romance and all its frilly edges are always on her mind, bringing new characters and plots to her on a regular basis. Being named one of three finalists in the 2003 Emma Awards was a highlight in her writing career and has increased her ambition to higher heights.

With her family's continued encouragement—especially hubby and the kids—she diligently moves from one novel to the next hoping to introduce new, entertaining and intriguing characters.

Artist loves to hear from her readers and can be reached via email at acarthur22@yahoo.com.

THE COLOR LINE

BY

LIZETTE G. CARTER

Release Date: May 2005

CHAPTER 1

Thank God, it's Friday!

I stepped off the elevator of my warehouse apartment building in Manhattan. It was a cool evening in New York—the first week in September. I was glad to be home. My arms were full of groceries and I was tired.

It had been a very exciting day at the office. We had given a going away party for my boss who was leaving our company to join another. I'd been an employee for five years and I was glad he was leaving. He wasn't the easiest person to work for. Now, at seven in the evening, all I wanted to do was put my feet up and relax and enjoy some peace of mind.

When I unlocked the door to my apartment, I noticed a stack of mail on my threshold. I knew my next door neighbor Robert had put it there. He's an attractive guy, but quiet and distant. Ever since I moved in, he's always been nice enough to put my mail at my door, but never once has he asked me out.

I was grateful that he'd brought my mail up, but figured it wasn't anything important, probably just junk mail or bills. That's why I hadn't looked in the mailbox. I needed no reminders of my liabilities.

With one free hand I picked up the mail and went into the kitchen to put the groceries on the counter. I looked at the mail for a few seconds without opening any. Oh yeah, it was junk mail. Not caring that I would eventually have to come back and look through it later, I slid the pile into the garbage. Frankly, I was too tired to be bothered. Unpacking the groceries, I noticed a small, white card on the counter, which I must have over-looked. When I picked it up, I immediately recognized the hand-writing.

Just a reminder about our date. I'll see you at eight tonight.
Love,
S.T.

S.T. was Steven Turner. We'd been seeing each other for approximately three months. We'd met on the job. I'm one of the top administrative assistants in a large investment firm and he's one of many financial analysts working there, hoping to become a partner.

Before Steven, I had made a point of avoiding relationships with any male co-workers, but when he asked me out, I didn't hesitate. He was attractive and I was twenty-seven and not get-ting any younger. I hadn't had a date in months and needed qual-ity time with a man. Why not go out and have some fun? So I went out with him. That was my first mistake. My second mis-take was letting him practically move in with me.

Every day Steve wanted sex. Now, I like sex. As a matter of fact I love it; but sex is not good if there is only one satisfied partner. I often wondered if he realized that I was even there. One time while we were in the act, I decided not to move a muscle, moan or anything—just to see whether he would notice. Well, he didn't. He just continued doing his thing.

Another thing that bothers me about Steve is that we have absolutely nothing in common. He rarely likes to eat out, because he's leery of eating restaurant food. Whenever we do eat out, there's only one restaurant that he takes me to. He hates going to malls because he says they're too crowded. And as long as we've been together, he's never taken me to the movies. "Why go to the movies when you can wait for the movie to come out on video tape," he'd say. Steve is cheap and insensitive and I've had it with him. When he finds the time to think about me, then maybe I'll find the time to think about him. Nevertheless, I was committed to this date.

My watch showed seven-thirty. I had a half-hour to get dressed. Damn! I didn't want to see him and didn't want to go out with him. Out of the blue, I heard a knock at the door. *It had better not be him.* When I opened the door I saw my sister Reneé with three duffel bags on her shoulders.

I took in everything and said, "What's going on, Reneé?" I knew what was going to come out before she opened her mouth and said the words that I didn't want to hear.

"Mom and I had a fight and she kicked me out," she answered. Brushing past me, she put her bags on the floor in the living room and sat down on the sofa.

I closed the door and walked over to her. "Okay, spill it," I commanded.

"You know my boyfriend Danny, right?" she asked.

I nodded my head. I remembered Mama mentioning him. I hadn't met Danny, but I knew that he was the only guy Reneé had been seeing for the past year and Mama wasn't too happy about it.

Reneé continued. "Well, Danny and I've been getting really serious and we decided that I should get on the pill—just as a precaution. So I asked Mama if she would take me to a gynecologist."

My jaw dropped.

"She started screaming about how she would not have her seventeen-year-old daughter having sex and said that she didn't want me to see him anymore. I tried to reason with her. I told her it wasn't fair for her to stop me from seeing him. Then she said she could tell me to do whatever the hell she wanted, as long as I was under her roof. So I packed up and here I am," she explained easily.

This was great, just great. I sighed and looked at my sister. She was looking at me expectantly. Damn!

"Okay, you can stay here," I mumbled reluctantly. Her eyes lit up instantly. "This is only for tonight, though. You can sleep upstairs in the spare bedroom. Now before you get comfortable, I want you to call Mama and tell her that you're here."

"C'mon, Lacie!" Reneé exclaimed. "I can't do that. You know how irrational Mama is. She's gotten even worse since Daddy passed away."

Daddy was Martin. He was Reneé's father and my stepfather. He's been gone for about a month now and since the funeral,

Mama's been giving Reneé a hard time. It was evident that Mama was having difficulty dealing with his death.

"Lacie, she wouldn't even listen to me," Reneé continued. Her eyes widened. "Why don't you call her? She won't yell at you. Please, Lacie. You know I can't talk to Mama when she's like this," she pleaded.

She had a point. If Reneé called Mama, she'd be over here in minutes, screaming her lungs out for Reneé to come home. If I called Mama, the chances were better for Reneé to stay.

Reneé followed me into the kitchen. I put my index finger to my lips, signaling her to be quiet while I dialed Mama's number. She picked up on the first ring.

"Hello?"

"Uh, hi, Mama. I'm calling to let you know that Reneé is over here. She wants to sleep over here tonight."

"Uh, huh. I figured as much," Mama mumbled. "I'm on my way to pick her up."

Oh, boy. Here we go. "Mama, why don't you come by tomorrow?"

"No! I want her back here tonight!"

"What's the hurry?" I asked gently. "Listen, why don't you just tell me what's going on?"

"Lacie, I don't need this right now. I'll be over in…," Mama began.

"Wait a minute, Mama," I interjected softly. "We need to talk this out and I don't think it's a good idea if you come over tonight. You know that as soon as you come over here, you two will start arguing and shouting and I don't need that. Why don't we let things settle down for the night?" I looked at Reneé and

275

shrugged my shoulders.

"I don't think so, Lacie. Reneé is getting too grown. She thinks she can get away with a lot of things and I'm not having it," Mama voiced.

"That may be true, but come over here tomorrow and we'll talk about it then, okay?"

There was a long pause. "All right. But you tell her to be ready to come home."

It was time to get off the phone before she changed her mind. "Okay, Mama. We'll see you tomorrow and we'll talk then," I said hastily.

I heard Mama mumble, "There isn't anything to talk about," as she hung up the phone.

I was so glad that was over. I hate being in uncomfortable situations. I glanced at Reneé. She had a huge grin on her face.

"Don't you dare smile at me, Reneé. You know very well what kind of position you put me in," I scolded.

"Oh, please, Lacie. You did great! All you have to do now is convince Mama to let me stay with you permanently." She got off the bar stool and went into the living room and sat on the sofa.

I know she didn't say what I thought she'd said. I followed her and stood in front of her with my hands on my hips, then caught myself and put my hands down. I'd suddenly recalled how Mama would always stand over me with her hands on her hips whenever I did something wrong, and how I hated to have to listen to her talk first and then beat my behind. I don't know which I hated most—my mother's mouth or her beatings.

"Reneé, what are you talking about?"

She looked at me dolefully. "I don't want to go back home. I want to stay here with you."

"What?" I heard an alarm go off in my head. No, it was the telephone. I ran to the kitchen to pick it up before the answering machine came on.

"Hello?"

"Hey, girl!"

It was Dawn Robinson. She was my best friend and just like another sister to me. We'd known each other since we were kids.

"Hey, girl, what's up?" I responded wearily.

She caught on instantly. "Girl, you sound awful. What's wrong?"

"Reneé is here. She had an argument with Mama and she wants to stay with me permanently," I answered.

"What!"

"Yeah, that's exactly what I said."

"What are you going to do?"

"I don't know. I haven't decided if I'm going to let her stay or not," I said loudly as Reneé crept up the stairs. "She is going to stay tonight, though."

"What happened?" Dawn asked.

"Girl, I can't get into that right now. Steven will be over here in fifteen minutes and I'm not even ready."

"I thought you were going to quit him?"

"Well, I was. I mean, I am. I just haven't done it yet." I sighed. "I really don't want to be with him tonight."

"So don't. Tell him you already made plans with me. Then we can go to the club."

"I don't know. He's already on his way," I started to say.

"I don't even want to hear it. I'm on my way over. See you in about ten minutes."

"Where are you?" I asked. Dawn lived in Brooklyn, so I knew it wouldn't take her ten minutes to get to my place.

"I'm here in the city, calling from my cell phone."

"So you went ahead and got it, huh?"

"Yeah. Ronnie thought it would be a good idea if I had one so he could call me whenever he wanted," she explained.

"Dawn, you already have a pager."

"I know, but let's not get into that right now. I'll be over there shortly," she said and hung up.

She never wanted to get into it. She knew I didn't care for Ronnie. Why would I? He was no good. He had tried to make a move on me when I first met him, but I didn't dare tell Dawn that. They'd been together for only a month and already he'd bought her a one-carat diamond ring, a new wardrobe and they were living together. I just didn't trust him.

The clock showed seven forty-five. I ran upstairs to my room to get dressed.

In ten minutes I was ready. I hate being in a rush for anything, much less a man. After glancing at my watch and seeing that I had five or so minutes before Steve's arrival, I decided to get something to drink. Seeing Dawn's behind blocking the refrigerator door when I walked into the kitchen was no surprise, considering she had a key to my apartment.

Dawn stayed hungry and stayed thin. I took one look at her skinny frame and got angry. How anyone could eat so much was beyond me. She was five-feet-ten with long legs, a chocolate complexion, and a very pretty face. Dawn worked for the same firm that I did, but on another floor. She was a struggling actress and model and vowed that her job at the firm was temporary.

Knowing that she hadn't heard me come downstairs, I snuck up behind her. "Just what do you think you are doing?" I yelled.

She whirled around with a fried chicken leg in her mouth. "Dammit, Lacie, you scared me! Why do you always sneak up on people?"

I laughed and reached into the cabinet for a glass. "Why do you always have to come over to my house and eat up all my food?" I teased. "I thought you were on a diet anyway. Although you don't need to be."

"I am on a diet," she declared. "I'm eating this only because it looked so good."

Although my back was turned, I could feel her eyes on me and turned around. "What?"

"Are you ready for your big date?" she teased.

If she weren't my friend, I would have punched her in the mouth. "Look, it will take some time to get rid of him, but I will, eventually. I just haven't had the nerve yet," I explained.

"Uh, huh," she murmured, still chewing on the now meatless chicken bone. "I'm sorry, Lacie, but I just don't understand why you ever gave him the time of day."

"I don't know either. I guess I was lonely and needed some sex," I shrugged. "I mean, he's a nice looking guy, but we just don't click and he doesn't give me the attention that I need."

"Then let's do something about it. Let's go out to the club."

"I told you. I can't. Steve and I already made plans. He should be here any minute now."

"Then we'll break them. You need a man and I need to shake it up. So we're going."

"All right, then you tell Steve."

"I will," she returned indignantly.

There was a knock at the door. I didn't even have my drink yet. When I went into the living room, Dawn followed and sat on the sofa. I looked through the peephole of the door and opened it.

"Hey, baby," Steve said casually as he came in and strolled right past me, without giving me a kiss or a hug. That's exactly why I was dumping his behind. I should have slammed the door in his face. "Hey, Dawn. What are you doing here?"

"Lacie and I have a dinner date with my mother and I came to pick her up," she explained innocently.

Steve turned toward me. "Lacie, I thought we were going out tonight?"

Dawn didn't give me a chance to answer. "I'm sorry, Steve, but Lacie forgot about it as well. She didn't remember until I came over."

"Can't it wait?" he asked.

"No, my mother and Lacie get along really well. She's looking forward to seeing Lacie and she'll be quite upset if she doesn't come. You know how these things are, don't you, Steve?"

"I guess we can do it another night. I'll hang out with Ronnie, then."

"Uh, Ronnie's out of town. He won't be back until next Saturday," Dawn lied.

Steve looked from me to Dawn. I thought he was going to object again, but he didn't. Looking me straight in the eye, he said, "I guess I should go then. I'll see you later, Lacie." He walked swiftly to the door and slammed it behind him.

I turned toward Dawn and caught her smile.

"You see, that wasn't so hard," she said triumphantly.

"He knew it was a lie, Dawn. You saw his expression."

She stood up and grabbed her coat and purse. "Well, Lacie, I got rid of him like you wanted to. Now let's go out and have some fun."

"I'll meet you downstairs. I'm going to check on Reneé," I said, already heading for the stairs.

"Okay, but don't take too long," Dawn said as she walked out the door.

Reneé was watching television. "Hey," I said. "Dawn and I are leaving. There's plenty of food in the refrigerator and the number to the club is on the table."

"How long will you be out?"

"Not too long, I hope. Call me if you need me," I said and closed the door.

I left the apartment thinking how much I wanted to stay home.

The club was small and hot. Dawn chose a table right in front of the dance floor so she'd be able to see the men. I wanted to sit in the back so I could just sit and watch, but I went along with what she wanted. Shortly after we ordered drinks, one guy came over and asked her to dance and she jumped at the chance. I drank my strawberry daiquiri and watched them, shaking my head. The guy was cute, but he couldn't dance a lick.

While I continued drinking my daiquiri and looking around,

I sensed someone standing alongside me. I looked up and blinked. This man was gorgeous! He appeared to be about six feet tall, maybe an inch or so taller, with the most beautiful brown complexion I'd ever seen. His muscles were everywhere.

"Would you like to dance?" he asked, offering his hand.

Was he serious? "Sure." I took his hand

As he led me to the dance floor, "Between the Sheets" by the Isley Brothers came on. *Damn!* I'd gotten into many compromising positions because of that song.

We started to dance and boy, did it feel good! He had one arm around my waist and held my hand against his chest with the other. He held me so tightly I could hardly breath.

He whispered in my ear, "My name is Joe."

"I'm Lacie," I replied.

"Lacie. That's an unusual name, but it's pretty."

"Thank you." He could have hated my name for all I cared. He smelled so good that I just closed my eyes and enjoyed the feel of his arms around me. The last thing I wanted was for our dance to end.

Once I opened my eyes, I noticed Dawn signaling me with wide eyes. Evidently she had been trying to get my attention for the past few minutes. I figured her eyes were wide because she saw how attractive Joe was, but when I looked where she was pointing, I saw Steve! He was standing on the side of the dance floor with his hands buried in his pockets. Oh, man!

Joe, feeling me tense up, looked in Steve's direction. "Boyfriend?" he asked.

"Kind of," I answered reluctantly.

"Do you want to stop?"

No, I definitely did not want anything to stop. I said, "Let's wait until the song ends; then I'll go over there."

We continued to dance and I avoided looking at Steve. After the song ended, we let go of each other slowly.

Joe cleared his throat. "I guess you'd better go over there before he comes over here. Don't be so hard on him, now. I can understand why he looks so mad. You're a beautiful woman and of course he would be upset if he saw you dancing with another man. I would."

I smiled wearily. "Thank you. It was nice meeting you, Joe"

He smiled in return and his teeth were beautiful. "It was my pleasure as well. I hope to see you again. Take care," he said before he walked away.

I walked toward Steve, my anger building as I did so. I turned back around to get a last look at Joe, but he was gone. I walked that mile to Steve and the first thing he said was, "I thought you were going to Dawn's mom's?"

"Change of plans," I replied nonchalantly.

He looked at me as if I were a child he'd just caught stealing a cookie from a cookie jar. "I knew this was where you would be. C'mon, we're going home."

"Wait. Let me tell Dawn I'm leaving," I said, already heading for the dance floor.

He came up behind me and grabbed my arm roughly. "No. I'm ready to go now," he uttered through clenched teeth.

Oh, no he didn't! Seeing the expression on my face, he immediately released my arm from his vice grip. *Calm down, Lacie. Play it cool.* "Wait here, Steve," I commanded and walked off.

Dawn met me halfway. "Girl, what's going on with Steve and

who was that fine looking man dancing with you?"

"Steve's taking me home and I'll explain everything to you later."

"Are you sure you don't want me to take you?"

I knew she was having fun and was only asking because she felt it was the right thing to say. I glanced at the guy she'd been dancing with and decided she should stay.

"No, I'll be okay. Just give me a call later. No, better yet, I'll call you."

"All right. If you say so," Dawn mumbled uncertainly, although I knew she was glad I didn't take her offer.

"I'll see you later on, okay?"

"Sure. Don't forget to call me."

"I won't."

I met back with Steve and we left the club.

I didn't say anything to Steve on the way home. I merely sat in his car and seethed. When we arrived at my apartment, I went upstairs to change, while he made himself comfortable on the couch. I checked in on Reneé and saw that she was asleep. Next, I changed my clothes and got ready to deal with Steve.

He had his feet propped up on my oak coffee table when I went downstairs. I slapped them off, sat in front of him and spoke calmly.

"Steve, what you did tonight was inexcusable. You really pissed me off. I have had it with you. Enough said, I want you to pack your stuff and get out." I stood up and headed into the kitchen for a drink.

Behind me, I heard him say, "Wait, Lacie. Can't we talk about this? Don't you think you owe me an explanation?"

I stopped dead in my tracks. *No, Lacie. Don't respond.* Then I continued en route to the kitchen.

"Lacie, I'm talking to you!" Steve yelled, following me.

Once in the kitchen, I grabbed a soda from the refrigerator, took one huge swallow and said, "Steve, I don't owe you a damn thing. I mean, I can't believe that you're even asking me for an explanation after the stunt you pulled tonight. I am not some child who will jump to attention and do whatever you tell her to do. You embarrassed the hell out of me making a scene like that! Who do you think you are?"

He looked shocked at my outburst. "I'm your boyfriend, Lacie. That means something, doesn't it? How do you think it made me feel to see you in another man's arms? What's even worse is that you lied to me."

"I didn't lie to you. That was Dawn."

"You know what I mean. You went along with what she said and you don't seem sorry about it, either."

"No, I'm not," I said defiantly. "All of a sudden you see me dancing with another guy and now you want to act like my boyfriend? Steve, give me a break. You haven't been acting like one since we've been together, so don't try it now."

"What are you saying? You don't want me anymore?"

I sighed. "Steve, we've known for a long time that this was over. We're not right for each other. You can't give me what I want in a relationship."

His expression turned bitter. "If that's what you want, fine.

I'll call you when I'm ready to pick up my things. I'm getting out of here."

When he closed the door behind him, I immediately felt as if a huge weight had been lifted from my shoulders. Steve wasn't right for me and I think deep down he knew it. Dawn was right. I had to be upfront with him. Too much of my time had been wasted with men that were not giving me what I wanted. It was time to get myself together and ultimately that was what I would do. But right now, I had to figure out what to do about tomorrow.

So much for a night of rest.

Knock. Knock.

"Lacie, wake up, Mama's here." I heard Reneé's voice on the other side of my bedroom door.

I turned over and looked at the clock. It showed eleven in the morning, but I turned back over.

"Lacie, wake up!" Reneé yelled.

"All right, all right. I'm on my way down," I mumbled into my pillow.

I heard the door open and close. Reneé was standing over me with her hands on her hips.

I raised my head and gave her a stupefied look. "Wait a minute. Did I tell you to come in?" I asked. "I said I was on my way down."

"Sorry, Lacie, but I couldn't hear you." She pointed to my pillow.

I looked at the pillow. "Oh." I pulled the cover off and sat up. "Well, what's up?" I asked with a yawn.

"Do you remember that you're supposed to talk to Mama for me?" Reneé asked.

"Umm, now how could I forget? She's right downstairs," I grumbled cynically and walked tiredly to the adjoining bathroom with her on my heels.

Reneé stood in the doorway of the bathroom with her arms folded and watched me squeeze toothpaste on my toothbrush. "When are you going to tell Mama that I'm going to live with you?" she asked after I started brushing my teeth.

I almost gagged on the toothbrush. "Excuse me?" I asked, looking at her with a mouthful of toothpaste.

"You know…we agreed that I could stay here," she said innocently. "So when are you going to tell her?"

I rinsed my mouth out. "Reneé, I didn't agree to anything except you staying for one night."

"I can't stay with her, Lacie. I'll have no life. Mama will lock me up and throw away the key. Please, Lacie. I promise I won't get in your way," she pleaded.

I rolled my eyes. She could be so dramatic. "Don't do this, Reneé. I'm not ready for this. I like living alone." After I washed my face, I walked to the closet to pick out something to wear. Reneé followed. "I mean, how am I supposed to take care of a seventeen-year-old? I'm not ready for that kind of responsibility. *I'm* not even through growing up yet."

"I'm not a kid. I'm a senior in high school and I don't need a baby-sitter. I can take care of myself," she insisted.

"That's what I'm afraid of," I retorted.

Reneé stamped her foot.

I whirled around and looked at her. "Now you see. That's exactly why I don't want your spoiled behind to stay here. If you're not a kid, then stop acting like one."

"I'll tell Mama you're on your way down," Reneé mumbled and closed the door behind her.

I finished dressing and looked in the mirror. I'd seen better days. I knew I'd get a lecture from Mama. I always did. But I went downstairs.

Reneé had tears running down her face and she and Mama appeared to be in an intense conversation. I took one glance at Mama and knew she was not happy.

Mama's full name is Josephine Brown Taylor. An extremely beautiful, slender woman standing five feet six, inches tall, at forty-three, she doesn't look a day over thirty. All of my life, people have told us that we look alike—despite our difference in complexion and hairstyles. Her complexion is a deep mahogany color and I'm a couple of shades lighter. She always wears her hair short and I've always kept mine long.

"Hi, Mama." I kissed her on the cheek.

"Hi, Lacie. I was wondering when you were going to come down," she said. "You look awful."

I ignored her remark and started walking toward the kitchen. "Yeah, well...I'm sorry. I had a long day yesterday and a long week. Do you want some coffee?"

"No, Lacie. We're getting ready to leave. Get your things, Reneé," Mama commanded.

I stopped. "You just got here. Don't you think we should talk?" I suggested, signaling for Reneé not to get up.

"Not really," Mama said dryly.

I guessed I had to start the conversation off. I took a deep breath. "Mama, Reneé feels as if she can't talk to you and she's not happy."

"I know how she feels, Lacie," Mama said. "However, Reneé is getting too hot and I'm having a time trying to control her hormones."

"Mama, that's not true," Reneé said. "All I wanted was to go to the doctor for…"

"I know why you wanted to go. You don't have to repeat it!" Mama snapped. "You don't want to listen and obey me—especially when it comes to Danny. I don't want you to see him anymore and that's that."

"I told you this would happen, Lacie!" Reneé exclaimed.

"Mama, she's seventeen years old. Most young adults her age are dating," I said in Reneé's defense.

"I said I don't want her to see him and I mean it!" Mama yelled.

"That's it. I've had it." Reneé jumped up.

"Reneé, sit down," Mama said sternly.

"No!" Reneé yelled.

"What!" Mama's eyes widened.

"I don't…," Reneé began, but didn't finish because Mama walked over to her and slapped her face so hard it echoed.

Reneé touched her face in disbelief. I couldn't believe it either. Sure, Mama had hit us before, especially when I was growing up, but never over something so small. I had to get them apart before things got worse.

"Reneé go upstairs. I want to talk to Mama alone for a

few minutes," I said softly.

Reneé ran upstairs crying and closed the door.

"Mama, what's wrong with you? Why did you do that?" I asked, once Reneé was out of earshot.

Mama sat down heavily on the sofa. "I don't know. I don't know."

"What do you mean, you don't know, Mama? Have you any idea what you did?"

"Yes, I know. This is becoming too much for me." She brushed a hand through her hair, a gesture I inherited from her. As if making a decision, she stood up with a drained expression. "Lacie, would you mind taking care of Reneé for a while? I need some time by myself. Ever since Martin died…"

Oh no, not again. I shook my head. "Mama, I can't do this. I'm too busy for a child."

"She's not a child. It'll only be for a little while. Reneé's old enough to take care of herself. She won't need a babysitter or anything."

"So I've heard," I mumbled and shook my head. I couldn't believe this. First Reneé and now Mama. I sighed. "How long is a while?"

"I don't know, really. I may need a few weeks or a month. I need some time to get myself together, Lacie," she uttered weakly.

All of a sudden I started to feel guilty. Mama was still mourning Martin's death and I wasn't being considerate.

"All right," I agreed reluctantly. "But let's focus on a few weeks." Her weary smile thanked me. "Where are you going?

What are you going to do?"

"I don't know…start getting rid of Martin's clothes, I guess. I may go back home to North Carolina. I haven't decided." She looked sad. I didn't know what to say. She breathed deeply, then said, "Well, I'm going to leave. I'll send Reneé's stuff over here sometime this week. Tell her that I didn't mean…"

"Sure, Mama. No problem. You just do what you have to do."

She smiled thinly. "Thanks, Lacie. I really appreciate this."

I went upstairs to Reneé's room after Mama left.

"Are you okay?" I asked gently.

"Yeah, I'm fine. Did Mama leave?" she asked.

I nodded. "She just left." I decided to break the tension. "You know what? You and Mama must have ESP or something, because she just asked me if you could stay with me for a while."

"What did you say?"

"I agreed, just as long as you had your shots first."

Reneé smiled and then we both laughed. I walked over to her bed and sat next to her.

"Hey, everything is going to be fine. Mama just has some things that she needs to work out for herself. Then, once she's better, I can kick you out and I'll have the place to myself again," I joked. "Listen, I'm kind of new at this stuff, but we'll try to make the best of this situation. I'll spend as much time with you as I can. How does that sound?"

"Sounds good," she replied, and gave me a hug.

"I'm hungry. Let's go out to eat so we can get your mind off all this."

"Where to?"

"Anywhere you want. Just not any place too expensive. I'm not used to having a dependent yet."

"How about Chinese? There's a nice little place here in the village that I know of. Danny's taken me there a few times and it's not that expensive."

"Chinese, it is then," I said.

2005 Publication Schedule

January

A Heart's Awakening
Veronica Parker
$9.95
1-58571-143-8

Falling
Natalie Dunbar
$9.95
1-58571-121-7

February

Echoes of Yesterday
Beverly Clark
$9.95
1-58571-131-4

A Love of Her Own
Cheris F. Hodges
$9.95
1-58571-136-5

Higher Ground
Leah Latimer
$19.95
1-58571-157-8

March

Misconceptions
Pamela Leigh Starr
$9.95
1-58571-117-9

I'll Paint a Sun
A.J. Garrotto
$9.95
1-58571-165-9

Peace Be Still
Colette Haywood
$12.95
1-58571-129-2

April

Intentional Mistakes
Michele Sudler
$9.95
1-58571-152-7

Conquering Dr. Wexler's Heart
Kimberley White
$9.95
1-58571-126-8

Song in the Park
Martin Brant
$15.95
1-58571-125-X

May

The Color Line
Lizette Carter
$9.95
1-58571-163-2

Unconditional
A.C. Arthur
$9.95
1-58571-142-X

Last Train to Memphis
Elsa Cook
$12.95
1-58571-146-2

June

Angel's Paradise
Janice Angelique
$9.95
1-58571-107-1

Suddenly You
Crystal Hubbard
$9.95
1-58571-158-6

Matters of Life and
Death
Lesego Malepe, Ph.D.
$15.95
1-58571-124-1

2005 Publication Schedule (continued)

July

Pleasures All Mine
Belinda O. Steward
$9.95
1-58571-112-8

Wild Ravens
Altonya Washington
$9.95
1-58571-164-0

Class Reunion
Irma Jenkins/John
Brown
$12.95
1-58571-123-3

August

Path of Thorns
Annetta P. Lee
$9.95
1-58571-145-4

Timeless Devotion
Bella McFarland
$9.95
1-58571-148-9

Life Is Never As It Seems
June Michael
$12.95
1-58571-153-5

September

Beyond the Rapture
Beverly Clark
$9.95
1-58571-131-4

Blood Lust
J. M. Jeffries
$9.95
1-58571-138-1

Rough on Rats and
Tough on Cats
Chris Parker
$12.95
1-58571-154-3

October

A Will to Love
Angie Daniels
$9.95
1-58571-141-1

Taken by You
Dorothy Elizabeth Love
$9.95
1-58571-162-4

Soul Eyes
Wayne L. Wilson
$12.95
1-58571-147-0

November

A Drummer's Beat to
Mend
Kay Swanson
$9.95

Sweet Reprecussions
Kimberley White
$9.95
1-58571-159-4

Red Polka Dot in a
Worldof Plaid
Varian Johnson
$12.95
1-58571-140-3

December

Hand in Glove
Andrea Jackson
$9.95
1-58571-166-7

Blaze
Barbara Keaton
$9.95

Across
Carol Payne
$12.95
1-58571-149-7

UNCONDITIONAL

Other Genesis Press, Inc. Titles

Acquisitions	Kimberley White	$8.95
A Dangerous Deception	J.M. Jeffries	$8.95
A Dangerous Love	J.M. Jeffries	$8.95
A Dangerous Obsession	J.M. Jeffries	$8.95
After the Vows	Leslie Esdaile	$10.95
(Summer Anthology)	T.T. Henderson	
	Jacqueline Thomas	
Again My Love	Kayla Perrin	$10.95
Against the Wind	Gwynne Forster	$8.95
A Lark on the Wing	Phyliss Hamilton	$8.95
A Lighter Shade of Brown	Vicki Andrews	$8.95
All I Ask	Barbara Keaton	$8.95
A Love to Cherish	Beverly Clark	$8.95
Ambrosia	T.T. Henderson	$8.95
And Then Came You	Dorothy Elizabeth Love	$8.95
Angel's Paradise	Janice Angelique	$8.95
A Risk of Rain	Dar Tomlinson	$8.95
At Last	Lisa G. Riley	$8.95
Best of Friends	Natalie Dunbar	$8.95
Bound by Love	Beverly Clark	$8.95
Breeze	Robin Hampton Allen	$10.95
Brown Sugar Diaries &	Delores Bundy &	$10.95
Other Sexy Tales	Cole Riley	
By Design	Barbara Keaton	$8.95
Cajun Heat	Charlene Berry	$8.95
Careless Whispers	Rochelle Alers	$8.95
Caught in a Trap	Andre Michelle	$8.95
Chances	Pamela Leigh Starr	$8.95
Dark Embrace	Crystal Wilson Harris	$8.95
Dark Storm Rising	Chinelu Moore	$10.95
Designer Passion	Dar Tomlinson	$8.95
Ebony Butterfly II	Delilah Dawson	$14.95

Erotic Anthology	Assorted	$8.95
Eve's Prescription	Edwina Martin Arnold	$8.95
Everlastin' Love	Gay G. Gunn	$8.95
Fate	Pamela Leigh Starr	$8.95
Forbidden Quest	Dar Tomlinson	$10.95
Fragment in the Sand	Annetta P. Lee	$8.95
From the Ashes	Kathleen Suzanne	$8.95
	Jeanne Sumerix	
Gentle Yearning	Rochelle Alers	$10.95
Glory of Love	Sinclair LeBeau	$10.95
Hart & Soul	Angie Daniels	$8.95
Heartbeat	Stephanie Bedwell-Grime	$8.95
I'll Be Your Shelter	Giselle Carmichael	$8.95
Illusions	Pamela Leigh Starr	$8.95
Indiscretions	Donna Hill	$8.95
Interlude	Donna Hill	$8.95
Intimate Intentions	Angie Daniels	$8.95
Just an Affair	Eugenia O'Neal	$8.95
Kiss or Keep	Debra Phillips	$8.95
Love Always	Mildred E. Riley	$10.95
Love Unveiled	Gloria Greene	$10.95
Love's Deception	Charlene Berry	$10.95
Mae's Promise	Melody Walcott	$8.95
Meant to Be	Jeanne Sumerix	$8.95
Midnight Clear	Leslie Esdaile	$10.95
(Anthology)	Gwynne Forster	
	Carmen Green	
	Monica Jackson	
Midnight Magic	Gwynne Forster	$8.95
Midnight Peril	Vicki Andrews	$10.95
My Buffalo Soldier	Barbara B. K. Reeves	$8.95
Naked Soul	Gwynne Forster	$8.95
No Regrets	Mildred E. Riley	$8.95
Nowhere to Run	Gay G. Gunn	$10.95

Object of His Desire	A. C. Arthur	$8.95
One Day at a Time	Bella McFarland	$8.95
Passion	T.T. Henderson	$10.95
Past Promises	Jahmel West	$8.95
Path of Fire	T.T. Henderson	$8.95
Picture Perfect	Reon Carter	$8.95
Pride & Joi	Gay G. Gunn	$8.95
Quiet Storm	Donna Hill	$8.95
Reckless Surrender	Rochelle Alers	$8.95
Rendezvous with Fate	Jeanne Sumerix	$8.95
Revelations	Cheris F. Hodges	$8.95
Rivers of the Soul	Leslie Esdaile	$8.95
Rooms of the Heart	Donna Hill	$8.95
Shades of Brown	Denise Becker	$8.95
Shades of Desire	Monica White	$8.95
Sin	Crystal Rhodes	$8.95
So Amazing	Sinclair LeBeau	$8.95
Somebody's Someone	Sinclair LeBeau	$8.95
Someone to Love	Alicia Wiggins	$8.95
Soul to Soul	Donna Hill	$8.95
Still Waters Run Deep	Leslie Esdaile	$8.95
Subtle Secrets	Wanda Y. Thomas	$8.95
Sweet Tomorrows	Kimberly White	$8.95
The Color of Trouble	Dyanne Davis	$8.95
The Price of Love	Sinclair LeBeau	$8.95
The Reluctant Captive	Joyce Jackson	$8.95
The Missing Link	Charlyne Dickerson	$8.95
Three Wishes	Seressia Glass	$8.95
Tomorrow's Promise	Leslie Esdaile	$8.95
Truly Inseperable	Wanda Y. Thomas	$8.95
Twist of Fate	Beverly Clark	$8.95
Unbreak My Heart	Dar Tomlinson	$8.95
Unconditional Love	Alicia Wiggins	$8.95
When Dreams A Float	Dorothy Elizabeth Love	$8.95

ESCAPE WITH INDIGO !!!!

Join Indigo Book Club©
It's simple, easy and secure.

Sign up and receive the new releases
every month + Free shipping and
20% off the cover price.

Go online to www.genesis-press.com and
click on Bookclub or
call 1-888-INDIGO-1

Order Form

Mail to: Genesis Press, Inc.

P.O. Box 101
Columbus, MS 39703

Name _____

Address _____

City/State _____ Zip _____

Telephone _____

Ship to (if different from above)

Name _____

Address _____

City/State _____ Zip _____

Telephone _____

Credit Card Information

Credit Card # _____ ☐ Visa ☐ Mastercard

Expiration Date (mm/yy) _____ ☐ AmEx ☐ Discover

Qty.	Author	Title	Price	Total

Use this order form, or call 1-888-INDIGO-1	Total for books _____
	Shipping and handling:
	  $5 first two books,
	  $1 each additional book _____
	Total S & H _____
	Total amount enclosed _____
	Mississippi residents add 7% sales tax

Visit www.genesis-press.com for latest releases and excerpts.

Order Form

Mail to: Genesis Press, Inc.

P.O. Box 101
Columbus, MS 39703

Name _____
Address _____
City/State _____ Zip _____
Telephone _____

Ship to (if different from above)
Name _____
Address _____
City/State _____ Zip _____
Telephone _____

Credit Card Information

Credit Card # _____ ☐ Visa   ☐ Mastercard
Expiration Date (mm/yy) _____ ☐ AmEx ☐ Discover

Qty.	Author	Title	Price	Total

Use this order form, or call 1-888-INDIGO-1

Total for books	_____
Shipping and handling: $5 first two books, $1 each additional book	_____
Total S & H	_____
Total amount enclosed	_____

Mississippi residents add 7% sales tax

Visit www.genesis-press.com for latest releases and excerpts.